HELLFIRE

A Hawk Tate Novel

DUSTIN STEVENS

Hellfire
A Hawk Tate Novel
Copyright © 2018, Dustin Stevens
Cover Art and Design: Paramita Bhattacharjee, www.creativeparamita.com

Truth, at the wrong time, can be dangerous.
—Michael Ondaatje

Remember not only to say the right thing in the right place, but far more difficult still, to leave unsaid the wrong thing at the tempting moment.
—Benjamin Franklin

Prologue

My father had turned the engine off and taken the keys with him, a conditioned response performed without the slightest bit of forethought.

Pull to a stop along the shoulder. Turn off the ignition. Remove the loose tangle of metal and shove it in his pocket as he exited.

Just from that one simple open-and-close of the door, I could feel a blast of cold air push inside the car. From the passenger seat, I could even see the loose collection of snowflakes that had sauntered in, settling on the indented cushion in front of the steering wheel.

And I could feel the temperature inside the car plummeting with each passing moment.

Framed in the jagged cone of light from the single overhead stanchion alongside the road, the small sedan he had stopped to help was plainly visible. No more than a foot off the side of the highway, it was dark in color, the rear flashers winking at me in even intervals.

Stooped alongside it was a single figure, their form masked from view by the swirl of bulky clothing enveloping them. Moving in slow, stilted motions, the person was going about the unenviable task of attempting to change a flat tire.

A task that was being made much more difficult by the elements.

A job that they might never have completed had my father not decided to stop.

As a boy of eleven, I remember not being able to fathom such a gesture. The weather outside was abysmal, growing worse by the moment. Our own car was in dire need of new tires, not exactly equipped for the storm.

Long before the days of cell phones, we were already late getting home, my mother no doubt terrified of what might have befallen us.

Of course, my father must have already known all that and a hundred other reasons why we should have kept going.

Not that a single one stopped him from doing it anyway.

Start to finish, the endeavor took more than twenty minutes. Under optimal conditions, I'd seen him change a flat in less than half that, but given everything going on, I'm willing to bet the swap was seen as a success.

By the time he was finished, the front windshield had frosted over, blocking my view. I was starting to feel a chill that resonated clear to the bone, meaning I couldn't even imagine how he must have been feeling as he wrenched the door open and swung inside.

Nor would I ever find out, as not once did he say a word about it. Instead, he merely brushed the collection of flakes from his coat and turned the heat up high, holding his exposed fingers to the vents.

Not until the flesh was wet with snowmelt and bright pink in color did he put the car in drive and start away.

By then, the car he had stopped to help had already done the same.

"Who was that, Dad?" I remember asking as we inched our way forward in the storm.

"A nice lady named Paula."

"Oh," I said. "So you knew her?"

"Not before tonight," he answered.

Again, as a child of that age, what had taken place was borderline incomprehensible. "So then, why...?"

"Sometimes in life, we do things simply because there's nobody else around to do them."

Not once did he even look my way, nor did we ever speak of it again after that night, but I'll be damned if it wasn't a story that resonated with me in a way he never could have intended.

Or maybe he did...

Part One

Chapter One

Edgar Belmonte was never much of a football fan. Despite it being known as the most beautiful sport in the world, despite it being viewed as the official pastime of Venezuela – the country he was now campaigning to become the leader of – the game had never really done it for him.

A heavy-set child, he had not cared for the constant running. It made it impossible to participate in, and not much more fun to watch.

If he was going to devote two or three hours to something, he wanted there to be a lot more action than one or two goals.

Some might call such a thing an attention deficit issue. To him, it was merely a matter of priorities.

Now a grown man in his forties, he still didn't particularly care for the game. Gone was any of the baby fat that had dogged him through his youth. In its stead was a body that was fit and trim, now proudly displayed by the Armani suit that was cut to perfectly mirror his shape.

Still, some preferences are established in youth, and his disdain for the sport was one that would stay with him through the end of his days.

But that still didn't change the fact that football *stadiums* could come in quite handy from time to time.

One such instance being on nights like this, when more than thirty thousand people were crammed tight into the space, all waiting for him to take his place before the microphone.

Tucked away in the underbelly of the structure, Belmonte and his team had acquired the home team locker room for the evening. A palatial area more than sixty yards in length, it was more than enough space for the tiny assemblage of people.

All dressed in dark suits and matching ties, they were a harsh contrast to the blue-and-green color pattern around them, every surface capable of holding paint covered in the team colors.

"This is fantastic," Giselle Ruiz said. Standing in the center of the room, her feet were set wide, one on either side of the dragon emblazoned on the carpet. "I can feel the vibrations of the crowd rising up through the floor."

Standing perpendicular to her a few feet away, Chief of Staff Hector Ramon placed his hands out to either side, mimicking her pose. "Just wait until Edgar takes his place out there. This whole damn place will be moving."

From across the room, Belmonte's only response was a thin smile, his lips pressed tight together. Tonight had been a long time coming. There would certainly be much more to do thereafter.

But it was a turning point for sure. A spot that schoolchildren across the countryside would one day read about in textbooks.

The night that a hero came forward, and Venezuelans moved toward finally taking back what was theirs.

The preparations for the night had been in motion since the start of the campaign a month prior, though the big surprise they had in store was something they had thrown together just a few days before. The brainchild of Ruiz, Ramon, and himself, it was something so bold that it would either submarine them or catapult them into the stratosphere.

No middle ground whatsoever.

Belmonte was betting everything he had on the latter.

Raising a bottle of water to his lips, he asked, "How much time do we have?"

At the sound of his voice, any hint of side discussion bled away. Every head turned in his direction.

"You go on in sixteen minutes, sir," Ruiz said.

"And how many people do we have out there right now?"

"There are still about a thousand waiting to file in from outside," Ramon answered. "They should all be in place in time."

Belmonte nodded. Tonight would be one of the most photographed and talked about in his nation's history. It was imperative that every image showed a full stadium behind him.

Sixteen minutes would be more than enough time to ensure that happened.

Chapter Two

The feed coming in was grainy and distorted. It jumped every few moments, reminding the people around the table of being inside a darkened room with a strobe light going at full capacity.

Brief pockets of darkness interspersed with snippets of light, each offset enough that things seemed to be jumping ahead instead of moving in smooth motion.

"Is this the best we can do?" Charles Vance asked from the head of the table. Despite the late hour, he was still wearing his full suit, the navy blue material free of wrinkles. With his chair twisted sideways, the heel of one polished wingtip rested on the corner of the table.

As Special Director for South American Operations, there was plenty on Vance's plate to keep him working ninety hours a week or more. In the previous year, the situation in Venezuela had escalated to a point that a country that had earned five percent of his attention when he started was now demanding almost a full day a week.

This tonight was just the latest example. One more in what had been an interminable slog through the sham known as election season in that part of the world.

"Let me see what I can do, sir," a young man in the corner said. His age alone would have been enough to demarcate him as the tech wizard in the room. The shaggy hair and eyebrow ring he wore drove home that assumption.

Despite all that, he was still wearing a suit. It was ill-fitting and the tie was loosened, but it was a suit.

Vance demanded as much from every person in his employ. Regardless of gender or time of day. Regardless of location.

If they were on the clock, they would look the part.

The room was one of several tucked away in the bowels of the Central Intelligence Agency spread outside of the nation's capital. Buried beneath three floors of concrete and soil, no more than a handful of people even knew the meeting was taking place.

Of those, most were present, a trio of people seated around the table before Vance. On his right were Peter Reiff and Dan Andrews. Both in the same age bracket as Vance, they had all started around the same time together.

These two had been brought in by him personally upon ascending to the Special Director seat.

With brown hair and olive skin, Reiff still held the ability to catch the stray glance from a passing female. A fact he was quite proud of, his suit was cut to enhance the effect.

Beside him, Andrews was different in every way, his extra weight causing him to sweat profusely. Taken together, his suit had been reduced to a rumpled mess, his thinning hair plastered to his head.

On the opposite side of the table sat Hannah Rowe, a woman several years their senior. In her early fifties, already her hair was trending toward silver, lines framing her eyes and lips.

Vance might have had to appoint a few females when taking his new position to keep the powers that be in Human Resources happy, but that didn't mean he had to bring on someone that would be a distraction.

Or a temptation.

"Who do we have on the ground there?" Andrews asked.

Vance glanced down to the printout before him but was cut short by Rowe getting there first.

"Ramirez," she said. Nothing more.

Cocking his head back a few inches, Andrews looked to Reiff in his periphery. "Ramirez. Which one is he again?"

Again, Vance began to respond.

Once more, he was cut short, the pattern fast growing to become an annoyance.

"*She* is Manuela Ramirez from Miami," Rowe said. "Thirty-one years old, she is posing as a local graduate student."

"Oh, right," Andrews said, pretending to understand completely.

It was clear from his tone and his expression that he didn't.

"She has joined up with a group calling themselves Libertate Loco," Vance added. "Just another nameless faceless young adult getting swept up in the movement."

There was plenty more he wanted to add. Comments about young people, about political movements, even about females in general. After a year in his post, forced behavior was finally starting to become a habit.

He bit his tongue.

"Probably in the cheap seats," Reiff said. "Might be tough to get much of a view of things."

"Which is why we have a backup in position," Rowe said. Her tone indicated no small amount of disdain, as if she didn't like being challenged. "John Farkus is there as well. He will be looking on from seats with a high vantage point."

"Basically," Vance said, fast growing weary of the conversation, "she's our ears and he's our eyes." Lifting his chin a few inches toward the tech in the corner, he said, "Speaking of which, how are we coming over there? This thing is set to go live in just a few minutes."

If the disjointed feed they were receiving was all that came through, they would make do. It wasn't like it was the first time he'd had to deal with such things.

These were third world countries, after all.

At the same time, if he could survive the ordeal without getting motion sickness, that would be a good thing as well.

Raising a single finger behind him, the tech said nothing. From his stool, all that was visible was his back, a thin trail of brown hair streaming down from the base of his skull.

If Vance had his way, removing the ponytail would have been a condition of hiring. Just like in the good old days, every male would wear their hair high and tight, as he did.

Ponytails would be the only accepted look for females.

Like a great many things, though, Vance had learned to loosen his grip on accepted norms over the years. Trying to classify someone by their haircut simply wasn't acceptable any longer.

The eyebrow ring the young man wore was a different story entirely, something he was fast trying to reach a solution on.

The thought rested at the front of his mind as the tech whirled around. Lifting his feet from the floor, he used the swivel chair to turn back and face them.

A satisfied look was on his features.

"All clear, we are a go."

Chapter Three

Normally the spot would be reserved for the home goal. It would have a metal structure stretched ten yards wide across it, a net draped over it. A series of lines would be scrawled on the grass, demarcating the end line and goalie box.

Bouncing around in front of it would be a long and wiry man with padded gloves, ready to keep any opposition at bay.

Tonight, the space was covered with an impromptu stage. Screwed together with 4x4's and sheets of plywood, it stood five feet off the ground. Ten yards on either edge, a red carpet covered the top surface. A skirt of yellow, red, and blue – the Venezuelan flag colors – was wrapped around the outside of it.

Beefy men in dark suits were spaced every few feet around it, patrolling the empty piece of grass that separated the stage from the crowd outside.

In the center of the stage was a single podium, a pair of microphones extended straight up from it. On the corners sat banks of speakers more than three feet in height.

A single barren flagpole rested beside the podium.

Just a few steps from the staircase leading up to the stage stood

Edgar Belmonte. Tucked into the corner of the stadium, the angle was poor for seeing the full expanse of the crowd on the field, though he had a clear view of the bleachers rising tall on every side.

Exactly as he and Ramon had discussed earlier, the sixteen minutes had been more than enough to fill in any remaining holes.

Not a single empty seat could be seen, the assemblage lit up by the powerful banks of lights lining the top of the stadium.

It was perfect.

"You sure about this?" Giselle Ruiz asked. Standing just a few inches from his shoulder, she had to practically yell to be heard.

On their previous campaign stops, they had approached events as if they were concerts. They had asked someone to serve as a master of ceremonies for the evening. That person had been in charge of keeping the crowd excited, whetting their appetite until Belmonte took the stage.

A few times, they had even used opening acts. Local officials or influential people from the party, anybody that could lend a kind word and a bit of credibility to the proceedings.

Tonight, such an approach had been abandoned.

There would be no sharing the stage. No asking the crowd's excitement to ebb and crest over the course of many hours.

This evening was about Belmonte. Everything before had been a prelude, building name recognition.

"Absolutely," Belmonte replied. Tucking his chin to his shoulder, he asked, "Do you have it?"

Ruiz kept her gaze out to the crowd, a collective buzz seeming to well up from the throng of people before them. Extending one arm his direction, she passed a simple plastic sack into his hand.

There was no outward reaction from Belmonte as he accepted it. There wasn't even the need to open the top and inspect the contents.

He already knew exactly what was there. Two simple items, both procured the day before, carbon copies to the ones they had used for a practice run that very afternoon.

"*Buena Suerte*," Ruiz said, just barely loud enough to be heard.

Belmonte didn't bother to respond. They were well past the point of believing in luck. Instead, he pulled back the cuff of his dress shirt and checked his watch.

It was time.

Chapter Four

There was definitely an energy to the crowd. Even while watching from a conference room three thousand miles away, that much was obvious.

Not that Charles Vance really thought much of it. In his forty-five years, he'd been involved in some capacity with hundreds of political campaigns. Starting with his own father's bid for sheriff in small-town Iowa thirty years prior, the list had grown to span multiple countries on multiple continents.

In that time, he'd seen virtually every possible permutation and compilation of things that a campaign could put together. He'd seen town hall meetings on street corners and heard stump speeches in empty airport hangars.

He'd even seen more than a few stadium events like the one he was now staring at.

And what every last one of them seemed to have in common was energy. Nobody that had ever run for office thought they were going to lose. In fact, many believed their election was a virtual lock.

So certain of it were many of them, they were able to impart that same level of expectancy to those gathered around.

Some would call such a thing optimism.

Vance preferred the term naivete.

Reclined in his high-backed chair, the emotion of the crowd was almost palpable. Broadcast through the camera hidden in the frame of John Farkus's glasses, the masses were spread across the opposite wall.

Not that it really registered with Vance. Energy meant nothing. Energy merely meant that their decision to stay late and monitor the event was vindicated.

Anything less, and he would have been angry he was missing the Celtics game at home again.

"So what are you expecting from this tonight?" Peter Reiff asked.

Vance cocked an eyebrow his way before looking over to Hannah Rowe, waiting for her to interject. A moment later, she did just that.

"Merely monitoring," Rowe said. "Right now Salazar still holds the lead, but the gap is starting to narrow. If Belmonte's going to make a move in time for the election, we expect it will have to happen soon."

Like a spectator in a racket sport, Vance shifted his focus across the table to Reiff and Andrews.

Under his watch, the entirety of South America was split into thirds. Each of the three people before him was tasked with overseeing one of those subsections, all reporting directly to him, who in turn reported to the Director.

From there, it was just a quick call across the Potomac to the White House.

Much higher up the food chain than Vance would have ever imagined, though he'd be lying if he said he didn't savor it every day of his life.

The division of the continent had nothing to do with size or even location, but rather importance level to the agency. Brazil might have been massive compared to the other nations present, but it would never rise to the level of Colombia as far as national interests were concerned.

At the moment, Venezuela was not at the top of the list, but it was rising fast.

Similarly situated to Vance in the pecking order, just a few rungs from the top, if one wanted to think of it in such a way.

"Does the Agency have a particular favorite at this time?" Reiff asked.

Having assigned Venezuela to Rowe long before, Vance was not surprised at the questions being fired her way. Had expected them, even.

"Not yet," Rowe said, "given that right now, Belmonte is still kind of feeling his way forward. He hasn't really taken a stance on any of the major issues yet, just trying to build a platform and get his name out there."

"Trade? Military? Terrorism?" Andrews asked.

Rowe gave a quick turn of the head. Her ponytail twisted to either side behind her.

"So far he's stumped for education and better food access. Neither one amounts to much for us-"

"But in Venezuela, they are paramount," Vance finished for her.

Even with so little information about Belmonte, it would be hard to imagine him not being an infinitely preferable option to Salazar. As the sitting president, the man had been in office for five and a half years now.

No less than five of those had been spent in complete and utter disarray. The value of their currency had plummeted, crime and poverty rates had risen exponentially. Graduation and birth rates were both sliding to their lowest levels in two decades.

As it currently stood, people had been handed identification numbers, their ability to do something as simple as go to the market dictated by the last digit on the number they were given.

To say social revolt was on the horizon might be an overstatement, but not by much. The country was in need of a change. But as was the case in so many instances like it, the question was whether or not they would be able to recognize that for themselves.

And for the people seated in the room, the question was if such a change would align with their own interests.

On the far end of their huddle, Reiff turned toward the screen.

The view from Farkus showed some movement in the stadium corner, the proceedings appearing ready to begin.

"What about Belmonte personally? Anything of note?"

"Nothing we'd be interested in," Rowe said. "Locally born, locally educated, now a local businessman. Basic bootstraps case, a guy trying to get his homeland turned around."

The choice of words was curious, enough to bring a smirk to Vance's face.

Just like the stadium event he was now staring at, such rhetoric also seemed to always accompany campaign events.

And for some reason, no matter how many times the crowds heard the same tired lines, they always seemed to eat it up.

Chapter Five

The night air was warm and moist. Being so close to the equator, rare was the evening when that wasn't the case, even in April. Despite it being now well after nine o'clock in the evening, the temperature still hovered close to eighty. The humidity was even higher than that.

Coupled with the intense heat of the spotlights aimed directly down at him, Edgar Belmonte's body was filmed in sweat. He could feel the cotton of his undershirt clinging to his back.

Even sense droplets of sweat running the length of his hamstrings.

A bright veneer of moisture covered his forehead. Rivulets ran down over his brows, burning his eyes as he stood at the lectern.

The taste of salt was fresh on his lips.

Not once did he dare do so much as raise a hand to wipe it away. To do so would insinuate discomfort, something he refused to allow.

Little by little, he had spent the preceding months getting his name out there. He had started in small pockets, building trust, sitting and having direct conversations.

This was now his chance to launch forward. To take his candidacy to the next level. To let people know they could put their trust in a man that would sit on their couch and listen one day, then go out and advocate to the masses on their behalf the next.

The first twenty minutes of his speech had gone exactly as planned. The crowd had responded where and how it was supposed to.

When he made a joke to open things, a chorus of chuckles had met his ears. When he spoke of the extreme degradation plaguing their citizens, people had reacted in kind as well.

Now it was time to ramp things up. To start slowly building the energy. To bring everyone to the precipice.

Only then could he pull off what he and Ruiz and Ramon had put together, effectively shoving them over the edge.

And propelling his campaign in a way that had never been seen before.

"So far this evening, we have talked about a number of things," Belmonte said. "We have discussed the hardships we are all facing. The reality of having to wait until a certain day of the week to get bread or milk. Of what it's like to wake up and not know when or how we're going to feed our families."

Beyond the glare of the bright lights, there was precious little Belmonte could see. Even at that, a few nodding heads were visible.

"We have touched on our education system. How we are failing our children, not putting them in a position to compete in a world that is fast changing around them."

A murmur of agreement came to him through the darkness. With each word, he could feel his own anticipation rising. More sweat came to his features. His heart rate increased.

"And we even went as far as to mention the rampant crime and poverty that have gripped our society. The one thing we haven't gotten to yet? How this has happened."

The sack Giselle Ruiz had handed him was balled on the ground by his feet. Casting a quick glance down at it, Belmonte felt a well of emotion settle in his stomach.

Flicking his gaze over to the barren flagpole beside him, he saw the pair of gleaming hooks affixed to it, waiting to be used.

And again felt another pang stir within.

"I grew up in this country," Belmonte said. He raised a hand, pointing to the west side of the stadium. "No more than a few miles from where we now stand. When I was a child, we never locked our doors at night. We were never afraid to walk wherever we wanted to.

"We never wanted for a single thing. If we were hungry, we went to the store and got food. Or we stopped at a neighbor's and asked for it. There was plenty to go around. Nobody was in competition. Everybody was happy to help."

Lowering his hand back to the podium, he said, "Now, I don't know about you, but I refuse to believe that all this change has happened here on its own. I cannot fathom that the wonderful, hospitable, beautiful people that I called my friends and neighbors just became this way on their own.

"They were influenced. Little by little, in ways that we didn't even realize until finally, we found ourselves in this position.

"And who was it that did the influencing?"

A host of random words and phrases floated in. Lobbed from every direction, they were tinged with anger, bitterness, some even a touch of sadness.

Not one was the correct answer. Not that he really expected it to be.

That was what made their plan so beautiful. The only way to truly get everybody behind him was to give them all something they could unite against.

And in order to do that, it had to be something that nobody could disagree with.

Bending at the waist, Belmonte let his question hang. Taking up the sack, he lifted it to the podium. The faint sound of a solid object hitting against wood could be heard as he set it down, the top half of the bag resting in a distorted heap.

Reaching inside, Belmonte grabbed at the hem running along one side of the item. Keeping the rest wadded into a tight ball, he pulled it free.

Taking just one step, he used the metal clasps and affixed the item to the flagpole before stepping back, allowing gravity to do its job.

By the time he was back to the podium, the square of material had managed to unfurl.

Revealing the stars and stripes of the American flag.

His hope had been that the sight of it would be enough to elicit an immediate reaction. That just seeing it would bring out a cascade of boos. That people would already be in agreement with him.

The fact that such wasn't the case was alright, though, the crowd seeming more confused than hostile just yet.

Not that that would be a problem. He had already managed to lead the horse to water. Now forcing it to drink would be fairly easy by comparison.

"This," Belmonte said. Curling his wrist back toward his shoulder, he extended a single finger and jabbed it at the flag. "This is what I believe has caused our downfall. Western culture – specifically, *American* culture – with their greed and their bullying and their antagonism.

"The Venezuela today isn't the one we grew up with. It's the one *they* want it to be. The one that's oppressed, that is in need. That can't fend for itself and needs their help."

Each word brought a bit more agreement. Assorted other sounds floated in from the crowd, letting it be known they were following him.

Just as he knew they would.

Belmonte slid a hand into the sack before him. His fingers touched on the only other item inside, the source of the heavy sound he'd heard a moment before.

"And it is my solemn vow that if elected your next president, I will bring an end to such influence. I will make sure that Venezuela's interests are always at the forefront. That our people are the only ones that matter when making decisions.

"And I promise that things like this will not plague us any longer."

The sound of the crowd grew to a deafening crescendo as Belmonte pulled the metal lighter from the bag. Running his thumb down the gnarled flint on the back, he sparked it to life, taking a step toward the flagpole.

The thin polyester material gave no opposition to the flame. In just an instant it was glowing brightly as the crowd cheered with everything it had.

Chapter Six

The heel of Charles Vance's shoe was no longer resting on the corner of the conference room table. Nor was his bottom planted square in the padded seat at the head of the room.

Instead, he was on his feet, standing in front of the enormous screen on the opposite wall. To either side of him, Reiff, Andrews, and Rowe all stood as well.

Standing with his arms folded over his torso, Vance didn't bother looking to any of them. He imagined they all wore the same expression he did – a mixture of shock and concern.

He didn't need to glance over to confirm it.

It wasn't like it would change anything.

This was bad, in a way he could not have imagined. Certainly not in any way he had encountered yet in his time as the Special Director.

Maybe if he dug back into the archives he would be able to uncover something similar that had happened somewhere in the region.

He'd just never heard of it.

The Agency's presence in Venezuela was growing, but it still didn't compare to some of the other countries on the continent. There were no cartels operating in broad daylight, controlling the government and everything else that went on. Nobody was trying to export copious amounts of cocaine or heroin out, most of it bound for Los Angeles or Miami.

Interest was largely predicated on the fact that it was a country that it was in the midst of a political and economic freefall. Interfering with such a thing didn't do much to serve America's interests.

Making sure it didn't turn into the sort of place that could easily become Colombia or worse did.

Monitoring the campaign was something Vance had decided on not long before. At the time, the decision was an easy one to make, even easier to justify.

Whoever was the next president – new or incumbent – would have a large role in how the country was shaped moving forward. Vance wouldn't be doing his job if he didn't know everything he could about the two candidates, including the promises they made along the way.

As any American could easily attest, things said on the campaign trail rarely came to pass in real life, but they did often serve as a starting point.

All of that circled in the back of Vance's head as he stood and stared at the screen. Keeping tabs on the election was necessary, but it wasn't supposed to be difficult.

It damned sure wasn't supposed to be shocking.

"Is that...?" Andrews began, his voice trailing away.

"A burning American flag?" Vance finished. "Yes. Yes, it is."

"And that crowd...?" Reiff asked.

"Eating it up?" Rowe said. "Absolutely."

On the screen before them, the flag was down to just a few loose strands of fabric. Most of the flames had receded to nothing more than glowing cinders. A few melted parts had already fallen to the ground at the base of the flagpole.

Over the years, he'd seen many pictures of the stars and stripes burning, most of them from the Vietnam War era, when such social protest was commonplace. Not once had ever seen one in person.

Never had he ever witnessed one being torched on foreign soil.

Especially by someone seeking the highest office in the land, looking to ascend there by playing on hatred of the western world.

"Has there been any indication of this sort of behavior before now?" Vance asked.

In his periphery, Rowe took a half-step forward. "Never. Like I said, he's a businessman. If anything, he's profited greatly from the global markets."

Under other circumstances, Vance might have smirked at the irony of a man trying to villainize the very thing that had allowed him to be where he was.

"What is the anti-American sentiment like in the region?" he asked.

"No more than anywhere else in the world," Rowe said. "There's some occasional grumblings about greed and such. Nothing that would seem to indicate this sort of rhetoric."

Both of the answers Vance had already known before asking the questions. He just had to make sure he did, and that his three ranking staff heard him do so.

The person he had to call next would ask him the exact same things.

On the screen, the man they were watching turned away from the flag. He raised a fist in the air and began to bellow, the crowd eating up every word he said.

Vance didn't hear a bit of it. Nothing that was said from this point forward greatly mattered anyway.

A line had officially been crossed.

There was no undoing that.

Part Two

Chapter Seven

The files were split into three distinct categories, one each for the trio of hard plastic cases piled on the desk before me.

On the right were the dry flies. Parachute Adams. Stimulators. A few elk hair caddis and foam beetles. Four full rows, all were filled to capacity without being overcrowded and risking damage in transit.

Opposite them on the right were the nymphs. Hare's ear, pheasant tail, and princes, each with their own row.

Set into the space between them were the streamers – my personal favorites. A little larger, they were designed for times when you really wanted to get a trout's attention. Muddler minnows, Mickey Finn, and several woolly buggers, all tied up and ready to go.

In total, it was a collection that a normal person could pick up at most any Sportsman's Warehouse in the greater Yellowstone area for a few hundred dollars. If someone was especially enterprising, they might even be able to find it for half that online somewhere.

For me, it represented more than a week's worth of effort, all of it sitting stooped over my tying station, squinting through a magnifying glass.

Originally tied in anticipation of the spring season, I didn't feel the least bit sorry for deciding to bring them along now. Was reasonably certain my client would feel the same.

Leaning away from the desk, I heard the springs on my desk chair groan beneath me. Giving them no mind, I laced my fingers atop the shaggy hair on my head, admiring my handiwork.

A moment that lasted just a few seconds before being interrupted by the sound of the bell on the front door announcing that I had a visitor.

Flicking my gaze from the spread before me to the door, I listened as heavy footsteps crossed the wooden planks of the front half of the building. Knowing merely by the sound and pace who it would be, I remained motionless as Kaylan Quick appeared in the doorway across from me.

Six years prior, I had moved to West Yellowstone and founded Hawk's Eye Views, a private outdoor guide company. Drawing on the training I had received first from my father, later from the navy, and finally, by the DEA, I had made a second career out of taking people from all over into the nation's largest playground.

In that time, I had hired only a single employee – Kaylan. For the first two years I was in business, most things were done by word of mouth. By extension, that meant finances were tight, at times barely covering what I alone needed to survive.

Over time, word got out and my clientele expanded, allowing me to purchase the building we were now sitting in.

A year later, the need for someone to answer phones and keep my calendar straight had precipitated the need to hire on.

At the time, she was nominally more than that, a local girl in search of work, thankful just to have something to do. In the few years since, both the business and her role had each grown tenfold.

Now if pressed on trying to give her a title, I would probably default to the clichéd Jack-of-all-Trades, a moniker that would include marketing whiz, computer expert, customer service guru, and a host of other things.

Not the least of which, friend.

"Why, hello there."

Kaylan's first response was a huff. The second was dropping the heavy shoulder bag she carried to the floor, the item landing with a thud.

Half a decade younger than me in age, she was freshly thirty, a fact she was still doing a good job of concealing. Carrying a few extra pounds kept her skin clear and full. A pile of curls extended from the back of her head like a blonde pompom.

Dressed for April in the park, she wore jeans and a hooded Montana State sweatshirt. In sneakers, she was just a shade above five feet in height.

"Hello yourself," she replied. She leaned her body against the door frame and folded her arms across her torso. "Nice to see you're here in one piece."

I knew exactly what the veiled reference was alluding to, a situation that I had been pulled into up north in Glasgow a few months earlier. The reports in the aftermath had been appropriately vague to keep any names or incriminating details out, but in a place like Montana, it didn't take long for whispering to occur.

And given that my own cabin had been destroyed in a similar dustup not long before that, it was only natural for my name to get mentioned.

Not that I – or the others involved – would ever confess to such a thing.

"Of course," I replied. "Winters up here aren't as hard as you guys try to make them out to be."

Opening her mouth to respond, Kaylan thought better of it. She settled with a simple nod of her head, a knowing smile on her lips.

Again, a friend.

"Thanks for coming in a week early," I said, shoving the conversation back to the present. "I really appreciate the help."

The look lingered another moment, letting me know she saw what I'd done there, before she waved a hand across her body. "You kidding me? By this time of year, I'm starting to crawl the walls at home. If I have to watch one more episode of *The Price is Right...*"

She didn't finish the thought, though she didn't have to. The previous fall, her mother had moved in with her and promptly commandeered the best seat in the house and the remote control.

At last word, there seemed to be no sign of her relinquishing either in the near future.

"Still," I replied, "spring cleaning and setup isn't exactly the most fun part of our job. I'm sorry I won't be able to lend a hand."

"No worries. Like I said, be nice to get out of the house for a while."

It seemed there was a great deal more she wanted to add but pulled up short.

Family has a way of doing that.

"Take all the hours you need," I replied. "This is all being billed as overtime, so feel free to milk the clock."

Chapter Eight

The sun was sitting at a forty-five-degree angle, exactly between the horizon and high noon. Shining in from the east, it blazed through the windows on the veranda, illuminating the office of Venezuelan president Miguel Salazar.

When he had first taken office, the veranda had been one of his favorite places in the world. Every morning he had taken his Cafecito there. For one solid hour, he would sit and sip it, perusing newspaper offerings from around the globe.

Now, on the heels of all that had transpired in recent years, it was determined by his security staff that presenting himself in the open like that would be a foolish and unnecessary risk.

Which meant he was now resigned to sitting in his desk chair and looking out through the thick plexiglass that had been installed over the windows to protect him.

Like a puppy in a pet shop staring out the window in longing, hoping to one day escape.

Down to the last dregs in his porcelain cup, Salazar pushed it and the saucer it rested on a few inches away. Turning sideways, he lifted his right ankle to his left thigh, his linen pant leg hiking up, revealing bare skin beneath.

If he had a major function that he needed to attend, the full regalia of suit and dress shoes came out. Over time, such events had become less frequent, a combination of both his post and the general apathy of the country as a whole.

In their stead, it was easier to cluster such things together on the same day, meaning that most of the time he was free to dress as he now was.

Linen pants, cotton dress shirt, leather slip-on shoes without socks.

The only acceptable business attire for a place where the temperature and humidity were both perpetually above seventy.

Especially in April, the hottest month of the year.

In his hands, Salazar held a copy of *The Guardian*. Just hours removed from the presses in London, he idly flipped through the pages, reading more of the usual offerings from the first world.

The stock market was continuing to stall in the wake of their exit from the European Union. A gunman had shot three people in a tube station.

On the far end of the room, a door opened and a woman with silver hair and a green skirt suit passed through. With her came a burst of background noise, all of it fading as she quickly closed the door behind her.

Walking on square-heeled shoes, she strode directly to the opposite side of his desk and stopped, a sheaf of papers clutched to her chest.

"Buenos Dias."

Salazar flicked his gaze from the newspaper to see his Chief of Staff standing before him. His own cousin, he had known her since birth, the two having grown up together and spent much of their adult lives working together.

Most people that were close to them assumed they were siblings, their constant company and close semblance making it a likely conclusion.

Both were on the smaller side in stature, standing with exaggerated precision, chests out. Each had thick hair that was once dark and glossy but was now trending toward silver. Both shared smooth olive skin.

The only major difference between them – save fashion sense – was the thin beard Salazar wore along his jaw and framing his mouth.

"Good morning, Isabel. How are you this morning?"

She ignored the question, nodding to the paper in his lap. "How is the news from around the world today?"

As always, she spoke in short sentences, the words clipped. More than once Salazar had thought it was like she was always racing to finish speaking as fast as she could.

Folding up the paper, Salazar sighed and tossed it on the table. "Same old stuff. Economies are hurting, madmen with guns, but people like to say we're the ones that are collapsing."

If she had any opinion on the matter, Isabel kept it to herself, offering only a terse nod. "Have you seen *our* newspaper yet this morning?"

Picking up on something in her voice, Salazar asked, "No, should I?"

"You should," she replied. Pulling a copy from the stack in her arms, she dropped it down onto the desk before him.

His gaze fixed on her for a moment, Salazar shifted his focus down to the newsprint. The way it was folded, he could only make out half the headline stretched across the top, though the picture below it was clear enough. Several inches tall, it was done in color, the subject framed to stare directly up at him.

His opponent, Edgar Belmonte, standing beside a burning American flag.

Again, he flicked his gaze up to her. "What the...?"

Expecting no response, he reached out and slowly unfurled the paper. Once it was expanded to full size before him, he scanned the article quickly, his attention eventually landing in the same place it had started.

On Belmonte standing beside the flag, a hoard of cheering people visible in the background.

"Any idea where this came from?" he asked.

"Sir?"

Gesturing toward the page, Salazar said, "You know, *this*. The burning flag, the anti-American sentiment, all of it."

As he asked the question, he leaned back in his chair, lacing his fingers over his stomach.

Taking the cue, Isabel slid to the side, lowering herself onto the seat across from him.

"Truth? No clue," she said. "We've been monitoring his campaign up until this point, and thus far it's been pretty vanilla. Traditional values, education, the same old stuff."

"Right," Salazar inserted. Still months away from the election, he had kept a very distant eye on what his opponent was doing.

Up to this point, he'd been quite unimpressed. Definitely nowhere near the point of feeling threatened.

This was a different tact entirely.

"Desperation play?" he asked.

"This early?" Isabel asked. "Hard to say, but I doubt it."

Salazar nodded. That would be his best guess as well. Crazy things like this were usually the sort of thing that occurred on the final weekend before polls opened.

To do something so outrageous so early seemed to indicate that Belmonte was going to use it as a platform moving forward.

For a moment, neither side spoke, both processing the information.

"This could be bad," Salazar eventually said.

"Extremely."

Given the weight in her tone and the instant response, he focused on her, unable to miss the signal she was handing him. "What do we know thus far?"

Isabel drew her mouth into a tight line. "Two things. First, we did a quick overnight poll. Just based on this, Belmonte jumped eight points."

Salazar felt his eyes bulge slightly. Eight points more than cut his lead in half. Eight points could make for a much more difficult election than he had anticipated.

That sort of a response to a burning American flag could also signify a starkly different public sentiment than he had realized.

"And the second?"

"We have a call with the White House set for this afternoon."

Chapter Nine

"So why am I here early this year?" Kaylan asked. She had pushed herself away from the doorframe and was now seated in one of the two visitor chairs on the opposite side of the desk from me.

Which effectively meant my office – despite comprising the entire back half of the building – could comfortably accommodate one more individual.

Provided they weren't too large.

Not that such shortcomings had ever had any noticeable effect on my business model.

"And does it have anything to do with the Montana jewelry cases you've got spread out here?"

It took a moment for me to realize she was referring to the fly boxes sprawled wide, their insides arranged in tiered rows. Once it clicked what she was saying, I couldn't help but smile.

"Montana jewelry boxes. Nice, I like it."

Kaylan bowed her head in acceptance of the compliment. "Thanks. Feel free to use it."

"Appreciate it," I said, knowing full well I probably would. "And to answer your question, yes. You remember a guy named Grey Rembert? Did a tour with us summer before last?"

A crease appeared between Kaylan's brow as she stared upward, trying to place the name. "Vaguely? I remember it being the first time I'd ever seen Grey used as a first name, but..."

"Older, heavyset guy from Georgia," I said, hoping to help jog her memory.

Of all the guests we'd ever gotten, Rembert might not have been the most memorable, but he was easily in the top ten.

The instant the word *Georgia* was out, I could see things settle into place for her, eyes going wide. "Oh! Him! The guy that was always saying *hellfire!*"

"Damnation!" I added, both of us bursting into laughter.

Most trips that fall under the guise of being worth recalling do so because they are a miserable experience. A family trying to find themselves in the woods and realizing they still didn't like each other. Folks from a major city wanting to see what it's like to rough it and finding out pretty fast they didn't like it.

People not realizing how damn cold it can get in the park.

Rare was someone like Rembert, a jolly guy that if his name wasn't already distinctive enough would have earned a nickname along the lines of Santa Clause.

"Hot damn!" Kaylan said, slapping at her thigh. "I always liked him. He's coming back up?"

Still quivering with laughter myself, I could feel blood flushing my cheeks. Warmth had passed beneath my sweater, raising my core temperature.

"Not exactly," I replied. "He actually called a few days ago and said he's heading down to Patagonia for a fly fishing trip. Supposed to be some of the best in the world."

"Depends on where you're at," Kaylan said. "Is he going to be in Argentina or Chile?"

To that, I offered only a raising of the eyebrows. When Rembert had first called, I knew about Patagonia only because I had spent an inordinate amount of time with the DEA working in and around South America.

Otherwise, I wouldn't have had the foggiest clue about where it was or what it encompassed.

"Don't give me that," Kaylan said, again waving a hand at me. "We do have schools here in Montana, you know."

Raising my hands to either side in submission, I said, "I didn't-"

"Didn't what?" Kaylan asked. "Didn't think I could read a map?"

Slowly, I lowered my hands. I slid the chair back a couple of inches, putting a bit more space between us, and said, "Easy, I never-"

"Never thought I would know about other places or cultures?" she snapped.

Unsure how to respond, where the sudden burst of vitriol came from, I merely sat and stared. Across from me, Kaylan did the same, holding the pose as long as she could.

Which was about fifteen seconds.

Her face splitting into a broad grin, she resumed her posture in the chair. "Man, it has been a long winter. You're losing your edge."

For a moment, I had no response, merely staring back at her, before slowly pushing out a breath. "Holy hell. I was trying to figure out what just happened there."

"What just happened was you made it too easy," Kaylan said. "Almost took all the fun out of it."

Looking away for a moment, I raised my right hand and dug at the inch-long growth of beard on my chin. The whiskers felt wiry beneath my fingertips as I scratched, making sure not to let her see me smile.

She had gotten me.

But I didn't have to be happy about it.

"My dad was a fisherman," she said. "Always talked about Patagonia, wanting to get down there, but he never made it."

"Ah," I said, my head rocking back slightly in understanding. Knowing better than to offer condolences, that she hated anything of the sort, I pushed ahead. "Well, Rembert is headed there, and apparently had contracted with a company out of Georgia to go with him and act as a guide."

"Oh-kay," she said, drawing the word out to signal she was not quite yet understanding.

Which was pretty much exactly where I was at during this point in the story when Rembert first called.

"And very long story short, they backed out on him at the last second and he needs someone to go with him."

A host of lines appeared around her eyes as she winced slightly. "Ouch, that sucks."

"That's what I told him," I replied.

For a moment, Kaylan cast her eyes over the array of flies spread around us. "But we don't work down there. I'm not even sure we have the proper permits and everything for that."

"I told him that, too."

"And his response?" she asked.

"Said he made sure when setting it up that all the paperwork was transferable. He has everything necessary, just needs someone to go down and do the day-to-day stuff."

Raising her eyebrows, Kaylan said, "*That'll* be fun."

I knew exactly what she was alluding to. More than once she'd had to hear me vent about such days. Hour after hour of listening to terrible stories. Unknotting one leader after another when they couldn't get their casting down. Watching flies I'd spent hours tying get tossed to the winds. Maneuvering the boat through rocky straits.

In terms of those things, Rembert was only a half-step up from most that I encountered.

But at least he was a nice guy about it.

A nice guy with extremely deep pockets.

"So you told him you'd do it?" she asked.

The fact that we were even having such a conversation made the answer to that clear, as was the fact that the question was purely rhetorical.

"Well, it wasn't quite that simple," I replied. "I did play a little hard-to-get."

Arching an eyebrow, Kaylan said, "Yeah? How fat a check are we talking?"

"Morbidly obese."

"Nice. And when do you fly out?"

"First thing in the morning."

Chapter Ten

The Director of the Central Intelligence Agency was a compact man with square shoulders and knees and elbows that all seemed to be jutting out at the same time. Even dressed in a solid grey suit and matching tie, his joints were all easily distinguishable.

As was the scowl that had settled onto his face, a hardened visage shaped like the inverted head of a shovel.

With short cropped steel grey hair and a faint scar on his right cheek, he looked to fulfill every last stereotype of what a former special forces soldier would look like.

And at the moment, all of that was staring fiercely at Charles Vance.

Standing just a few feet away from the closed doors of the Oval Office, the pair was sequestered in a small holding room. An antechamber no larger than the average water closet, they could hear the faint din of office business taking place through the door on one end.

Could hear absolutely nothing through the door on the opposite side, the one that would open for them at any moment, beckoning them forward.

Wedged into the tight space with them was Hannah Rowe, Vance choosing to leave his other two senior personnel behind in favor of the sole one with actual direct knowledge of Venezuela.

Three times in the last twelve hours Vance and Director Horace Joon had been through the events of the rally.

The first was in the immediate aftermath. Joon had listened in silence as Vance relayed the proceedings of the evening. Had stayed that way as he pondered what it might mean.

After a full two minutes of thinking on things, he had then rattled off a litany of questions. The first two were the ones Vance had asked Rowe in the conference room. Content with the responses, a back-and-forth had then opened up about the best way to handle it moving forward.

Less than ten minutes after making the connection, it was agreed by both that a meeting with the president needed to be set for first thing in the morning.

It was also agreed that neither side was especially happy about it.

The second and third trips through the information had been made during the car ride. With both Vance and Rowe before him, Joon had rattled off every question he could think of twice.

A list that included some things that could not possibly be relevant, but Vance knew he had to ask about in the name of saving his own hide should it come to that.

Which everybody hoped it would not.

Standing inside the small room, the pressure seemed to build by the second. Nervous energy rolled from each of them. It filled the small airspace, threatening to blow the doors on either side from their hinges.

Until, mercifully, the door to their left opened. Through it, White House Chief of Staff Max Hemmings appeared and said, "We're ready for you now."

Without another word he disappeared, followed in order by Joon.

Casting nothing more than a quick glance to Rowe, Vance followed third. A moment later, the door closed behind them.

It was the first time Vance had ever been to the White House, let alone near the Oval Office itself. Stepping inside, it had all the familiar trappings one might expect, the Hollywood professionals having done a masterful job of recreating it a hundred times over.

Framed along the back wall was the Resolute desk. On the floor was the presidential seal, standard shades of blue the chosen color scheme.

On the wall was a framed portrait of Thomas Jefferson, a popular choice as the favorite for the sitting president.

In the interior of the room was a pair of sofas facing each other. On either end of them were armchairs, Hemmings staking a claim to one. Opposite him stood President Mitchell Underall.

A contrast in almost every way to the Director, Underall was tall and lanky. Light brown hair was worn long enough to comb to the side. Skin sagged slightly beneath his jawline.

As the trio entered, he stepped forward, shaking each of their hands in turn and exchanging introductions, before motioning to the sofas.

"Please, be seated."

Not until everybody was positioned – Joon on one side, Vance and Rowe on the other – did Underall assume his seat as well.

"Mr. President, thank you so much for meeting with us on such short notice," Joon opened. Per usual, he spoke in a quick cadence, rattling the words off.

"Max here informed me that it was a most urgent matter that demanded my attention," Underall replied. "It is my experience that the CIA doesn't label such things unless it is warranted."

From the opposite side, Vance watched the mutual preening with a slight level of detachment. While never had he intended to rise to his current station, never did he try to deny it either.

Men like him didn't get to where they were without a certain amount of motivation and ego.

That being said, not once had he ever had any wanting of climbing higher, the exchange he was witnessing being a perfect example why.

Every account he had ever heard sold President Underall as a reasonably likable man. More than once in his five years in office, he had been an ally to the Agency.

Which was to say, he didn't offer too much resistance, followed their advice, and provided cover where he could.

Again, a reasonably likable man.

Even as such, never would Vance be able to arrive hat in hand on a weekly basis to deliver a briefing or ask some sort of favor. It just wasn't in his makeup.

"No," Joon agreed. "And we know you are a busy man, so we'll be brief. Charles, would you please?"

Having been warned beforehand that the floor would be his, Vance jumped directly in. He stated everything in a short and orderly fashion, beginning with why they were monitoring the event and finishing with the spectacle of the flag burning for all to see.

As he spoke, not a single person in the room gave a reaction of any kind.

Clearly, everybody had been prepped ahead of time, his delivery of the information merely a formality so that everybody was on the same page.

More of the necessary box checking that seemed to fill government work.

The first two questions Underall asked were the same two that Vance and Joon both had, referencing Belmonte personally and if there was any prior mention of America. When both of those turned up negative, he shifted gears slightly.

"What has been the reception of the event in the time since?" he asked.

"His numbers have climbed eight points," Vance said.

"Which puts him where?" Underall asked.

Turning his chin toward Rowe, Vance deferred in silence to her expertise.

"That takes President Salazar's lead from fifteen points down to seven," she stated.

For the first time since their arrival, Underall gave some form of visible reaction. His eyebrows raised as a low, shrill whistle from his lips. "Down to single digits? Just like that?"

Vance knew exactly how the president felt.

It was the same initial reaction he'd had as well.

"Belmonte also has rallies scheduled for tonight and tomorrow night," Vance said. "Our team believes that this was meant to be the jumping off point for his campaign."

"Spearheaded by introducing a new platform of blaming America and burning our flag," Underall said.

More a statement than a question, Vance chose to respond anyway. "It would appear that way, sir."

Shifting his focus from the Agency officials to Hemmings on the far side, Underall raised his hands to his face. He rubbed both palms over his cheeks vigorously, and by the time he lowered his hands, both showed bright pink.

"You mentioned that we have a call set up with President Salazar later this afternoon, right?"

"That is correct," Hemmings said. "Three o'clock."

"Three o'clock," the president repeated. "That gives us just over six hours to figure out exactly what we want to say to him."

For another moment, he and Hemmings sat in silent conversation, matching each other's gaze, before Underall turned to face the Director. "I assume you folks have some suggestions on the best way to proceed?"

Chapter Eleven

The previous evening had been a raucous one. After the events in the stadium, it had taken more than two hours for the cheering crowd to disperse.

Another two before Edgar Belmonte and his team were able to be whisked away.

Forced to hole up in the underbelly of the stadium, the time had been split into two equal parts. The first was a celebration of sorts. Food was brought in. Jackets and ties were stripped. Congratulations and handshakes were offered all around.

It was still early, too early to truly be counting the night as a major step toward victory, but there was no denying the effect that the display had had on the crowd.

The goal had been to get a solid visual. To get some energy from the crowd and translate that into a platform they could build on moving forward.

What they had gotten was a full-fledged launching pad for the next few months.

Once the initial euphoria had worn off, the tone of the room had tempered slightly. Empty food cartons were shoved to the side. The chalkboards in the locker room were put to good use.

They had momentum. It was important not to squander it.

The event was the first in a trio that was planned, the week meant to launch Belmonte into the national consciousness. Having achieved that goal on the first outing, they needed to recalibrate on the fly.

Already they had what they were after. Now it was time to go bigger, bolder.

By the time the crowd was finally gone, the chanting falling mercifully silent, the team filed home bleary-eyed and weary. Six hours later, they were back at campaign headquarters, ready to start another day.

As ready as six pots of coffee could make the small contingent crammed into the meeting room in the back of the office anyway.

Seated at the head of the table was Hector Ramon, a pair of clipboards spread before him. On either one was scads of blue ink, a hundred different thoughts and ideas jotted down on every bit of available space.

As people filed in, he sat pouring over them, intently committing everything he could to memory.

To his right was Giselle Ruiz, making an impassioned effort to speedread every newspaper article she could. One atop another they were stacked in front of her, the tip of her finger skimming each one as she passed through.

Every few seconds, the slap of a new paper joining the stack could be heard.

Not once did she bother to even look up at the haphazard pile.

Filling in the remainder of the seats stretched wide in either direction were a handful of aides and staff. Some had been present the night before. A few of the more junior in the room had managed to slide their way in that morning, no doubt anxious to be a part of whatever was about to take place.

Standing in the doorway, his shoulder leaning against the frame, Edgar Belmonte couldn't begrudge them in the slightest. The events of the previous evening had been a powder keg. It was only natural for them to want to get their piece of it.

Just as it was only natural that he drew all the labor he could from them in the process.

Casting a glance at the opposite wall, he saw it was now exactly eleven o'clock. Taking a half step forward, he pulled the door shut behind him, letting the rattle of the frame call the room to attention.

At once, any residual conversation bled away. Every head turned his direction.

"*Buenos Dias,*" he said. "Thank you all for being here today after such a late night." Pausing, he let a slight smile cross his face, "Though if ever there was a day to get in early, this would be it."

To that, several smiles appeared around the room. Bright white teeth glimmered against tan skin.

"For those of you that weren't on hand last night, I'm sure you've all read the recaps in the papers. As I haven't yet seen many of them, I trust they are going well, Giselle?"

"Beautifully," Ruiz said from her spot in the corner. "Better than we could have ever hoped for."

For a moment, Belmonte said nothing. He merely let the words resonate in his mind. Allowed them to pass through his body, filling it with warmth.

The move had been calculated for sure, but it was still a bit of a risk.

For it to have played out so well was something he never would have imagined.

Turning back to the room, he said, "Which gives us all the more reason why we need to be sure to capitalize on it. This has given us a tremendous start, but we can't let that energy dwindle."

Around the room, a couple of heads began to nod.

Again flicking his gaze to the clock on the back wall, he said, "In exactly three hours, we will all be boarding our caravan bound for Maracay. Tonight is the second in a trio of stadium visits planned, this one slated to hold almost twenty thousand people.

"Last night was a start, but this will be what truly puts us on the map."

Pausing, he again measured the people sitting before him.

Just like the crowd the previous evening, all were leaning forward, eagerness and anticipation practically seeping from their pores.

"Last night, we began preliminary discussions on how to best do that, but I want to take some more time here this morning to open the floor back up. Any suggestions you might have for how to proceed moving forward, how to really make a splash, throw them out there now.

"Remember, no idea is too big or small, and nothing is off-limits."

Chapter Twelve

The trio of fly boxes were snapped shut and stowed, just three more items in the jumble of equipment that was piled high beside the door in my office. Taking up the sole bit of open floor space between a bookshelf containing every book ever published on Yellowstone and the chair Kaylan had sat in earlier, the mass was quite the eyesore.

Even if it was just for the afternoon.

Crossing from the front half of the building – where the desk and reception area were – into the office, it was quite jarring. An immediate reminder that things were out of place, like a family portrait that had suddenly gained a few extra people.

Holding a cup of the radiator fluid that doubled as coffee in our establishment, I scanned the jumble of equipment for the fifth time. One item at a time, I tried to determine if it was necessary.

After each piece was indeed deemed vital, I then tried to make sure that what I had was sufficient for the trip.

Eight days on the water, after all, was a hell of a long stretch.

"You're worse than a woman packing for vacation, you know that?"

A smile came to my face, the only reaction I gave as I continued to stare at the gear. The source of the voice I didn't need to turn to see, knowing Kaylan's tone well enough to recognize it anywhere.

How she had managed to appear behind me without my hearing it I wasn't sure, chalking it up to being deep in thought on my travel checklist.

"You realize the sum total of that heap that's actually mine is about a third of a duffel bag, right?" I asked.

"Great, so you'll be the smelly guy on the plane ride back, huh?" Kaylan countered.

The smile in place grew a bit larger. Based on the feistiness she was now unloading on me, it *had* been a long winter.

Not that she was especially wrong.

"I'll be returning from eight days of fishing. If I come back smelling like a basket of roses, it means the trip was a failure."

Behind me, I could hear Kaylan snort. "Or that you'd have some serious explaining to do."

To that, I cocked an eyebrow and looked over my shoulder, an impish grin on Kaylan's face.

"And while I'm sure you have a wicked retort all lined up for me, Rembert's on hold for you."

Keeping the look on my face a moment longer, I raised my coffee to her in salute. Taking a step forward, I swung the door closed behind me before heading toward the desk.

Finishing the last of the thick sludge in my cup, I tossed it into the wastebasket and lifted the receiver from the phone. With one finger, I pressed the glowing red button letting me know a call was waiting and fell back into my chair.

"Mr. Rembert."

"Hawk! Damnation, how are you, my friend?" Just as was the case when speaking in person, the volume used was several decibels louder than necessary.

I held the phone to my ear just long enough to reply, "I'm good, and yourself?" before pulling it away.

An instant later, it was proved to be a solid choice for the future of my auditory health.

"I'm more wound up than a dog with two dicks," Rembert

boomed. "So damned excited to get down on the water, I can barely hold my piss."

Unsure how to even begin unpacking the amount of imagery packed into the two sentences, I opted to not even try.

The last time we had spent time together had proven how futile such an attempt could be.

As an angler, the man was passable at best. Any skill he lacked was more than compensated for by extreme enthusiasm and a willingness to lend a hand wherever he could.

Two things that were in far shorter supply than one might expect.

"I'm excited as well," I replied. "First time down that way to catch fish."

Which was, technically, the truth. I'd spent plenty of time in Argentina and Chile over the years. As a member of one of the preeminent FAST – Foreign Deployed Advisory and Support Team – groups working out of the American Southwest, I'd been in and out of the region more times than I could remember.

If I hadn't decided to walk away when I did, Lord only knew what the count would be up to by now.

"Hellfire, me too!" Rembert said. "Once I got back from Yellow-stone, everybody I knew said that was the place to go."

"That's what I've always heard."

"Good, good," Rembert said, his voice trailing slightly. Already it was clear the man had called for little more reason than to have someone to share his eagerness with, though I decided not to stifle his moment.

For the rate he was paying me, a little awkward phone time was a reasonable trade-off.

"Welp!" he said after a moment, his voice again causing me to wince. "I will see you at Atlanta International in the morning?"

"I'll be there."

Chapter Thirteen

T he seating arrangement inside the Oval Office was an exact copy of the previous meeting. President Mitchell Underall took the chair at the head of the group, his back just a few feet from the front edge of his desk.

Seated eight feet away was his Chief of Staff Max Hemmings. With his legs crossed and his gaze averted, it was obvious that his role was merely as an observer.

The look on his face hinted that even that was more than he really wanted.

Split to either side on the sofas between them were the contingent from the Central Intelligence Agency. Director Horace Joon again chose to go solo, sitting to the left. Across from him sat Charles Vance and Hannah Rowe, each looking about as comfortable as Hemmings beside them.

The second gathering of the day thus far, it was the culmination of a sequence of events that had escalated quickly. What had started as viewing a long-distance campaign event the night before had turned into a meeting with the highest-ranking official in the country just a few hours later.

Now, it had progressed even further, becoming an international ordeal.

How Charles Vance felt about that, he wasn't yet completely certain. On one hand, the events could be a serious boon for his career. If there turned out to be a real threat in the form of Edgar Belmonte, his quick and decisive action would be praised endlessly.

It was, after all, government work. No victory, no matter how small, ever went without receiving proper recognition.

By the same hand, if it turned out to be a false alarm, that too would be deposited at his feet. Taking the blame was not the sort of thing men like the Director of the CIA or the President of the United States ever did unless they absolutely had to.

And Vance was under no illusion that his presence was for any other reason than making sure they didn't have to.

The only difference in the office since their prior meeting was an ovular coffee table that had been positioned between the sofas. Recently polished, it had a bright gleam and the faint smell of cleaning solution.

On it sat a handful of water glasses and a speakerphone, a series of red lights already glowing on its face.

Having arrived five minutes before the hour, every person sat in silence, avoiding eye contact, until the shrill sound of a paging tone was emitted. Jerking the focus of every person toward the phone, Underall reached out and pressed a single button.

"Mr. President, I have President Salazar on hold for you."

The voice was female, so mechanized Vance couldn't tell if it was real or another of the new automated phone assistants.

Not that it mattered either way.

"Put him right through," Underall said. A moment later, a single ring could be heard before he again pressed the same button. "President Salazar, how are you?"

Despite the grim look on his face, the question was asked with plenty of faux buoyancy.

"I am quite well, my friend, and how are you?" Salazar replied.

Despite being the Special Director for South American Operations, Vance had nothing more than a passing familiarity with Salazar.

While it was true his country was in the midst of a tragic backslide, they had also done nothing prior to elevate them to the status of being an active threat.

Had they been speaking to the President of Colombia, Vance would have been able to recite a full resume from memory.

For this particular meeting, it had taken quite a bit more brushing up.

"Well," Underall said, "as I'm sure you're aware, there was an incident down your way last night that we're a little bit concerned with."

After delivering the line, Underall glanced to each of the people in the room. He didn't bother adding anything further, a standard move to see if Salazar would seize the bait.

To Vance's surprise, he did.

"I assume you are referring to my opponent Edgar Belmonte and his little display," Salazar replied. Bitterness seemed to bely his words. "And you're right, I was made aware of this first thing this morning."

"Mhmm," Underall said. "So I don't think I need to point out then how concerning we find this."

This time, a moment passed. Long enough for Vance to glance between Joon and the president before returning his focus to the speakerphone.

"No," Salazar eventually said, "you do not. I would feel the same way in your position. But I can assure you, this was nothing more than a campaign stunt."

"That may be," Underall replied, "but we're not so much worried about it as an isolated incident as what it could escalate to. You know as well as I that once anti-anything sentiment takes hold in a country, it's a tough thing to reverse."

Beside him, Vance could see Rowe's fingernails grow white as she pressed them into the sofa between them. It was the same reaction he'd had.

The words were formulated carefully, delicately even, but the sentiment behind them was pretty clear.

For a decade, groups like the Taliban or Al Qaeda had based their existence on mining hatred for the United States. In recent years, ISIS had managed to take that to an entirely different level.

Never before had such a thing surfaced in Venezuela, but that did not mean the United States would not be proactive in keeping it that way.

"I can understand your concern," Salazar said, "but I assure you, no such thing exists in this country. Times are hard here right now, but my people are not the kind to point a finger or assign blame.

"The United States has nothing to worry about."

Chapter Fourteen

T he night before had been beautiful. A mid-air collision of luck, timing, and perhaps even a bit of magic, it had gone so much better than Edgar Belmonte could have ever imagined.

The key was that they had not tried to do too much too soon. They had started small. Spoon fed the crowd a concept and allowed them to come around on it by themselves before hitting them with a visual they could take back to their friends and family the next day.

And even at that, they didn't try to do too much.

There were no giant video screens, no fireworks bursting in the night sky. Certainly not a bloody spectacle, or even a single human face to attach to things.

Nothing more than a simple square of fabric and a lighter.

And just like that piece of fabric, the country had found itself ignited. Every radio station, every newspaper, every television program was showing it on loop.

Belmonte was even willing to bet that most of the people on the street had spent the day rehashing it.

Which was exactly the point. His entire campaign was predicated on being a man of the people. On lifting up the native sons and daughters of Venezuela and making them realize that their plight was through no fault of their own. They were merely victims of a larger force than they could ever imagine.

And it would have to be someone just like them to help elevate them above that influence.

The Estadio José Pérez Colmenares in Maracay was much smaller than the previous night. Officially listed at holding just over fifteen thousand, the grounds had been opened up for seating, allowing them to cram in an additional five thousand.

Unlike the sprawling expanse of the prior soccer facility, this one was designed for baseball, giving the entire affair a much more intimate feeling.

Standing on the stage positioned just over home plate, Belmonte stood with his back to the home bleachers. To either side, people seemed to be looming close.

In the air was a charge that was unmistakable, a clear response to the night before already starting to take hold. What had started as something of testing the waters was already proving to have a positive effect.

No doubt the trajectory for their entire campaign was going to be evolving on the fly with it.

"Sons and daughters of Venezuela," Belmonte said. More than halfway through his talk, his brow was saturated with sweat. His eyes were beginning to burn from the glare of the overhead lights.

Neither so much as registered with him.

"I trust that by now many of you have seen what happened last night. Some of you might have even shown up today hoping for an encore."

Pausing, he assessed the crowd.

It was clear his words were correct. Whether many of those in the audience had come wanting to support him or merely to see a spectacle was something he would concern himself with later.

Right now, all that mattered was they were present, their energy palpable.

"To that, I must confess I am sorry, but there will be no flag burning here this evening."

A slight groan could be heard. He pushed right on despite it.

"And the reason for that is, I don't want this to become about burning flags or outlandish behaviors," Belmonte continued. "My point last night was not to create a scene, but to share with you all something I strongly believe.

"The problems of our country are through no fault of our own. They are the result of outside influences, and if we are going to rise above them, we must break free from that presence."

A series of whoops and calls went up from the crowd in response. Enough that it sparked a few more, a swell starting to take hold.

It was time.

"Which is why this afternoon, as I was standing in my office, trying to figure out the best way to convey that message to you all, I had a realization. I took a good, long look at myself in the mirror, and I had an epiphany right then and there."

Pausing, Belmonte took a half-step back from the podium before him. He raised his right foot and peeled off his shoe. In turn, he did the same with his left.

Gripping them both by the heel, he held them at shoulder height for all to see.

"I realized that the very shoes I was wearing were manufactured in New York City."

Spreading his fingers wide, he let the shoes fall to the stage floor.

The gesture was rewarded with a spur of cheers as he shrugged his shoulders, the suit coat he wore sliding down over them.

"And this suit. I checked the label and found that it was produced by a company in Los Angeles."

Around him, the night air became electric. People seemed to edge closer as he peeled away the garment and tossed it into a heap atop the shoes.

Their calls became louder. The intent behind them more pointed.

Seizing on that vigor, Belmonte grabbed for his tie, pulling the perfect knot he'd folded an hour before from his neck.

"And I realized what I was wearing around my neck wasn't a tie. I realized that it wasn't even a piece of cloth. What I realized was this thing, this item made in Miami and sent down here, was nothing more than a noose."

Again, the crowd responded just as he had anticipated. Standing barefooted and in shirtsleeves, he had but a precious few seconds. Nothing but a few instances to make one final point before the place erupted, swallowing up any chance at him being heard again.

"Nothing more than a symbol for us to wear around our necks every day. A visual reminder of their control over our lives.

"Well, I say that ends now! I say no more, from this day onward!"

Chapter Fifteen

President Miguel Salazar's day had started twelve hours earlier. At the time, he had had no reason to believe it was going to be anything out of the ordinary.

His schedule was clear, allowing him to dress in his preferred attire. The morning coffee was hot and fresh, the spring sun warm without being oppressive.

Then, Isabel had arrived with the morning paper and news that a meeting had been set with the President of the United States for later in the afternoon.

And things had just spiraled from there.

Raising his left wrist, Salazar checked the face of his watch to realize that half the day had passed since then. The sun that had shined so bright was now a distant memory.

The dinner his wife had planned for them was just another set of canceled plans he would be forced to apologize for.

In their stead, the half-eaten remains of a plate of rice and beans rested on his desk beside him. A few feet away, an untouched plate of the same sat in front of Isabel.

On the opposite corner of the desk, a third plate was completely clean, scraped free of even the slightest residue. Two feet beyond it sat the man that had taken down the meal with aplomb, General Renzo Clega.

Far removed from the front lines, it took nothing more than a glance to understand the empty plate before him. More than twice the width of Isabel, his form seemed to wobble on the narrow chair beneath him.

In his early fifties, his hair and mustache were dyed coal black, the color made even more pronounced by his ruddy cheeks.

Dressed in an ill-fitting uniform, he had kept his napkin from dinner, using it to wipe sweat from his face.

"And that was all that was said?" Clega asked.

"Yes," Salazar replied. "A few veiled comments, but nothing that would rise to the level of an outright threat."

Salazar had listened to the recording of his conversation with President Underall more than a dozen times since hanging up. Each time he had strained for some hint of overt hostility. Something that would make his next step an easy decision.

And each time, it had been just as he'd reported to Clega.

A whole lot of innuendo, but nothing more. The sort of thing the American was famous for.

Saying a great deal without actually saying anything at all.

"I see," Clega said. Nodding, he ran the napkin along the side of his neck. The look on his face appeared to intimate queasiness. "But you seem to think otherwise."

Salazar flicked his gaze to Isabel. Received just the tiniest of nods in return.

"I do. Edgar Belmonte might not be affiliated with us, but he is still looking to incite violence – or at the very least hatred – on the heads of Americans.

"There's no way they can let that stand."

In his five years in office, Salazar's dealings with Underall had been virtually non-existent. Given the state of affairs in his own country, there had been little reason to extend much effort beyond their own borders.

And as Venezuela posed little advantage to the western world, they had been largely ignored by the outside powers.

Still, not once had he ever deluded himself into believing that wouldn't change quickly if the need arose.

"No," Clega said. "Given their interaction with other parties around the globe, they'll want to be especially certain not to allow another faction to pop up against them.

"If ISIS has taught them anything, no movement is too small to become a thorn in their side."

Turning his chair sideways, Salazar nodded. Just that afternoon, he'd had that exact thought, the reality of it putting them in a very peculiar situation.

"So we agree they didn't come out and say anything overt," he said. His tone indicated he was thinking out loud more than engaging in conversation, the other two recognizing it and remaining silent. "And we also know they won't sit back and allow things to escalate."

For a moment, nobody spoke. Each thought on things in silence, superimposing what they knew with what they suspected.

The cumulation of which didn't seem really appealing to Salazar.

"General, I asked you here this evening for your counsel, and because if something were to arise, you would be our first line of defense."

To that, Salazar added nothing more, allowing Clega to infer the rest.

Nodding slightly, the general seemed to do just that. He pressed his lips tight, taking a moment, before tilting the top of his head to either side.

"With all due respect Mr. President, I think you are right once, but wrong twice."

A tiny flare of animosity rose in Salazar. It was not often that such things were said to him, especially while sitting in his office.

Flicking his gaze to Isabel, he saw a similar look of surprise cross her features.

Just as fast, they both squelched the reaction. They had asked the general there for his advice. They at least needed to hear him out, even if they did later choose to ignore it.

"Please," Salazar said. He extended a hand and waved his finger toward himself, signaling for Clega to continue.

Clearing his throat, Clega adjusted his bulk on the chair, the wood straining slightly.

"I think you are correct in that the Americans will not let this go. They have never been a country to employ a wait-and-see approach, and their style of diplomacy is something akin to – what is the expression – a bull in a China shop."

One corner of Salazar's mouth flickered as he nodded in assent. The words weren't exactly what he would have chosen, but there was no way to even insinuate that they were wrong.

Never had he heard the Americans accused of being overly delicate.

"But I think you are incorrect if you believe my men will be the ones to deal with it," Clega continued. "If past history is any indicator, they will not use full military force. To do so would be ugly, would provide too much fodder for their eager media."

Aligning points in his head, Salazar could see where Clega was going.

And that he was right.

"So they'll bring in a small contingent," he said. "Look to nudge things in their favor without making a big deal out of it."

"Nudge might be a bit of an understatement," Clega said, "but yes, that is what I believe."

Again, Salazar glanced at Isabel.

Again, his cousin nodded in agreement.

The logic was solid. In the wake of the earlier call, he had waffled between incredulity and uncertainty, which had clouded his thinking. Hearing it now laid out so clearly, things were pretty obvious.

"And the second thing I was wrong about?" Salazar asked.

To that, Clega's first response was a thin smile. Leaning forward, he rested his elbows on his knees before looking to Isabel and Salazar in turn.

"The second is thinking that our only course of action here is purely as a response."

Chapter Sixteen

The feed coming up from South America was a bit better, though the mood in the room was no less somber than it had been a night before. Whereas in that meeting, Charles Vance had been the centerpiece of the proceedings, this time he was relegated to the sidelines.

Nothing more than an observer as President Underall and Director Joon stared at the blank television monitor. Wheeled into the office for that specific purpose, the video transmission had ended a few minutes prior, though nobody had said a word.

The events of the previous night were unmistakable. Burning a flag bore a symbolism that was universal. There was no greater representation of a country than its colors.

No greater disrespect than to burn them in effigy.

Tonight was a different tenor. It didn't only speak of deep-seated animosity for America as an ideal. Lashing out at the products it produced and exported was a clear casting aside of everything it stood for.

And if the crowd reaction was any indicator, it was a notion that everybody present seemed to be in full agreement with.

"Well now, that was..." President Underall began, seeming to search for the proper word. "Something."

Seated in the same chair he'd used for most of the day, he had one leg folded across the other. His blue suit showed a few wrinkles behind the knees, but was otherwise unmarred.

"It was," Joon agreed, if only so that somebody responded to the comment.

Flicking a glance between the two men, Vance then looked to Hemmings and Rowe, finding both to be staring at the table. Each looked to be intensely avoiding eye contact at all costs.

They had officially reached the point in the day where giving advice and collecting information was over.

It was now time for the senior officials in the room to make decisions and everybody else to carry them out.

"Tell me, what was the reaction tonight versus last night?" Underall asked.

Tracking his focus to Joon, Vance waited until the Director matched the look, only then realizing that the question had been aimed in his direction.

"The crowd was smaller," Vance said. "This was a baseball stadium, so it didn't hold near as many people. At the same time, this was a markedly different demographic."

The president shifted slightly. He propped an elbow on the arm of the chair and rested his chin on his palm.

"Go on."

"Last night," Vance continued, "they were catching everybody by surprise. Nobody showed up expecting anything more than a standard speech, so you had – to put it bluntly – a standard crowd.

"Older folks, families with children, your average voting demographic."

All of this he had gleaned from extensive conversations with both Manuela Ramirez and John Farkus in the wee hours of the morning, his two assets inside the stadium.

"And you have to consider the element of surprise. They weren't expecting a damning statement like that, so it took a while for everybody to realize what they were seeing."

"Right," Underall said. "And tonight brought out the crazies. They were looking for a show, and he gave them just that."

Vance nodded. "Which begs the question..."

"What happens tomorrow night," Joon finished, seizing back control for their side of the table.

Content to let him do just that, Vance slid his attention to Underall. He watched as the president debated things in silence, wrapping his mind around what they knew.

Which was that a situation had gone from non-existent to escalating quickly in record time.

"When he has his third speech in as many nights scheduled in the nation's capital," Underall muttered.

"In a stadium as large as the first two combined," Joon said.

The looks and tones used by the men brought a tangle of emotions of Vance. To the positive, their trepidation validated his decisions and swift actions.

To everyone's detriment, it presented a very contentious situation they all were now forced to deal with.

Removing his chin from his palm, Underall extended his left arm before him. Folding it back at the elbow, he checked his watch.

"Okay, it is now half past nine. If we're going to do something, we have to get moving. Give me the full list of options once more."

Already they had been through the list twice, but the latest stunt by Belmonte had elevated things tremendously. What had previously been a conversation in the ethereal was now as real as the room they were sitting in.

"Option A," Joon said, "we do nothing. We continue to monitor the situation, hope for the best."

Vance knew that not a single person in the room put even a tiny bit of faith in such an approach. Just as the president had said to Salazar that afternoon, once anti-anything sentiment was implanted, it never managed to recede.

If they allowed Belmonte to continue on this path, they would be forced to deal with it at one point or another.

The only question would be how large it had gotten by that time.

"Option B," Joon said. "A press assault. We go on the airwaves and attack Belmonte and his rhetoric. We offer support to Salazar and his regime and trust that will be enough to stem this thing."

This one Vance recognized as Joon merely going through the motions. There was no way the Director had any interest in such an approach, but he had to at least mention it before going forward with the third option.

"And Option C?" Underall asked.

Raising his eyebrows, Joon said, "Option C is, we do something a bit more proactive."

Part Three

Chapter Seventeen

Five years ago, I lost my wife and daughter.

Actually, a more accurate way of putting things would be to say, my wife and daughter were forcibly taken from me.

By the hired henchman of a Russian drug czar I didn't even realize my DEA team and I were investigating.

I don't bring that up to try and invoke sympathy or to demand that any amount of leeway be given to me. At thirty-six years old, I am responsible for my own actions.

More than a year ago, I finally tracked down the men that killed my family. In the ultimate of ironies, I wasn't even looking for them. Rather, they came looking for me.

And I'd venture to say the outcome was surprising to everybody involved.

Again, that's not the point of things. Neither the beginning nor the ending is the reason why I bring up the event, but rather the five years that transpired in between.

After burying my family, I spent two months in what the DEA deemed a *mandatory paid leave*, which was the nice way of saying they refused to accept my resignation until enough time passed that they knew I was serious about it.

If all the days I spent staring alternately at a bottle of Jim Beam and a loaded Glock 19 were any indicator, I was.

Luckily for me, I didn't succumb to either one.

What I did do was trade in my badge and cash out the meager retirement savings I had. Went north to Yellowstone and translated the decade of government training I had into a profitable business.

And did everything I could to stay as far off the grid – and away from social interaction – as I could.

There are still plenty of times when I have to put on the face and go through the motions. I wouldn't be worth much as a guide if I couldn't act pleasant and smile at all the appropriate moments.

Over time, I've even learned to let my guard down enough to pal around with Kaylan. But that doesn't change the fact that there's a reason my off-season home is a one-room cabin eight miles outside of a Montana town of just over three thousand people.

All meaning that for a man like me, stepping off an early morning flight into the Hartsfield-Jackson Atlanta International Airport is only a step up from being in hell.

Even at nine-thirty in the morning, the place was a veritable zoo. Food courts and shopping options beckoned from every available inch of floor space. People were lined fifteen deep to get their daily shot of liquid caffeine.

Frazzled parents and screaming children seemed to have been ordered in bulk and positioned in every empty seat.

With my travel duffel on one shoulder, I walked through the terminal, the world a cacophony of sound and energy around me. Setting my jaw, I let the look on my face part the crowd before me, leaving it in place until the very last possible moment.

At which point I let it fall away, replaced by a smile I only hoped appeared sincere.

"Mr. Rembert," I said, finding my client perched on a stool that was entirely too small for a man his size. One of just a handful of clients in the makeshift sports bar, a plate of eggs and bacon was on the table beside him.

The last remains of a Bloody Mary was in his hand.

Upon hearing his name, the man turned in surprise, the look

lasting for just a moment before recognition set in. Dropping the glass back to the bar, he stood, extending both hands before him.

"Damnation! Hawk!" he said. He clasped both hands around my right, his enormous paws enveloping it completely and shaking vigorously. "So good to see you."

Turning toward the bar, he said, "See, this is the guy I was telling you about."

A few feet away, a middle-aged woman in a white dress shirt and auburn curls gave me a quick once-over. Seeing the beard and shaggy hair, she offered a dismissive shrug and said, "What'll it be?"

Whether the clear disinterest was a product of my appearance or just annoyance with Rembert, there was no way of knowing.

Probably fair to say, a little of each.

"Oh, you've got to have a Bloody Mary," Rembert said. "Got to."

"Oh, no thanks," I replied. Not once in my life had I ever had one, the last minutes before a fifteen-hour flight not seeming like the best time to start.

Never mind the fact that it was still technically breakfast time.

"Mimosa?" Rembert asked. "A beer, maybe?"

Already I could tell it was going to be a long eight days.

"Cranberry juice," I said, the woman again shrugging before setting off to fill my order.

Her disdain was palpable.

"So," Rembert said, slapping a heavy hand against my shoulder as he lowered himself to his seat, "how was your flight?"

"Early," I replied. Sliding my bag from my shoulder, I took the stool beside him.

"Yeah, sorry about that," Rembert replied. "The only other option would have been for you to come in last night, and with short notice and all..."

"No worries," I said. "I had to be around yesterday to help my partner get things up and running for the season anyway."

I didn't. Kaylan was more than capable of handling everything at this point, but there was no need to tell him that.

We were about to be spending eight solid days together.

And I actually did like the man. I just needed to get out of Atlanta and back to someplace a little more my speed.

Someplace with trees and water and a whole lot of silence.

Or at least a lot less people.

Lifting his fork, Rembert pushed around the last scraps of his breakfast as my cranberry juice arrived. Nodding thanks, I took a sip as he thought better of eating any more and shoved his plate away.

"I don't know about you," he said, "but I could barely sleep last night. It was like I was six years old waiting for the swimsuit edition again."

Considering that my night had been about three hours of rest in a cheap hotel outside the Bozeman airport, my experience had been a bit different.

But I knew the feeling he was referencing intimately well. The winter had been long and hard, as most tended to be in Montana. Living the way I do necessitates a certain level of being outdoors, but there comes a point when the wind chill forces one inside.

As winter had chosen to linger a bit longer than usual this year, it was only in recent weeks that I'd really been able to get out and about again.

Which meant that I was aching for the activity and climate a trip to Patagonia promised.

"Yeah?" I asked.

"Hellfire," he said. "Just think, by this time tomorrow, we'll be two guys in the middle of nowhere, just enjoying the moment. Can you imagine anything better?"

At the instant, just getting out of the Atlanta airport would have been a welcomed respite.

Though what he was talking about didn't sound all that bad either.

"No sir, I really can't," I conceded.

Chapter Eighteen

Almost fifty hours had passed since Charles Vance had felt the warmth of his bed. His face was shaved clean and he wore a new suit, but there was no denying the fatigue he was under. Dark circles hung beneath his eyes. His legs felt heavier with each step.

The cause of his first night without rest was the flag burning incident. In the wake of it, he'd stayed up the entire night gathering as much information as he could in anticipation of his morning briefings at the White House.

The second was spent in planning, he and Director Joon looking to carry out the decisions made therein.

The unanimous choice of the group was that something had to be done. Too many times in the preceding twenty years, the country had been slow to react, and they had paid dearly for it.

Mogadishu. Baghdad. Even 9/11.

Those days were now past. If anti-American sentiment was brewing, it needed to be contained as fast as possible.

Once that part was decided, the conversation had turned to the decidedly more difficult aspect of how to best act. A large-scale invasion of any form would violate all sorts of treaties and conventions, not the least of which was the fact that it would be considered an act of war, which was constitutionally allotted to Congress.

Even worse, it would effectively render the CIA moot.

Any sort of on-the-ground involvement would have to be a precision strike. What that would look like had been cause for debate for another hour, Vance watching as the president and Joon analyzed everything from a myriad of angles.

And watched again as, true to government form, they reanalyzed everything a second time for good measure.

Not until after midnight had the group disbanded, a plan in place.

A plan that had immediately put Joon and Vance on a plane south, which was why they were now standing in a private hangar on the outskirts of the Atlanta International Airport. Standing in front of them was a quartet of men in jeans and polos. All between the ages of thirty and forty, they were each fairly bland in appearance.

Two had blonde hair, another brown. The fourth had black hair, his skin a dark tan that could pass for Latino. Aside from that, there was nothing particularly remarkable about any of them, a look that Vance knew the Agency worked hard to cultivate.

Leaving behind nothing to remember made their job that much easier.

Standing four across, they held their hands loose by their sides, small duffel bags by each of their feet.

"Good morning, gentlemen," Joon said. Like Vance, he had had time for a change and shower, but no rest.

Something they both anticipated being the norm for the foreseeable future.

"Thank you all for being here on such short notice," he said. "My name is Director Joon. A couple of you I have met before, for the others, this is the first encounter.

"Along with me here this morning is Special Director of South American Operations Charles Vance."

Vance gave no outward movement beyond a small nod of the head.

None of the others returned the gesture.

"At your feet is a duffel bag containing passports and flight tickets to Punta Arenas, Chile. You will depart in exactly one hour, and you will all be scattered throughout coach."

He paused, passing his gaze over the men, as if awaiting questions.

Nobody said a word.

"Also in your bags are assorted clothing and toiletry items, none of which are of any consequence," Joon said.

The inclusion of the bags was something Vance and Joon had discussed just a few hours before. The sight of anybody stepping onto a fifteen-hour flight without something would raise curiosity, if not outright suspicion.

Again, not something the Agency looked favorably upon.

"Six hours into your trip, the plane you are traveling on will experience a mechanical error. It will be non-serious and not induce panic, but it will be cause for an unplanned landing in Caracas, Venezuela."

The briefing was a long way from what Vance or Joon would have preferred, but it was the best they could do under such tight time strictures. It wasn't as if the Agency had loads of agents sitting around, ready to be deployed. A good bit of the evening had been spent scrambling to select the right men and get them to Atlanta.

Part of that being because departing from Washington, D.C. would be too obvious to anybody paying attention.

The remainder because it was the only major port with a direct flight to South America that passed anywhere near Venezuela before Edgar Belmonte took the stage for his final speech.

"When you land in Caracas, everyone will be asked to exit the aircraft. At that point, you will all make your way out of the airport and rendezvous three blocks northeast at a bus station. You have all been given the contact phone number.

"Young Latina, activation sign Mockingbird. At that time, you will be filled in on your objective, provided with anything else you might need."

The choice to go with Ramirez over Farkus was something Vance and Joon had initially disagreed on. The Director had wanted Farkus because he was two decades senior and had a longer working relationship in Venezuela.

The exact reasons Vance had argued against it.

In the end, the Director had capitulated, an act induced in no small part by the truncated timeframe they were under.

"This will be a short operation," Joon said. "If all goes to plan, you'll be out of the country by this time tomorrow, back home in the States within the week."

Again, he paused. One at a time he looked the men over, meeting their gaze.

"Are there any questions?"

Not one person said a thing.

Chapter Nineteen

A few months ago, I had a cabin, in every sense of the word. It wasn't a vacation retreat. Certainly wasn't one of the sprawling monstrosities found in Vail or Breckenridge.

It was a simple wooden structure I'd built myself. Fashioned from the very trees it stood tucked into, never would it win a beauty contest, but it was always useful for serving its primary purpose.

Keeping the Montana winter out.

Inside, the furniture was mostly things I'd built myself as well. Roughhewn wood frames with padded seats covered in old Pendleton quilts. A table and chairs for the eating area. A sofa, coffee table, and armchair for the living space.

In total, I spent six years in that cabin before it blew up.

Or rather, before I blew it up during a melee with a drug cartel that had tracked me and the girl I was protecting north from Southern California.

Not once in those six years did I ever feel like I was lacking in comfort. My needs were met, whether I was reading an old Lee Child paperback or sprawled out watching reruns of *Friday Night Lights*.

Of course, that was before I flew first class on the largest jet in the LATAM Airlines fleet.

More than three feet in width, there was space for the seat to lay flat, an alcove carved out more than seven feet in length. On either end were partitions separating me from other passengers.

The seat itself was made of memory foam, forming a perfect mold around my body as I eased myself down into it.

As far as I was concerned, it was like being in a semi-private bubble, the sole point of contact with the outside world being Rembert seated beside me. Taking the aisle seat, his attention was aimed down at an oversized electronic device in his hands. Using both thumbs, he was jabbing at is if it was a console for one of the old Atari game systems.

"Pretty nice, huh?" he asked, barely casting a glance my direction.

"More comfortable than my last home," I replied.

To that, he chuckled, acting as if it had been a joke.

"Yeah, figured if we were going to spend the better part of a day in the air, might as well enjoy ourselves. No point in showing up so sore we can barely get on the water."

Unable to argue with the logic, I simply nodded.

Not every statement needs a verbal confirmation.

Continuing to work at the device in hand, Rembert grunted softly. "I don't suppose you have any experience with one of these, do you?"

Shifting my focus down to the item, I saw that it was large and square. Vaguely resembling one of the new iPhones I'd seen some of my clients use as cameras in the park, it had a smaller screen and a lot more buttons.

"I'm not even sure exactly what that thing is," I replied.

One corner of his mouth lifting up, Rembert smirked, his head rocking back slightly. "You and me both, brother."

Stabbing at it for a few more minutes, the color in his face continued to climb. Monosyllabic mutterings of various kinds spilled from his lips before frustration won out.

Snapping forward at the waist, he shoved the item back into his carry-on and extracted something I was at least nominally more familiar with – a basic cell phone.

"Hellfire," he spat, powering the phone to life. "Thing is supposed to be the newest and fanciest satellite phone on the market, but damned if I even know how to turn the thing on."

Glad he had stowed it before giving me a go, I only nodded.

"Wife got it for me when I booked this trip," he explained. "Said she didn't care if I went, but she wanted to know I was safe while I was gone."

Shifting slightly to look at me full, I could hear his seat groan beneath him. "You'd think she'd forgotten that most of my career was spent on business trips all over the country for days at a time. If I can survive that, I think I can handle a few days of fishing."

I didn't bother commenting on the first part of the statement. I'd always liked Rembert. Didn't want to dwell on if he'd had dalliances in the past or if his wife's concern was about something more than his safety.

Even less did I want to examine the fact that he was hovering somewhere near sixty. The inevitabilities of time and all that.

Instead, I merely offered, "Can't really blame her, though. I've seen some mighty bad cases of sore thumb from removing hooks from the mouths of trout."

An impish grin appeared on his face. "Is that right?"

"It is. Just one after another all day can become quite taxing on the hands. She's right to be concerned."

Chapter Twenty

The sun was again streaming through the glass on the far end of President Miguel Salazar's office. Refracting up off the polished Spanish tile that lined the floor, it gave the space a light, ethereal glow.

For five years, the place had been his home. Not his second home, as the cliché so often liked to point, but his primary residence. The spot in the world where he spent the bulk of his waking hours. He took most of his meals there, quite often even used the shower and cot that were set up in the small room adjoining it.

Even for a country as far down the international pecking order as Venezuela, being president still carried a heavy burden.

A burden that felt even more pronounced as Salazar sat at his desk this particular morning. With his elbows resting on the front edge of it, he could feel the morning sun on the side of his face. With it came the promise of another steamy day, his shirt already sticking to his skin in spots.

By his left forearm sat his untouched Cafecito, a precise stack of newspapers before him.

None of that mattered at the moment.

All that did was the constant rehashing of everything that had transpired the day before.

The morning visit from Isabel, sharing with him the events of Belmonte's campaign speech. The call from President Underall later in the afternoon. The evening conversation with General Clega thereafter.

The discussion long into the night with Isabel about if what they could soon be embarking on was the right decision.

The general had of course been right. If something was going to happen on Venezuelan soil, they had to be the ones to respond to it. Already Belmonte was seeing a surge just from burning a flag and stripping half-naked in the middle of a baseball stadium. He had tapped into something in his countrymen that Salazar had only vaguely been aware even existed.

If news of what was now taking place were to get out, and he did nothing, it would provide a perfect vehicle for Belmonte to strap the remainder of his candidacy to.

A vehicle that would be near unstoppable as it careened forward.

At the same time, the situation wasn't without some serious foibles. Chief among them would be having to act on something that they did not yet know the full extent of. And doing so against a country that they had at least passable relations with.

A country with many more resources – both in terms of military and media heft – that could be brought down on him.

Not to mention, if all that were to happen and they were still left standing, figuring out how to use it to their own advantage for the upcoming election.

One after another, the various thoughts swirled through Salazar's mind. Like an unending vortex, one idea would push to the surface, only to be replaced an instant later by another.

So immersed in these thoughts was Salazar, his eyes glassed over, that he didn't notice the door on the far end of the room open. Didn't pick up the sound of Isabel's square heels clicking against the tile.

Failed to even acknowledge the flash of her blue suit as she came to a stop less than two feet from him.

Not until she gave a small throat clear did he jerk himself to attention. Snapping his attention up to her, he shook his head sharply, pushing aside the swirl of information in his mind.

"Sorry."

Ignoring the apology, Isabel said, "We just received a call."

Salazar folded his hands over his stomach. A frown formed on his face.

"Okay."

"It was about the, um, *request* we sent last night."

Six hours prior, the two of them had decided to put out a bulletin to all airports, train stations, shipping docks, and bus depots in the country. In it, department heads and overseers were asked to keep a watch for anything unusual and to report back discreetly if something caught their attention.

The fact that somebody was already calling either meant somebody was getting jumpy and looking to make a name for themselves, or the Americans were moving faster than he anticipated.

"Already?" he asked.

"It would appear so."

"Where?"

"Bolivar," Isabel replied.

The Simón Bolívar International Airport was the largest airport hub in the country. Situated no more than twenty kilometers from where they were now sitting, it offered daily flights throughout the Americas and even Europe.

"Christ," Salazar muttered.

Again, Isabel ignored the statement. "A transmission was received a few minutes ago from a LATAM flight requesting an emergency landing."

Salazar felt his eyes narrow. Already, he could cross someone getting jumpy from the list of possibilities.

This was exactly the sort of thing he'd asked facilities to be on watch for.

"What kind of emergency?"

"They cited a mechanical problem," Isabel said. "Halfway into their flight from Atlanta to Punta Arenas."

The last line was said without inflection, though there didn't need to be anything extra for Salazar to catch the implication.

"Has this sort of thing ever happened before?"

"I asked the same thing," Isabel replied. "And was told that in the director's eleven years, this was the first time for such a thing. Now, that could be because we don't sit on many common flight paths..."

"Or it could be because this one in particular has a vested interest to stop here," Salazar said, finishing the thought.

Resuming his stance on the front edge of the desk, he bobbed his head slightly. A bitter taste rose in his mouth.

His hope all morning had been that America would simply opt to wait and monitor the situation. That over time Belmonte would prove nothing more than a minor blip.

The sort of thing that pops up every election season in various places, but never has the staying power to amount to much.

If already the man was presenting enough of a problem to warrant foreign interference, that also meant that he was a much bigger worry than Salazar had realized.

Faced with two new concerns in as many days, he raised his palms to his forehead. Closing his eyes, he rubbed them in slow concentric circles.

From the window nearby, the morning sun continued to get warmer. Sweat droplets began to form on his brow.

It was going to be one of those days.

"How long before the flight arrives?" he asked.

There was a brief rustle of fabric, presumably as Isabel checked her watch. Salazar didn't bother opening his eyes to check.

"On the ground in fifty-eight minutes."

"Get me General Clega."

Chapter Twenty-One

My father was an army lifer. From a very young age, he used to instill in me a great many of the maxims that he learned there, not the least of which was always eat and sleep when you can.

You never knew when the next opportunity might be.

While I would never liken the situation I was in to anything he might have faced in the military, I was coming off a night where I only received a few hours of rest. I had then followed that up with a cross-country trip and was staring at a flight almost fifteen hours in length.

And I was in a seat that doubled as one of the more luxuriant beds I had ever been in.

Shortly after the wheels lifted from Atlanta, I left Rembert to go back to wrestling with the satellite phone. Reclining myself to completely horizontal, I barely heard the captain give the standard welcome shtick shortly after takeoff.

Flat on my back, I melted straight to black, not to move until a stewardess put a hand on my shoulder an indeterminate amount of time later and gave me a hearty shake. Giving no outward reaction beyond opening my eyes, I looked up to see short dark hair and too much lipstick peering down at me.

"I'm sorry sir, but you'll have to return to your upright position for landing."

As fast as she'd arrived, she was gone, leaving nothing behind but a plume of perfume.

Pausing for just a moment to rub my hands over my face, I raised my seat back to vertical. Unable to hide the confusion I felt, I glanced at Rembert. "Sorry about that. Didn't realize I was asleep that long."

"You weren't," he replied. "We have to make an emergency stop."

Feeling my eyebrows rise slightly, I shifted my attention to the window. In the distance, I could see the Atlantic Ocean, multiple shades of blue all melded together.

"What sort of emergency?" I asked.

"Didn't say. Only that we would need to deplane briefly, but that we'd be on our way shortly."

A host of responses came to mind, but there was no point voicing any of them. It was already clear that a long trip had just gotten longer. No point in dwelling on the obvious.

Given what I was looking at, and the general route from Atlanta to Punta Arenas, there was no way to definitively know where we were. All that was for certain was that we were still on the front half of our journey, almost all of that flying over the Caribbean before reaching the mainland of South America.

Not the worst of places to be making an unscheduled visit, for sure.

"Where are we stopping?" I asked.

"Caracas," Rembert replied, "Venezuela." Beside me, he leaned forward to see out through the window. "Never been before. You?"

Despite there being no earthly reason for it, my core tightened slightly. My breathing slowed just a bit, my body's natural defense mechanisms stepping into action.

In a different lifetime, my DEA team and I had made untold forays all along the northern coast of South America.

Most of them ended as they were supposed to, but that wasn't to say they were without their share of close scrapes.

Compared to some of the other hellholes in the region, I wouldn't put Venezuela at the top of the list, but I wouldn't put them at the bottom either.

And that was before the last few years, when it sounded like nothing good had befallen the country.

"A few times."

Chapter Twenty-Two

Being an unexpected landing, there was no available gate for us as we landed at the airport in Caracas. I'm sure there was a fancy name given for some famous patron or historical figure, but in my previous trips to the country, we didn't exactly fly commercial.

To me, they were all just airports, even the tiny hubs in Montana bearing the added moniker *international* in their title to accommodate the fact that once a day they sent a turboprop plane over the border into Canada.

From the tarmac, I could see the front of the building, a glass and steel structure that deserved more credit than I would have initially given it. Gleaming under the harsh light of the sun, it seemed a beacon wedged tight amongst jungle foliage to one side and dense urban landscaping on the other.

Which likely meant that, like most cities, the airport had been originally constructed far outside of town. Over time, urban sprawl had connected the two, filling in the gap with strip malls, hotels, and anything else that might make a buck.

Some truths being universal and all that.

Outside, I could see a bus approaching. Constructed to be twice the length of a normal vehicle, it had a divider in the middle that expanded and contracted like an accordion.

Long ago I had seen such a thing on the streets of Washington, D.C. Even a few other times in places like Los Angeles.

Years had passed since I'd encountered one in person, though, most places shoving them aside in favor of public transit of more economical or environmental means.

This one, in particular, looked like a castoff from someplace like Miami, having last seen a regular tune-up sometime during the nineties.

"Looks like our chariot has arrived," I whispered.

Pushing forward a few inches to see out, Rembert said only, "Hellfire," before dropping back against his seat.

Well put.

"Ladies and gentlemen," the captain announced over the PA system, drawing my attention away from the window. "As this is an unscheduled landing, air traffic has asked that we deplane here. Once they have a gate open up, they'll be able to get us in and have their team check things over for us.

"Nothing to worry about, just a gauge that we need to get looked at, and then we'll be back on our way. Shouldn't be more than a couple of hours."

"Nothing to worry about," Rembert muttered. "Don't those sound like famous last words."

Raising my eyebrows slightly in agreement, I said, "I thought it was originally supposed to be an hour?"

"That's what the man said."

Again, I could feel the clench in the pit of my stomach tighten slightly. Why it was there, I had no way of knowing. Perhaps it was nothing more than muscle memory, a natural reaction to being back on South American soil.

A psychosomatic response to memories and experiences buried long ago.

Regardless, I knew better than to completely disregard it. The body was designed to perform a particular set of tasks, automatically programmed to prioritize and handle certain functions in order.

And none had a higher natural ranking than survival.

"Feel free to leave your carry-ons and personal items onboard," the captain said. "A bus will now take you folks over to the terminal, and you'll all be right back on board soon enough."

The feeling within grew slightly stronger. Perhaps I was just being paranoid. Maybe I was superimposing past experiences onto a current situation that didn't call for it.

But I'd rather be overprepared than not at all.

Ahead of us, the front door opened. Bright light streamed in as the same stewardess that had woken me smiled and motioned for people to begin exiting.

"Hey, you ever get that phone working?" I asked.

Beside me, Rembert paused, his hands on either arm of his chair. "No, not yet. Damn thing is like trying to operate a nuclear surfboard."

Doing my best at a forced smile, I said, "Why don't you bring it along? We're going to have some time, might as well see if we can't get it up and running."

For an instant, he simply looked at me, people filing by us in the aisleway. Eventually, a smile split his features as he lowered himself back to his seat and grabbed for his bag.

"Damnation, that's a good idea. One call now is one less we have to mess with while we're out there on the water, right?"

The smile felt awkward on my features, though I managed to keep it in place.

That was not at all my thinking, but I'd be damned if I let him see that.

"Right."

Chapter Twenty-Three

At one point, the small warehouse had been used as a shipping hub. Erected and maintained by one of the small transport businesses in the country, it was tucked away into the far corner of the airfield. No longer than the average office building, it was two stories in height. Most of the first floor was an open design, meant for loading and unloading cargo.

The second was parsed off into offices, capable of housing all the necessary personnel.

Tucked into one of those offices, General Renzo Clega stood with binoculars raised to his eyes. Dressed in jeans and a nondescript polo shirt, there was absolutely nothing about his appearance to denote his title or even his employer.

An employer that was currently on the other end of the speaker-phone placed on the table by Clega's hip.

"What is going on right now?" President Salazar asked.

Clega gave the focusing nobs on the binoculars a slight twist. Before him, the image blurred for a moment before coming into sharp relief.

Less than a half mile away, the bus they had commandeered just minutes before was pulled up parallel to the LATAM jumbo jet. In a steady line, people were streaming down the staircase that had been pushed up beside the plane.

Like cattle, they moved in an endless slog, covering the few steps across the asphalt and into the bus without so much as a second thought.

"The plane is on the ground," Clega said. "Passengers have been told that there is no room at the gate and that they are to be shuttled to the terminal."

A small grunt was the first response. "So they are loading onto the shuttle now?"

"As we speak," Clega said. "Once they are all onboard, they will be brought to the old International Shipping warehouse in the corner of the grounds."

"And then what?"

The binoculars lowered a few inches as Clega glared at the phone. Keeping the look on his face, he glanced at the young man in the room beside him, a staff sergeant dressed in similar attire that acted as his personal aide.

Every aspect of this operation had been discussed in minute detail the night before. And again that morning. And a third time just a few minutes prior.

Salazar wasn't asking questions because he needed the information. He was asking because he was searching for holes that he could exploit if the need arose.

In most instances, Clega would have shied away from spearheading such an operation. It was easy to see the various ways things could go sideways, especially for someone like him.

If this became an ugly international hostage incident, the president would not be the one bearing the brunt of it.

That honor would go to the military leader in charge, salacious words such as *rogue* and *vigilante* thrown around at will.

At the same time, with an election fast approaching and an opponent that had no affinity for Clega or the military in general, Clega had no choice but to back Salazar's play. For the time being at least, they were in things together, however they may play out.

"And then they will be kept under surveillance by my men," Clega said.

Again, a grunt was the only response.

Choosing to ignore it – or rather, not trusting what he would say in response – Clega lifted the binoculars back to his eyes. He watched as the last few stragglers made their way down the ramp toward the bus.

His grip tightened on the plastic frames as he saw a stewardess appear at the top of the stairway and wave, a signal that everybody on board had been cleared.

"Have you had a chance to look at the flight manifest yet?" Salazar asked.

"Yes," Clega replied. "It appears that just this morning, seats for four men were obtained within twenty minutes of each other. All middle-aged, they were seated throughout the cabin."

"Hmm," Salazar replied. "Four, that's more than we anticipated."

"It is," Clega agreed, "but we have their pictures now. It shouldn't be too hard to isolate and neutralize them."

On the last few words, he felt a smile come to his lips. For years, various American agencies had been a problem, an unwanted presence in their country, no matter how small. Finally, he had been given a chance to return some of the angst they had caused him.

And the best part was, there would be no way for America to retaliate. Doing so would mean having to acknowledge that they were ever here.

"Just, be careful," Salazar said. There was a clear sigh in his voice, fatigue obvious.

Or possibly just a deference to what it was they were doing.

"A jammer has been installed to block any attempted transmissions," Clega said. On the far end of the tarmac, the bus looped wide, beginning its return to the warehouse. "I will be in touch as soon as they are found."

Chapter Twenty-Four

With the exception of the few strides it took to get from my seat to the front door of the plane, the terminal of Caracas airport was always in my sight. Bright and shiny, there was no way to miss it.

A monument rising up where there was no business being one.

Which made the fact that once on the bus we were looping wide in the opposite direction all the more obvious.

Starting in a lazy circle, we moved in a long arc. Instead of circling toward the terminal, we headed in the opposite direction. What should have been on my left was suddenly on my right, growing smaller as we rolled forward.

"Something's not right."

The words were low, so much so I barely even realized I had said them out loud. Just enough to cause Rembert to lean in beside me, he asked, "What was that?"

The interior of the bus was jammed tight, more people inside than a vehicle of its design was ever intended to hold. If out on the street, there was no way a driver would have been allowed to proceed.

I didn't know how many people were on the plane, just that it was a large liner. I couldn't imagine them sending such a jet that far without at least fifty percent capacity, which put us well over a hundred people in total.

All wedged into the bus, pressing against both sides and my front.

Casting a quick glance around, I could see a couple of folks looking my way, though nobody seemed to be too interested in our conversation.

Not that there was a lot I could do about it anyway.

"Something's not right," I repeated. Still, just loud enough to be heard by him and as few others as possible. "We're moving away from the terminal, not toward it."

Lifting his chin to see past my shoulder, Rembert said, "Damnation, you are right. Where the hell are we going?"

Raising his face another inch or two, he yelled, "Hey! Driver! The terminal is the other direction!"

Warmth crept to my face, a veneer of sweat coming to my features.

So much for trying to keep things quiet.

"Driver!" Rembert called again.

Around us, a murmur went up from the crowd. People began to twist their bodies so they could see out, many coming to the same conclusion I already had.

More still chose to go the route of Rembert and voice their displeasure to the driver.

Not that it mattered. Onward we went, pushing straight ahead for another couple of minutes before slowing slightly.

From my perch in the back end of the oversized bus, I didn't have an unobstructed view. All I had was my one window, chosen originally to keep an eye on the terminal. With that now gone, I could see just a chain link fence rising more than ten feet from the ground. A coil of barbed wire was wrapped around the top of it.

Beyond it, nothing more than dense trees, a canopy so green it was almost black.

Definitely not the sort of place we wanted to be going, in Venezuela or anywhere else.

"Can you see up ahead?" I asked Rembert. "Any idea where we're headed?"

Leaning back at the waist, he managed to open a couple of extra inches. Straining for an angle, he rose to his toes before dropping back to flat feet beside me.

"No," he said. "Too many people. What do you think is going on?"

Around us, people continued to voice their dismay. A couple had even taken to trying to force their way to the front.

"Nothing good."

Beneath us, the engine slowed further, the bus decelerating down to a crawl. In a steady pace, darkness moved back over the length of the bus.

Too dark to be merely a cloud, or even a shadow, it was clear we had moved inside some sort of structure.

Again, the feeling in my stomach grew more pronounced.

With each passing moment, it was becoming more obvious that the mechanical problem on the plane was nothing more than a ruse. An excuse to get us on the ground and nothing more.

The only questions that remained were why, and who had the sort of juice necessary to force down an international flight exactly where they wanted.

This time, the feeling extended clear to my face, a frown forming on my features.

None of the people on that list were particularly appealing.

Nor were the people standing outside my window as we came to a stop, all of them dressed in jeans and casual attire, all of them carrying automatic weapons at the ready.

Chapter Twenty-Five

I was the first to see the weapons, but only by a split second. While my mind immediately delved deep into the recesses, searching out the places I'd spent five years trying to bury, others around me went to the most basic of human responses when seeing a firearm.

Fear. Panic. Pure, unbridled terror.

The first sign of it was a gasp. Second in order was a woman asking if the people outside were armed.

Third was a shriek, a shrill, brittle sound so close to my ear it almost rattled my teeth. A noise that instantly brought about a dozen more just like it.

By the time the door on the front end of the bus opened, the interior of the space resembled a disco. Loud noises and lots of sweaty bodies crowded in close.

"Listen up!" a voice just barely audible over the din of the crowd called out, completely disembodied from this angle. "Hey! Quiet down!"

The second attempt was no more effective than the first. Which meant the next move was fairly easy to forecast as well.

Inside whatever structure we were now parked in, the gunshot sounded extraordinarily loud. Like a steel sound tunnel, the noise reverberated through the space, managing to silence the crowd instantly.

To either side, I could see people panting. Women stood clinging to their husbands, wide-eyed.

For me, a steady drip of adrenaline seeped into my system. Hearing gunshots where they're not supposed to be has a way of doing that.

"Now then," the man began anew, "as I was trying to say!"

He paused, as if daring someone to say anything. Classic power move.

Already I could tell I was going to supremely dislike this man.

"You are all now our guests. Do not ask who we are, do not ask where we are. Do not even look us directly in the eye. Do as we instruct and my men will not hurt you.

"Do not, and I cannot guarantee your safety."

The faces around me continued to register extreme terror. Everybody seemed to edge their way toward the sides, people crowding closer from every direction, recoiling from the intruder.

Which was exactly the wrong thing to do in such a situation.

Not that any of them had a single reason to know that.

"Okay," the man said. "Right now, you are all going to follow me out of here. You are going to move in a slow and ordered fashion and you are going to listen to everything my men say. Is that understood?"

A couple of heads nodded slightly. Most stood in complete silence, shock apparent.

A quick glance around the place showed that most of the people on board had been like Rembert. They were a little older, with the kind of financial standing to afford such a trip. Many had probably built a life with a nice home and all the furnishings a person could hope for.

This sort of thing didn't happen to them. This sort of thing was reserved for the evening news. It was the kind of event that they sat and watched on television, shared their sympathies for, and maybe wrote a check to charity to ease their conscious about after the fact.

It was not something they'd ever fathomed facing in their own life.

Given my position, I couldn't see the man doing the speaking as he stood at the front of the bus. Not until he stepped off could I grab a glimpse of him through the side window.

Shorter than I would have expected, he had thick hair and a matching mustache, both dyed a ridiculous midnight black. His middle was quite prodigious, emphasized by a polo tucked tight into jeans.

No uniform or insignia of any kind on his person, or those of his men.

Meaning he didn't want to be identified.

Taking a few steps to the side, he stood with his arms folded as his men waited at the ready, weapons held before them.

A couple of feet away, passengers filed off the bus, their gazes averted and their shoulders rolled inward. Standard submissive stances, whether they even realized it.

The same exact one I would soon be taking.

No use in provoking anybody, or even having them look my way, until I'd had time to gather some more information.

Namely, who these men were and what they wanted.

Extending one finger out from my side, I jabbed it into Rembert's hip. "Leave the bag."

Flicking his gaze my way, his eyes narrowed slightly. "Hmm?"

"Leave the bag," I whispered a second time. "No point in giving them a reason to look your way."

Confusion came first to his brows before spreading over his face. "You sure?"

"Positive," I said. "But give me the sat phone first."

Chapter Twenty-Six

The trip from Atlanta back to Washington D.C. had taken just over an hour. Most of that Charles Vance and Director Joon spent in conversation, trading first impressions and trying to troubleshoot what they envisioned moving forward.

Upon arriving back at Langley, they both agreed to break for three hours to rest. Given the stretch they were both coming off of, and what the coming day or two promised, they agreed that a bit of sleep would be for the best.

Two hours and forty minutes of that, Vance spent on a twin sized cot deep in the underbelly of the building. Sequestered in a closet-sized room made for that purpose, it was a timeless environment, completely dark and free of noise from the outside.

An instant after laying down, he was unconscious. Not bothering with REM sleep, his body succumbed straight to darkness until the alarm beckoned him a few hours later.

At that point, he rose and shook off as much off the grogginess as possible. The rest he left for twelve minutes under the hottest water he could stand.

Exactly three hours after stepping off the plane, he entered the central conference room on the main floor. Wearing the suit he'd grabbed before heading to Atlanta, his hair was still damp, his eyes clear.

Arriving at the same time and in the same attire, Joon looked to be much the same.

"Director."

"Vance," Joon replied, nodding curtly.

Side by side, they stepped into the room, a staff of more than a dozen already assembled and waiting for them. Together, they were clustered around a conference table twice the size of the one Vance and his crew had used two nights prior.

Made of dark wood, it was polished to a shine, the CIA emblem embossed in the center of it. Placed at two different intervals was a tray of coffee and all the necessary extras.

The smell was borderline intoxicating.

Pushing the scent aside for just a moment, Vance instead focused on his team sitting on the far side. Closest to the head of the table was Hannah Rowe, followed in order by Peter Reiff and Dan Andrews.

Each stared at Vance as he approached the table, though nobody said a thing.

Across from them were a trio of individuals Vance had never seen before, each looking to Joon.

Around the outside of the room was another half-dozen extra hands, each young and eager to track down anything that was needed.

All the makings of a war room if there ever was one.

Getting straight to business, the assembled mass had fallen to compiling everything they knew and everything they could possibly speculate on. With a constant eye for the clock, they worked steadily through the afternoon, all waiting for the appointed time.

A time that, as far as Vance could now tell, had come and gone.

Standing off to the side, he had his arms folded over his chest. Time and again he glanced at the red digital clock on the opposite wall, the numbers telling him that the plane should have landed more than twenty minutes earlier.

"Are we absolutely certain that there has been a touch down?"

Joon asked. Assuming the same stance as Vance, he paced at the far end of the table.

The question was aimed at nobody in particular, a bevy of people all rushing to provide an answer.

"Yes," a young woman with dark hair pulled into a bun said. "LATAM Airlines flight 681 is confirmed to have landed at Bolivar International Airport twenty-one minutes ago."

Again, Vance flicked his gaze to the clock.

Twenty-one minutes was a lifetime. Long enough for an entire cabin to have deplaned. Or have been abducted. Or mass murdered.

Certainly long enough for one of their contacts to have checked in.

"And as yet, we have no word from any of our guys?" Joon asked.

This time, the question was fielded more as rhetorical. Each person on his side of the table averted their gaze, nobody wanting to be the one to state the obvious.

Of course there had been no word. Every last person in the room would know by now if there had been.

"How about our asset in the field?" Joon asked.

This time, it was Rowe's turn to respond. "Agent Ramirez last made contact three minutes prior. No word from anybody yet."

Only a few feet separating them, Vance and Joon exchanged a glance. This was one of the many things they had discussed on the way up, an eventuality neither had wanted to acknowledge.

President Underall had not shared with his Venezuelan counterpart what exactly would be taking place, but it was known that something would likely be attempted. That conversation was made under the highest of classifications, a pact that was only as good as the two sides taking part in it.

On their end, neither worried about the president sharing something he shouldn't have.

As for Salazar and the leaks that could be present in a country such as Venezuela, neither had wanted to speculate.

Now, it looked like they would have no choice but to do just that.

"No messages in or out," Joon said, the comment directed at Vance.

"Which could mean that our guys were found and silenced in the air-" Vance began.

"Unlikely," Joon inserted.

"Or that the airport − or rather, the people on that flight - are now being jammed," Vance finished.

He didn't bother expounding further. The director would know exactly what he was referring to.

The best they could hope for was that the passengers were being held somewhere with transmission signals blocked.

A muscle twitched in Joon's cheek as he stared at Vance. Slowly, his head rocked up and down slightly, no more than a few millimeters in either direction.

Neither man could say much more out loud, but it wasn't that hard to envision it playing out. Salazar knew something was imminent, especially with Belmonte set to give his final speech in just a few hours.

All he would have had to do was keep an eye on traditional modes of transportation, be prepared to spring if something unusual surfaced.

Something like an aircraft bound from Atlanta to Punta Arenas suddenly needing to make an emergency landing.

At the time, sitting in the president's office, every person present had been in favor of the idea. It gave them the most plausible mode of entry, especially on such a short timeframe.

Now looking at it in retrospect, it was borderline foolish. The sort of thing that would be a glaring aberration to anybody looking for one.

"Who else do we have in the area?" Joon asked.

Vance knew he already had the answer, though he said, "Just Agent Farkus, who is currently getting ready for tonight's speech."

The same bitter look returned to Joon's face as he glanced at the clock on the wall. Pulling Farkus off without compromising him at this point would be nearly impossible.

And it would completely nullify any assistance he might be able to provide with Belmonte later on.

"Christ," Joon spat. Swiping a hand at the table, he sent a stack of papers flying, sheets spreading in a wide arc across the floor.

After, he stood staring down at them for a moment, saying nothing, before shifting his attention back to the table.

"Keep trying to get our guys on the line. I have to go brief President Underall."

Chapter Twenty-Seven

The sat phone went down the front of my pants. Not the back, as that would cause an unnatural bulge that would be noticed, especially given the stance I was taking upon exiting.

Much like many of the people that stepped off the bus at the beginning, I chose to adopt a posture of complete submission. My shoulders were rolled forward. My head was tilted downward, allowing my shaggy hair to hang down over my eyebrows.

Adding a little extra was the fact that I was coming out right beside Rembert, the man's girth making me look even smaller by comparison.

At a six-foot-four, I was by no means a small man. Living and working in the wilderness meant that my frame still much resembled what it did when I left the DEA years before. Designed more for function than form, overinflated weight room muscles didn't really do much for me.

All of those things were now playing in my favor. Years of working in the region had shown me two incontrovertible truths about many of the men that lived there.

That they tended to be a bit on the smaller side, and that they were aggressively aware of it.

Given the current situation, they would be looking to flex their dominance over us. They would look with blazing hostility as each person exited, almost daring us to match the glare.

From there, it was anybody's guess how exactly they would react.

The only certainty would be that it wouldn't end well for whoever was on the opposite side.

Still much too early in the process to be antagonizing anybody, I chose to appear as meek as possible. Hidden beneath my hair and beard, I cast sideways glances as we passed from the bus into the space.

Not once did I stare at anyone directly, or let my gaze linger longer than necessary.

The place appeared to be an abandoned warehouse of some sort. With a low ceiling and a staircase running up the side wall, it looked to be the loading portion of some sort of shipping facility.

Adding to that impression was a stack of crumbling pallets in the back corner. On the ground were rubber streaks from forklifts used long ago, the lines punctuated by the occasional spot of oil.

In the air, faint traces of fuel and cardboard could be detected.

Despite more than a hundred people having crammed into the bus, over half were already gone by the time we made it off. Of those, a decent percentage was moving in a loose gaggle toward the stairs, men with automatic weapons walking on either side like ranch hands leading cattle to pasture.

Moving along in what could best be called a zombie slog, they reached the foot of the stairs and began to ascend. To their credit, nobody seemed to be putting up any resistance.

Tears streamed down many faces, both men and women.

An understandable reaction, for sure.

"All of you, come together and stand right here," the man from the front of the bus said. Even shorter up close, he stood with his hands on his hips. His extended chest accentuated the bulk of his midsection.

As did the pair of guards standing with Kalashnikovs beside him.

Obeying his command, the group shuffled toward him. Totaling maybe thirty, my furtive glances confirmed that it was comprised of a two-to-one female-to-male ratio. Of those, no more than a handful appeared to be minors.

Luckily, there were no babies or children too small to run should it come to that.

Once everyone was in position, the man said, "My men will now lead you to your room. Like I warned you before, if you try anything, we will shoot you.

"The other groups did as they were instructed, and they are all now safely upstairs."

In a slow and measured movement, he swung his gaze across the group. Partially tucked behind Rembert, he seemed to barely notice me, instead lingering on a pair of young college co-eds a few feet over.

Something that helped me in the immediate, but could be a problem for all of us in the long term.

"What is going on right now," he said, "it does not concern you. If all goes to plan, twelve hours from now you will return to your plane and be on your way."

The words were meant to be placating, but for me, they only served as an added warning. A harbinger of heightened danger for sure.

Most people would hear what he just said and assume that was a good thing. Any quarrel was not with them. Soon enough, they could be on their way.

Having spent time around men like him, all it told me was the fact that we presented no actual value in the slightest.

Once whatever leverage we could provide was exerted and completed, we would be cast aside without a care.

Chapter Twenty-Eight

The structure was two stories in height, but the space was not divided equally between them. While the first floor was fifteen or more feet in height, the ceiling of the second floor looked closer to eight. If I was to reach up, my fingertips would likely be just shy of it, bringing with it the effect that the walls were closing in tight from every direction.

An impression that seemed to heighten the fear of every person present in the room.

Moving in a loose queue, we exited off the staircase into a hallway. Made of bright white walls and matching tile floors, a yellowing effect had set in with age and going unused.

Entering from the side, we were just short of one end, double doors a few feet away.

Spaced evenly along the hall in the opposite direction were a handful of doors, more than half a dozen by my count. Three of them stood closed and barricaded, a pair of armed guards standing outside each one, eyeing us as we passed.

For our part, we were led to the last door down on the left. The lead guard took us as far as the threshold before stepping to the side. Using the tip of his gun as a pointer, he gestured for us to go through.

One at a time, people disappeared within. Those of us at the end did our best to continue giving the impression of movement, lifting our feet and putting them right back down, avoiding eye contact the entire time.

Toward the end of the line, I eventually stepped into the room to find it a barren square no more than thirty feet on either end. The walls and floor matched the same aged appearance as the hallway.

Located in the corner of the structure, the windows were covered with sheets of plywood, shiny screw heads visible every few inches.

Whoever had cobbled this together had certainly put in some prep work ahead of time.

Above, the ceiling was standard office fare, Styrofoam squares laid out in a grid interspersed by tubular lights hidden behind frosted glass.

Otherwise, there was no furniture of any kind. Not even chairs for people to sit on.

And certainly nothing that could be fashioned into a weapon.

Maintaining the same pose I had since exiting the bus, I walked directly to the back corner and pressed my shoulder into it. Using it for support, I slid my body down a few inches, making myself seem even smaller.

There, I waited.

Once the last of the file was inside, the lead guard stepped into the room. He bandied about in excited Spanish for a few moments, waving his hands and jabbing his weapon our direction.

Each time he did, it elicited the reaction he wanted, someone inside giving an obligatory squeal.

Prattling on for several minutes, the guard eventually ran out of steam. Panting slightly, he gave his best angry glare before turning on a heel and exiting the room.

In his wake, the door was slammed closed. A moment later, a series of screws being inserted into the wood could be heard, securing it from the outside.

Working his way toward the back of the room, Rembert managed to nudge aside an older couple. Ignoring their withering glare, he positioned himself so he was facing me, both of us tucked tight into the corner.

"You still have it?" he asked.

Already, I could feel a few stares move our direction.

Now was not the time to be pulling out the phone. Most likely, we were currently being held in this place because it was set up for containment. That meant there was no way we were getting a signal in or out.

Even trying would only incite the people around us. It would draw attention in a way that we weren't yet ready to handle.

Which was why I merely shook my head at his question. "No. Couldn't risk it."

Chapter Twenty-Nine

The tone of the room was quite jovial. After the events of the last two nights, optimism was palpable in the air. Everybody had witnessed in real time the shift of the conversation in Venezuela.

For the first time in ages, there was a feeling that bordered on hopeful. People were starting to consider that there might be some alternative other than the status quo.

And most importantly to those present, that Edgar Belmonte – and themselves, by extension – might be the ones to make it happen.

Knowing that there was still work to be done for the night ahead, the feeling was somewhat measured. Every smile was kept in check. Every excited comment was held to a whisper.

But it was undeniable.

Which was what made the look on Hector Ramon's face that much more recognizable the instant he walked in.

Standing in the back office, Belmonte saw him as soon as he entered through the front door. Walking fast, his jaw was set in a grimace. His hair and tie were disheveled from the wind.

He made no effort to fix either as he wound his way through a sea of volunteers toward the back.

Standing at his desk, Belmonte felt the smile on his face fade.

Watching his Chief of Staff enter in such a manner, a pang of something sharp jabbed into his stomach. It continued to do so as his breath grew shorter and sweat formed on his brow.

In the middle of a phone call, Belmonte cut it short, offering only a perfunctory, "Let me call you back."

Dropping the receiver without waiting for a reply, he was out of his private quarters by the time Ramon made it to the back of the office. The look on his face matched that of his employee.

"What happened?"

Giving a terse shake of the head, Ramon shot his gaze toward the conference room. Picking up on the signal, Belmonte followed him inside, closing the door behind them.

As he did so, the cacophony of movement and conversation outside fell away to nothing.

As did any pretense of cheer in the air.

"What happened?" Belmonte asked again.

"I just got a call from a friend of mine over at Bolivar," Ramon reported. "It seems that about an hour ago, a flight going from Atlanta to Chile was grounded due to a reported mechanical problem."

Belmonte felt his eyes narrow. That alone shouldn't have been enough to warrant the reaction Ramon was having. "Was it legit?"

"I don't know," Ramon said. "Nobody does, because the plane still hasn't made it to the gate. Right now, it's just been taxied off to the side."

The crease between Belmonte's eyes deepened. "They're keeping a full plane just sitting out on the tarmac?"

"No," Ramon said. He looked like he might be ill. "They deplaned the passengers and whisked them away to a private warehouse on the back of the grounds half an hour ago."

Small pinpricks of light began to ignite behind Belmonte's eyelids. Even through the enormous confusion that he felt, his every faculty seemed to be telling him that something wasn't right.

What was being described didn't really happen, even in a place like Venezuela.

"So it was a private flight?"

"No," Ramon said. "LATAM Airlines, more than a hundred people on board, most of them American citizens."

With those final words, a bit of dawning settled over Belmonte. His chest tightened as he raised his hands, lacing them over the top of his head. Using the upright posture, he drew in deep breaths, pacing at the head of the table.

"Jesus," he muttered.

Opposite him, Ramon nodded in agreement, remaining silent.

A hostage situation was bad enough. Even in a place like Caracas, it would be enough to attract a swarm of local media.

To have it be an international flight full of Americans, though, took things to an entirely different level.

"Any idea who's behind it?" Belmonte asked.

"Speculation," Ramon answered, "nothing certain. Whispers have said it's Salazar, some call it a rogue military operation. Others..."

He let his voice trail off. For a moment, Belmonte stood waiting for him to finish, before piecing together what was being intimated at.

"They think we're behind this."

"Some do," Ramon confirmed. "Especially given-"

"The events of the last couple of nights," Belmonte said, finishing for him.

Not once had he seen this coming. So focused on putting together the events, on determining how to maximize effect, he'd never once considered that someone might just as fast turn it on him.

Especially someone with as much to lose as his opponent.

"Has to be Salazar, right?" he asked.

Ramon merely spread his hands, shrugging slightly. "One would think, but again, only speculation."

Belmonte knew his Chief of Staff was merely being diplomatic. Always careful to avoid hyperbole or pursuing the salacious, he was making sure that no hasty conclusions were drawn.

Though at the moment, he wasn't quite in the mood for such evenhanded tactics.

"If not him, then who?" Belmonte asked. "And please, for the love of God, speak freely. It's just us in here."

The statement came out a bit stronger than intended, but that didn't mean it was wrong. The manner in which Ramon had entered made it clear that a brewing crisis could be at hand.

Which meant their best course of action would be to head it off rather than trying to manage it after the fact.

"There is the other side to consider," Ramon said.

Not sure exactly what that meant, Belmonte motioned for him to continue.

"Which is to say, it is a plane headed south from America, carrying a full load of Americans."

Again he fell short, leaving Belmonte to sort through things on his own.

"You think someone from up there forced the plane down?" Belmonte asked.

"Maybe," Ramon said. "Possibly. I mean, Caracas is many hours in the air from Atlanta. It seems curious that a plane with a mechanical problem would make it this far before needing to stop."

Again, Belmonte nodded. Not only was it a long way from origin, there were plenty of other airports throughout the Caribbean that would have been much friendlier locales than Venezuela.

"You think this had something to do with us?"

"I think it is certainly possible," Ramon said. "My contact said this is the first time on record a plane from the U.S. has *ever* emergency landed here."

"And just two days after we burned an American flag in the open," Belmonte finished.

To that, Ramon didn't respond. Both men understood the enormity of what was happening, both from an international crisis standpoint and from within their own campaign.

They were now just hours from heading out to the final leg on their own coming out party.

And they were potentially facing opposition from the United States, Salazar, or both.

"Can your friend get eyes on the passengers?" Belmonte asked. "We need to know what's going on over there."

Chapter Thirty

Panic comes in a predictable sequence. Much like the famed stages of grief, there are steps that most people work through. Different ways that the human mind computes what is happening and translates it into a usable medium.

Once the door to our room was slammed shut, the first step was confusion. A hushed murmur went up from the crowd. People turned to each other, openly speculating as to what was happening.

From what little I could hear around me, the list they came up with was wide-ranging, spanning from plausible to the genuinely ridiculous.

About what one might expect.

Some gave the standard response that this was all a mistake. All we needed to do was flag them down and explain who we were and where we were headed. After that, they would feel compelled to put us right back on the plane and send us on our way.

At the extreme opposite end of the spectrum were those that were certain we were going to die. That we were going to be lined up in the hallway and executed just like they'd seen in ISIS videos online.

Such speculation often gives way to the second part of the process, which is when emotions start to polarize. Some become hysterical, bringing out tears and grief and such. Others became angry. They start looking for something or someone to lash out at.

Ten minutes after the door was closed, most of the people in the room were fully entrenched in that state. A few had slipped directly out of the progression and moved into catatonia, but by and large, they were expressing themselves to whoever would listen.

Of which, I had zero interest.

My focus was instead aimed at the room around me. Pushing myself away from the corner, I left Rembert in animated discussion with an older man with a thin ring of white hair and sloped shoulders beside him. Neither looked my way as I made a quick loop of the place, avoiding eye contact, taking in everything I could.

Much like the first pass through, no form of weapon presented itself. The doors and windows were secured tight. If pressed, the overhead ceiling tiles might present an option, but it would be a longshot at best.

A last resort in every sense of the word.

Nowhere was there a sign of food, water, or restroom facilities. As clear an indicator as any that this was either put together in a hurry or they had no intention of keeping us for long.

Of the people around me, I counted twenty-four in total. Six were minors and four looked to be north of seventy-five years old. That left just fourteen able-bodied adults, that number split between five males and nine females.

Of those, only a handful looked to be in top physical condition should a tussle break out.

Not good odds, all things considered.

Working back to my original spot, I had just made my way to the corner when the whine of power tools started again. As it did so, all conversation fell away. People recoiled in tight around me, a natural reaction to put as much space between them and the door as possible.

And in my own form of natural reaction, I worked my way through the crowd to the side, not wanting to have my movements constricted by the combined weight of people pressing in from every angle.

Just as they had put the screws into the door a few minutes prior, one at a time the guards removed them. With each wail of the tool, I could see people reacting, the sound cutting through the air.

Regardless what state those inside were in a few moments prior, all seemed to hold a collective breath.

In total, fourteen screws held the door and its assorted bindings in place. Once they were done and the wooden barricades stripped away, the hinges whined as the door swung open.

One last gasp was heard as I again rolled my shoulders forward, making myself as unimposing as possible. Flexing my knees, I lost a few inches of height, casting a sideways glance to the door.

Through it walked the same excitable guard that had given us the screaming session earlier. Moving with a bit of a swagger, he held a small caliber handgun in one hand.

Screwed onto the end of it was a noise suppressor, extending the barrel almost twice as long in length.

Beside him was a second guard, this one with an AK held loosely across his waist. Seeming to gain confidence from the man beside him, he tried to match the slow strut.

It was a poor attempt, at best.

In their wake, the door swung back into place. Slamming home, the sound sent a jolt through the crowd, many of them overexcited by the sudden sound.

"I hope you have all been enjoying yourself here in Shangri La," the lead guard said. Gone was the Spanish he'd used before, replaced by heavily stilted English. "Nice digs, no?"

Spreading his lips into a wide grin, a gold tooth glinted from the top row.

"I mean, this is sure nicer than my house. How about you, Cruz?"

The man named Cruz seemed to be surprised at being drawn into the conversation. He looked at Gold Tooth before nodding. "Yes, much nicer."

"And do you know what all these people have done in response to our hospitality?" Gold Tooth said.

"What's that?"

The smile slowly slid from Gold Tooth's face. A glower replaced it as he passed his gaze over the room.

Basic scare tactic. Use faux friendliness to thinly veil overt hostility.

"They have lied to us. They have made up a story about some damn mechanical problem just so they could touch down on our soil."

Gold Tooth paused there. He folded one arm across his stomach, using it to prop up his opposite elbow. That hand he brought to his cheek, tapping the side of the gun barrel against it.

"And you know what that is?" he asked.

"Disrespectful," Cruz replied.

Nodding, Gold Tooth said, "You damn right it is. And you know what we do in Venezuela with people that are disrespectful?"

Starting in the opposite corner, he again panned the length of the audience before him. Looking out through the long hair hanging over my brow, I could see the intense pleasure he was getting from the show of fear before him.

Could feel my own animosity for the man rising with each moment.

"Oh, I know," Cruz said, playing his part in the two-man show to perfection.

A smirk lifted one corner of Gold Tooth's mouth. "Yeah, I know you do, but I think it's about time they all learned."

Three-quarters of the way through his survey of the room, his head stopped. The smile returned, his tooth peeking out at us again.

For a moment, he just stood like that, staring at a man in jeans and a blue polo shirt, before snapping the gun out straight before him.

And, without reason or warning, firing two direct shots into his chest.

Chapter Thirty-One

The noise suppressor screwed onto the end of the gun was more for the benefit of the outside world. It was to make sure that anybody that hadn't seen the odd sequence of an oversized bus load up a plane full of passengers and take them to an abandoned warehouse didn't suddenly hear gunshots and come looking.

For those of us in the room, the sound was just as imposing as it otherwise would have been. In an enclosed space with tile floors and barricaded windows and doors, the twin pops sounded like cannon fire.

And they elicited the exact response that would be expected.

A shrill scream went up the moment the bullets struck home. Emitted by no less than half of the people in the room, a sea of movement seemed to sweep everybody back.

In their stead stood the man in the jeans and polo, his body uneven and swaying, held upright only by the fact that there were too many people bracing him up by proximity when he was first hit.

Staggering in place like a real-life marionette, twin blossoms of red steadily crawled down the front of his shirt. Blood spatter dotted the white tile in front of him.

Already, his face was ashen. Saliva dripped over his chin.

He didn't have long, if any time at all.

"Did you think we would not notice?!" Gold Tooth bellowed. The gun he continued to hold at arm's length before him. "Did you think we were so stupid you could just come in here and do as you please?"

Around me, people back away to either side. They continued to rush back, leaving the man alone in the center of the room.

For his part, he made no effort to respond, or to even move. His every effort seemed to be on merely staying upright, locked in a battle with gravity.

Until, slowly, the nerve endings in his body began to fade, taking with them what little muscle function remained. Seeming to melt directly to the floor, he went flat to his back, landing with a slap.

On cue, the crowd yelped again as blood smeared in wide streaks beneath him.

There was no way of knowing who the man was. Five minutes prior was the first time I'd ever seen him before in my life. I hadn't noticed him as he boarded the plane, or even as we were on the bus to the warehouse.

Which was precisely the point.

The man was unremarkable in every way, except for the fact that he was a man. A middle-aged, able-bodied, man.

And in that moment, reality and clarity both collided in my mind.

They didn't give a damn about any of us. They were going to keep us in a state of perpetual fear. They were going to extract whatever they could from us. And in the meantime, they were going to pick us off one by one, starting with the most capable looking in the bunch.

Which meant for all my attempts at making myself small, for my every effort to hide behind a beard and shaggy hair, it was only a matter of time before my number was called.

And once that realization settled in, a second arrived soon thereafter.

I'd be damned if I was just going to let this Gold-Toothed bastard walk in and mow me down.

Pushing off the side of my foot, I slid forward. Moving in the opposite direction of everybody around me, I went to a knee, coasting over the smooth tile.

The polished floor gave no resistance save the smear of blood that striped the front of my jeans as I came to a stop beside the man.

Grabbing at the hem of his shirt, I wadded it into a ball, pressing it tight it against the closest of the two wounds. Gripping it in my left hand, blood soaked through the thin cotton, coating my fingers.

"How do you like this, Cruzie?" I heard behind me. "Looks like we've got ourselves a hero."

The mocking tone made my pulse rise, acrimony spiking within. Pretending to ignore it, I focused on the pale blue eyes before me. On the lips parted slightly, fighting to pull in air.

The man was gone, or at least would be soon. It was unfortunate, but it was a reality. For all his faults, Gold Tooth seemed to know how to shoot, putting both rounds into the left breastplate, shredding the man's heart.

All that was left to do now was wait.

The faint squeak of rubber against tile told me that Gold Tooth was moving closer.

"Hey, asshole, you want to be next?"

The sound of his voice gave me his exact position.

Unarmed, I had only one chance at things. If he decided to pull up short and just open fire, there was nothing I could do. I was exposed, had no way of defending myself.

What I needed to do was pull him in close. To bank on the fact that he would be looking to make an example of me, a visual reminder to all of what happened when somebody dared oppose him.

Ignoring him, I continued to look down at the man on the floor. The fingers on my left hand curled into a tight ball around the wad of cotton.

Beneath it, the flow of blood seemed to slow, the man down to his final few gasps.

"Hey," Gold Tooth repeated, "I said..."

He paused. The dense touch of steel pressed against the side of my skull, the end of the noise suppressor flush against my head, still warm from the shots a moment before.

"You want to be next?"

The man had made three mistakes. Actually, he had made many

more than that, but in that moment, there were only three that really mattered.

The first was his arrogance. He had earned my ire the instant he'd walked into the door, making himself a target by his mere presence.

The second was calling me an asshole. Twice.

Far and away his worst mistake, though, was the third one, and that was pressing the gun tight against my head.

While the move might have looked good, may have made him feel like he was in control, what it really did was bring him within easy reach.

Snapping my right hand up in one quick movement, I snatched his wrist, driving it straight toward the ceiling. Rotating on my knee, I released the wad of cotton and drove my left palm into his exposed knee.

A bloody print was left on his denim jeans as the sound of a tendon snapping was heard, the man gasping in pain.

Pulling my hand straight back, I balled it into a fist and snapped it straight into the soft tissue of his groin.

An egregious foul in most any situation, but extremely effective for what I needed in the moment.

Above me, I could hear the man expel every bit of air from his lungs, his body becoming flaccid. Rising straight up, I slid my hand over his wrist, ripping the gun from his fingers.

Pulling him tight against me, I used his body as a human shield, poised to protect me from his counterpart.

There was no need. Three feet away, Cruz stood with his jaw open, shock painting his features.

Even as I put two rounds into his chest and a third in his head, not once did the Kalashnikov rise above his waist.

Nor did Gold Tooth put up any further defense as I pressed the smoking tip of the barrel to his temple and pulled the trigger.

Chapter Thirty-Two

Five minutes after leaving the conference room, Director Horace Joon was back. Leaning in just long enough to motion for Charles Vance to join him, he was gone again before saying so much as a word.

Not surprised in the least, Vance had positioned himself closer to the door. If a lifetime working for the Agency hadn't driven home one key point, the last two days certainly had.

Government work, especially at a certain level, was all about mitigating risk.

Sometimes, that meant parachuting into another country to curb a potential candidacy based on anti-American rhetoric.

Others, that meant bringing along a patsy when reporting a potentially colossal error to the most powerful man in the world.

Jogging a few steps to keep pace, Vance caught Joon halfway down the hallway. There he fell in beside him, both men moving quick, the heels of their dress shoes clicking against the tile.

On either side, people drifted to the edge of the hall, letting the Director-led convoy go where it may.

Bypassing the elevator, they took the stairs up two floors, passing into the Director's palatial suite. Neither so much as glanced at the aging secretary behind the front desk as they entered.

For her part, she did the same, the unexpected entrance just one more in the life of the Director's appointed gatekeeper.

The inner sanctum of the Director's office was every bit as austere as one might expect. Done in marble and polished oak, not a single thing was out of place. The scent of disinfectant was in the air.

Nary a personal touch was visible on the desk or shelves, nothing that wasn't directly issued by the Agency itself.

"Follow me," Joon muttered. Padding across the thick carpet underfoot, he moved past his desk, passing through a door on the rear wall. "Shut the door behind you."

Doing as instructed, Vance moved just inside a much smaller space and closed the door. Equipped only with a small round table and a trio of chairs, a host of electronic equipment made up one entire wall.

In the darkened space, the various lights and switches seemed especially pronounced.

Settling down at the head of the table, Joon went to work on a keyboard before him. Glancing up at Vance, he said only, "This room is fully encrypted, the most secure line in the country not in the president's direct possession. Have a seat."

Nodding slightly, Vance again did as instructed.

Many times over the years he had heard of such a place. Long thought of as nothing more than a rumor, he assumed it was just another of the untold stories that floated out there about the Agency.

Exploding cigars. A second gunman on the grassy knoll. An ongoing blood feud with the Soviet Union.

Of those, this one seemed more innocuous, though no less impressive.

"Needless to say, you were never here," Joon added. Without waiting for a response, he completed the sequence he was entering. A moment later, the sound of ringing could be heard.

A moment after that, President Mitchell Underall appeared onscreen.

"Gentlemen," he said, nodding in greeting.

"Mr. President," Joon said.

"Mr. President," Vance mumbled.

"Please tell me you're calling already to tell me this has been resolved."

Even knowing that he was there for nothing more than window dressing, Vance could do nothing about the warmth that crept to the surface. He could feel it passing over his features, threatening to force him to start sweating at any moment.

"Not yet, sir," Joon said. "Rather, we're calling to give you a status update."

"Which is?" Underall snapped.

"Which is, as if this time, the plane is on the ground in Caracas."

"And?"

"And," Joon said, flicking a quick glance to Vance, "no word yet from our agents."

The background on the screen before them showed that the president was seated at his desk. Leaning back, he rubbed a hand over his face. A series of muttered words were heard, all too low to decipher.

"And how long have they been on the ground?"

"Just over an hour, sir."

"At which point...?" Underall asked.

Every bit of this had been gone over in painstaking detail the day before. True to form, though, everything needed to be spelled out explicitly.

One could never be too careful these days, especially in the age of nonstop media coverage.

"At which point they were to have rendezvoused with Agent Ramirez on the ground," Joon said. "As of five minutes ago, she hasn't heard from them either."

A host of emotions seemed to flood over the president's face. None of them seemed especially positive.

"Do we have eyes on the airport?" he asked.

"No, sir," Joon said. "We have a very limited presence in country, which is why we needed to send in help. Two agents, both merely observe and report."

Again, all of this had been gone over repeatedly.

Not that Vance wasn't reasonably certain it would all be repeated twice more before the situation was resolved.

"What is the status now?" Underall asked.

"The status now is, we're reporting to you before taking further action," Joon replied.

The scowl on Underall's face deepened. Whatever collegiality he had extended the day before evaporated, his eyes flashing.

"You CIA guys are a real piece of work, you know that? This was supposed to have been a foolproof operation."

Knowing better than to say a thing, both Vance and Joon sat in silence, waiting.

It wouldn't be the first time they had to weather a temper tantrum from an elected official fearful of tomorrow's headlines.

"Get somebody over to Bolivar right now and figure out what's going on," Underall spat, "before we go making an even bigger mess."

Chapter Thirty-Three

If the two shots that Gold Tooth put into the man on the floor was a shock, what I did to him and Cruz was a full-on electrocution. Unsure what they had just seen – even less what to make of it – I turned to see every last person retreating toward the corners.

Some seemed to defy even basic human anatomy, contorting themselves into spaces much too small for their frames.

Not that their actions registered very high on my priority list. Fresh blood spatter was still on my cheek. The smell of gunpowder filled my nostrils.

Adrenaline pulsated at a level that threatened to spill from every available orifice.

Nobody said a single thing, everybody staring in abject horror.

"Grey, get over there and put some pressure on that man's wounds."

Using the barrel of the gun, I gestured to the man lying on the floor, still clinging to life by the thinnest of threads.

"Grey!" I snapped, the sound of my voice causing some to wince, others to wake from their trance. "This man doesn't have long, and neither do we."

From the corner, it took a moment for Rembert to pull himself into motion. Slowly, he extended his hands, nudging people to the side.

All of them did as told, nobody putting up the slightest hesitance.

Emerging at the front of the group, he gave me a look that showed he didn't quite know what to make of what just happened. With his jaw clamped, he dropped to both knees, pressing his bulk down on the man's chest.

Looking back to Gold Tooth, my mind swam. What I'd said to Rembert was the truth. We didn't have long before somebody came looking for him and Cruz. I couldn't expect anybody inside the room to lie for me, and I didn't foresee them taking too kindly to losing two of their own.

Which meant I needed to get moving. I needed to get away from the warehouse and get somewhere that I could use the sat phone to bring in help.

It also meant I needed to do whatever I could to buy a bit of a head start in the meantime.

Tucking the gun into the waistband of my pants, I bent over Gold Tooth. A quick pat of his pockets produced a folding knife and a spare magazine of ammunition for the weapon I'd confiscated.

Nabbing both, I rolled his body onto its side, grasping the back hem of his jeans and digging my opposite hand into his armpit. Given the charge roiling through my system, his body seemed to weigh nothing at all as I lifted him from the floor.

Carrying him the same way Cruz had carried the AK a few minutes before, I hefted him across the floor, depositing him quietly at the foot of the door.

Turning and going straight back, I avoided the uneven blood trail across the floor his open head wound had left behind. Taking just a moment to check Cruz's pockets, I found nothing of value, instead hefting him from the floor and taking him over to join his partner.

As quietly as possible, I deposited him atop Gold Tooth, hopeful that their combined weight would at least provide some modicum of defense to keeping someone from marching directly in.

All I needed was a couple of minutes.

Twisting Cruz's body so it sat flush against the frame of the door, the sleeve of his t-shirt rode up over his shoulder. Beneath it flashed the dark black smudge of a tattoo, the shape of it just catching my attention as I rose to head in the opposite direction.

Feeling a bit of dread seep into my stomach, the feeling mixing with the adrenaline into a volatile cocktail, I pulled myself back. Squatting beside his body, I extended my index finger, shoving the cloth a few inches higher.

Son of a bitch.

Jerking my attention down, I moved Cruz's leg to the side. Beneath it, Gold Tooth's arm was tucked up tight against his body. Using the same finger, I pushed the sleeve of the shirt he was wearing back a few inches to reveal the same thing.

The matching tattoos featured a shield in the center, a crown sitting atop it. Crossed behind it were what looked like a missile and a rifle with a bayonet.

Enveloping everything was a furled banner.

Otherwise known as the seal of the Venezuelan Army.

Dropping Cruz's leg back into place, I repositioned the bodies, my mind swimming to compute what I'd just put together.

The way we had been forced down for a mechanical problem could be discounted as a rare happenstance. Unlikely, but possible.

For us to have landed in Venezuela was even more unlikely, but not completely unheard of.

For there to have been armed men waiting for us on the tarmac meant that we were all unwitting accomplices in something much larger than we could have fathomed.

Something that apparently involved the Venezuelan military, even if their attempt at civilian attire was trying to hide it.

Turning back to the room, I was intensely aware of every last person staring at me. The looks on their faces ranged the full spectrum, not that I was particularly in the mood to try and decipher them.

Nor did I want to endure the litany of questions and comments that would arrive as soon as their minds started firing anew.

At the moment, my most pressing concern was getting out of the room.

"Listen up," I said, my voice only as loud I dared make it, "I don't know a damned thing more about this than any of you do. I don't work for the government, or the military, or anybody else that might be affiliated.

"What I do know is, there's no way these guys are ever going to let us out of here alive. Not if they can help it. Which means we have to make them."

In the movies, this would be the part where the hero made a big speech. He would rally morale, give a stirring rendition of what the coming hours held in store for everybody.

After that would come a montage, all the people arming themselves with whatever was around, preparing for an impending fight.

I had no time or interest in any of that.

"Hawk."

The voice belonged to Rembert. Across the room, he kept his focus on the man beneath him. There he stayed for several moments before jerking his attention my way, strain painted across his features.

"I think this guy's trying to tell you something."

Chapter Thirty-Four

The man could not speak. He was too far gone for that, having to retain whatever tiny bit of oxygen reserve he had left to keep his heart and brain working.

Sliding to a stop beside him, I could see there was no way I was going to get any useful information from him through direct communication.

His eyes were nothing more than slits.

"Pen and paper," I said, spewing the words over a shoulder. When I could sense nobody move, I looked out again, waving a hand. "Pen and paper, somebody, now."

Despite the low volume, urgency dripped from every word. Sweat lined my beard and brow.

Every second now was precious.

I had no idea who it was that finally came forth. I didn't bother to turn and look. The moment a pad was thrust into my outstretched hand, I jerked it forward, pulling an ink pen from the spiral wire binding at the top.

Making a quick swirl in the corner, I made sure ink was ready before pushing it into the man's hand. Holding the paper up flush against it, I stared at the page, waiting.

Little by little, he managed to construct the wobbliest collection of lines I'd ever seen. Looking like something from a poor attempt at a Halloween decoration, he scrawled seven distinct figures before dropping his hand back to his side.

As it did so, the last of his strength seemed to give, the pen falling from his grasp and rolling across the floor.

With Rembert still pressing down on his chest, he looked up at me, his features listless.

"What is it?" Rembert asked.

Running my gaze over what was written, it took a moment for me to decipher it. To string together each of the distinct images and what they meant.

"It's a telephone number," I whispered.

"For who?" Rembert asked.

"I don't know, but I have to get out of here," I said. "I'll try this number, and if it doesn't work, I'll think of something else."

His visage drawn tight, Rembert's eyes traced my face. His mouth was pulled into a tight line, droplets of sweat standing out against his skin.

"You've still got it, don't you?" he asked.

To that, I gave only a slight nod of the head.

"In thirty seconds, I'm going to step on your back and go up through the ceiling," I said. "As soon as I'm through, pull the tile back into place."

This time, he gave only a nod.

"I can't take the AK with me. It's too big, makes too much noise," I said, gesturing over to Cruz. "I will take the firing pin with me, though."

In no way could I leave an automatic weapon lying around, begging for somebody to do something foolish.

"Do not touch it, do not let anybody else try to either. It will only end badly for everyone."

Again, he bobbed his head.

My plan was to somehow get to the roof. From there, I could clear the fence on the edge of the grounds, work my way through the woods until I could call out for help.

How things went after that was anybody's guess.

All I knew for certain was I damned sure wasn't going to sit in a room and wait for them to come back and shoot me.

"Do what you can, keep everybody calm."

Whether he was even the right person to be saying all this to, I had no way of knowing. All I knew for certain was that he was a friend, and he wasn't slowing me down with loads of questions I had no way of answering.

"I'll be back. I promise."

Rising to full height, I stood on my toes. Lifting the foam tile from its track, I slid it to the side, a dark gaping maw occluding everything above from view.

It would either work or it wouldn't.

Not a damn thing to be gained by waiting to see.

Chapter Thirty-Five

My initial assessment of the building turned out to be correct. The place was a former warehouse that had been repurposed, meaning that a second-floor office complex had been retrofitted inside the space.

It also meant that it was more or less floating inside the original structure. The entire floor was built on independent supports, housed under - rather than built into - the larger shell.

Pushing myself up off Rembert's back, I was able to reach past the track that the ceiling tiles were sitting in. Grabbing hold of the metal rafter frame a foot beyond it, I wrapped my hands around the rusted beams and pulled myself upward. Once my upper body was through, I twisted to the side and pulled my feet up, lying perpendicular to the beams.

Fashioning myself into a human plank, I lay suspended above the ceiling tiles below. Reaching down, I slid the tile I'd come through back into place, Rembert watching me.

Inch by inch, it moved into position, taking his profile and the last bit of direct light I had with it.

Once the tile was back in place, I remained motionless, forcing my breathing and heart rate to slow. Under the metal roof just inches above me, I could feel the sun beating down. Sweat coated my body, burning my eyes.

Still, I waited, listening for any sound, letting my eyes adjust to the darkened world around me.

From what I could tell, the rafters were arranged parallel to the front of the building. That meant they were running in the same direction as the offices on the second floor, my body now at a ninety-degree angle compared to them.

To my left was the outer wall, the same one that had windows boarded up on it in the office below.

More than fifty yards to my right was the opposite wall, nothing but darkness stretched in that direction.

The design of most warehouses was meant to be as impregnable as possible. The place was likely meant for shipping, meaning they wouldn't have wanted the elements getting in from a host of places.

At the same time, they would have needed at least some bit of ventilation.

Trying to work my way around in the dark would be a fool's errand. The distance between me and the ceiling below was barely a foot, the structure not designed to hold any real weight.

Trying to fumble my way forward in the darkness would mean eventually I would either be heard or I would misplace a step and go tumbling through the thin foam tiles.

That wouldn't do a damned bit of good for anybody.

Given where I knew my position to be, my best bet was to work my way along the outer wall. At some point, I would have to find a vent.

Getting through it would be tough, but it was infinitely preferable to any other option I had. Certainly, more so than trying to go back to the ground level and getting out that way.

With my body braced, I did a quick inventory of what I had. A tap to the small of my back confirmed that the gun I had lifted from Gold Tooth was still intact. Ditto for the extra ammunition and the folding knife.

Still stowed deep in my jeans was the sat phone, the hard plastic digging into the tender flesh of my inner thigh.

The final thing was the phone number I'd received just a few minutes before, stowed in its own pocket for safe keeping.

Who waited on the other end of it, I had no way of knowing. Why he'd chosen to give it to me, even less.

The answers would come soon enough.

In the meantime, I had to get my ass outside.

Chapter Thirty-Six

Working in the dark, moving one painstaking foot at a time, there was no way to know how far I'd gone. I did know for certain that I was far enough along that my body was aching. My knees were pissed about being braced against the metal railing of the rafters. Flakes of rust dug into my palms.

Sweat started high on my head and ran down over my scalp. It burned my eyes, the briny taste bringing thirst to my throat.

My breathing became rapid, the clock in my head ticking with increasing intensity.

Thus far, there had been no sound from below. No indicator that Gold Tooth or Cruz had been found. No spray of bullets up through the thin ceiling panels, strafing fire meant to finish me without much effort.

That didn't mean somebody wouldn't soon come looking for them. Which in turn meant I needed to be well on my way by then.

The lives of Rembert and more than a hundred others depended on it. The man downstairs had already intimated that we were of no consequence to them.

Gold Tooth mowing down the man in our room was just the latest example of that.

Wedged on all fours between two parallel tracks, I had a system worked out. Moving my hand and knee on the same side in tandem, I would go forward about a foot. Then I would repeat it with the other side.

From there, I would pause, extending my right arm out through the triangular support struts. Leaning over a few inches, I would trace my fingers along the corrugated metal of the outer wall, feeling for any break in the smooth surface.

It was slow, terrible, grinding work. The sort of thing I hadn't done since I was a grunt in the navy, forced to perform unholy acts as part of various initiation rites.

In the dark, every other sense became heightened. I was acutely aware of each sound I made. The smells of bat shit and mildew filled my nostrils.

Still, I moved on, working until finally, mercifully, I found what I was looking for.

The first sign of it was a vertical metal casing. So immersed in my task, my body had slid into a state of auto-pilot, a charge roiling through me at the change. Pulling back my hand, I repositioned myself so I was directly perpendicular to it before reaching back, assessing what I could.

From the feel of things, the opening was approximately two feet across and about the same in height. Covering the space were metal slats shingled atop each other, louvers that could be opened on command from below.

Starting at the top, I felt my way down, counting an even dozen in total.

Digging the tips of my fingers into them, I felt more rust beneath the pads. Clearly, it had been some time since they were installed.

How long it had been since they were last opened was anybody's guess.

Moving my hand clear to the bottom, I leaned far to the right, bracing my shoulder against the metal rafter. I curled my fingers back into a fist and placed the ball against the bottom louver, pressing as hard as I could.

There was no response. Years of rust and corrosion had sealed the metal tight.

Drawing my left leg up beneath me, I braced it against the rafter beside me, using it for leverage. Sweat coated my body as I drew air in and held it, pressing as hard as I could.

For several moments there was still no response before slowly it started to move upward. A millimeter at a time, it nudged away, bringing with it a thin strip of light that was almost blinding in the total darkness.

Wincing, I pinched my eyes shut and turned my head to the side, pushing with everything I had. Little by little it continued to move, culminating with something I had never expected.

The sound of metal snapping.

As fast as I had slammed my eyes shut, I popped them open, jerking my head to the side. Convinced I had heard wrong, there was no stopping the tiny pulse of adrenaline that leaked in as I looked over to see the left side of the louver hanging at an angle.

Apparently, the building was older than I had thought, years of exposure to the elements and the sea nearby having worn down the thin metal rod holding the slat in place.

Feeling the exhilaration pass through my core, I instantly moved my fist upward. Without the slat beneath it, this one worked a bit easier. Unlike the one below it, the metal support rod stayed intact, but still, I had a four-inch window to work with.

That alone wouldn't be enough to get me through, but it was a start.

In what seemed to be blinking bright red numbers, the clock in my head continued to tick as I worked. Sweat poured from my body as one by one I went through the slats. Three I was able to break loose merely by exerting well-aimed pressure.

The others at least moved upward, forming a grid that as a whole would be more than enough for me to get through. Light poured in, plainly illuminating me, interspersed only by the few stray bands of metal cutting through it.

By the time I was done, most of my oxygen was depleted, my

shoulder aching. Pulling my arm back through, I rolled the joint twice, working a bit of stiffness out, staring at the opening beside me.

As it stood, the largest gap I had was eight inches tall. It was a good start, but that alone would never be enough for someone of my size to fit through.

If I was going to get out and up onto the roof, I needed to make it at least twice that size.

Which meant I needed to get the remaining few slats cleared.

Keeping my foot wedged to support my weight, I stared at the problem before me for a moment.

In a perfect world, I would have a blow torch. Or a pair of bolt cutters. Or one of the many other tools I had left behind in Montana. Any one of them would make easy work of the brittle metal, sending me through in a matter of seconds.

Having nothing of the sort at my disposal, I did a quick inventory of the items I had on hand. The note and the phone were worthless in this situation, for obvious reasons.

Ditto for the gun. Given the design of the place, where I sat was essentially an echo chamber. In the event that a bullet didn't ricochet and maim me or worse, I would basically be painting a target on myself for every armed guard below.

Which would defeat the purpose entirely.

The knife I considered briefly before again remembering the two dead guards downstairs and the dwindling timeframe I had before they were found. Chiseling away with the blade would probably eventually get me out, but at a time cost too great to bear.

Which meant I had only one option.

Far from ideal, I felt my core tighten at the notion. Dread passed through my system.

But there simply wasn't another way.

Fighting to keep my body wedged between the rafters, I pushed my upper half in the opposite direction. Once it was in place, I moved both knees to the other side before snaking my right leg through the triangle formed by the rafter supports.

Extending it to full length, I saw I had more than enough length to reach through the horizontal louvers.

Knowing it was going to be loud, that once I committed, I had no choice but to move as fast as I could, I pulled my heel back. In my head, I counted slowly to three before thrusting my leg out straight as hard as I could.

On contact, the metal of the bottom two louvers sheared loose, sending the slats hurtling outward.

And sending the God-awful screech of metal breaking loose out around me.

Chapter Thirty-Seven

Once my foot first made contact, I had no choice but to go with it. I couldn't stop and listen for anybody that might have heard. I damned sure wasn't going to make myself a stationary target, letting the guards downstairs figure out what was going on.

After the first contact, I drew my leg back and fired it again. And again. Like a piston, I lashed out six times, managing to clear the bottom nine louvers.

Figuring that eighteen inches was more than enough space, I pulled my leg back through. Again, I managed to wrestle my weight across the opening between the rows, working my head and right arm through the rafter.

Pushing with my legs, I extended outward, grabbing hold of the bottom ledge of the vent. Squeezing tight, I fashioned my hold into a horizontal pullup, tugging my body through.

I had no doubt the outside air was still tepid and humid, but it felt blessedly cool as my shoulders passed into the opening. A world that had just moments before been total darkness swung to the opposite end of the spectrum, bright light illuminating everything around me.

Exposing my head just far enough to get a full visual, I took in my surroundings, seeing it play pretty close to what I'd witnessed on the bus ride in.

The warehouse was positioned in the rear corner of the airport facility. Below, I could see a chain link fence running along the perimeter, coils of razor wire intertwined along it.

Beyond that, heavy vegetation pushed up close, the bright green treetops looking almost close enough to touch.

For a moment, my focus stayed on the puffy bursts of leaves, imagining the best way to work down to the ground, before my attention shifted. Rather than looking at the bright sun amplifying color saturation, I instead focused on the shadow line of the building I was now peeking out of.

With the sun coming down at an angle behind me, it cleaved a straight line across the ground, unnaturally straight save the one vertical intrusion not ten yards away. Upright and inching forward, a horizontal arm was extended directly in front of it.

A guard carrying a weapon.

Feeling my body clench tight, I watched as it moved closer, pausing every few feet.

So worried about being heard from below, I had failed to think about who might be waiting above. No way could someone have gotten up to me so fast, meaning they had to have been positioned there from the beginning.

Which also likely meant they didn't yet know where the sound was coming from, the stilted movements meaning they were stopping often to look and listen.

Threading an arm to the small of my back, I extracted Gold Tooth's gun. I gripped it tight in my right hand and braced with my left, rolling my weight a few inches at a time until my shoulder blades rested on the bottom ledge of the vent.

With my legs wedged into the rafter across from me, I was perfectly positioned, gun extended before me. In that post, I could wait as long as it took, practically willing the guard to come forward.

As far as I could tell, he was alone, but that didn't change anything. Already I had killed two men. I was attempting to crawl out through a side vent and had a satellite phone and a number to something stowed on my person.

Killing one more wouldn't make my situation any more dire. And it was only a matter of time before the rest of them found out about me anyway.

My only option was to continue pushing straight ahead. To charge onward, even at the expense of flailing at times, and hope for the best.

Or, as I had been taught countless times before, to always err on the side of aggression.

The gun was a standard 9mm, the slide well-oiled, the suppressor of high quality. Holding it in both hands, I extended the weapon to arm's length, counting off seconds.

With my back to the ground, I could no longer use the shadow as a reference, instead waiting for my opponent to appear.

Which, in total, took less than a minute.

Whatever cautiousness the man had been showing earlier had faded. Without my beating against the louvers, all had grown silent, his AK lowered from shoulder height to his waist.

Stepping close to the edge, he peered out over the side, his expression approaching bored as he glanced down.

Even as the pair of rounds slammed into his body, hurtling him backward, the look failed to shift.

The instant the shots were fired, I let go with my left hand. Pressing it tight against the top ledge of the vent, I slid my torso through, the metal almost scalding to the touch.

Remaining horizontal, I shifted my weight out far enough so my backside could rest on the bottom edge of the vent, hooking my feet under the rafter inside to brace myself. Once my haunches were square on the ledge, I sat upright, holding the gun at eye level.

Able to just see across the surface of the roof, I swept the weapon from left to right. Moving fast, I checked every surface, seeing no immediate threat.

On the ground a few feet away was the body of the guard, the Kalashnikov sprawled beside him.

Training the 9mm on him, I fired twice more, his body spasming slightly on impact, but having no real reaction. Content that he was dead, I placed the gun on the roof and grasped the top edge with both hands.

I unhooked my toes from beneath the rafter and slowly edged my way through. The heat of the metal burned my palms as I clamped down. Little by little I drew my feet out until they were on the bottom edge of the vent, my body perched in an awkward squat along the side of the building.

From where I was, I had two choices. I could scrabble my way up onto the roof. From there, I could pillage the guard, maybe take a look around and see if there were any other exits or anything of use.

As tempting as it might have seemed, I didn't give it a ton of thought. The clock in my head was continuing to pound ahead. Already I had killed three guards. Somebody inside had surely heard the sound of me tearing out the vent louvers.

Time was my most precious commodity now, even more than an extra gun or bit of ammunition.

Releasing my right hand, I snatched up the weapon and returned it to the small of my back. Keeping the hand free, I twisted and again examined the tree line below.

The fall from where I was to the top of the canopy was no more than eight feet. Thick and dense, it was hard to determine what the support structure was beneath it, but the trees looked like hardwoods.

Which meant they would have plenty of thick branches, any of which would give me a good base to work with.

The majority of the last five years, I had made a living working in the wilderness. Doing so had imparted certain skills in me, things far beyond what any amount of government training ever could.

The top of the list being the fact that I was good in the forest, and I knew it.

Standing on an exposed rooftop, my chances were mediocre at best. Working under the concealed protection of the forest floor, there was nobody better.

And it was time to act like it.

Steeled with that knowledge, I flexed my knees twice, building a tiny bit of momentum, before pushing myself outward in a free fall away from the building.

Chapter Thirty-Eight

Caller identification told President Miguel Salazar who was on the other end of the line. He had been waiting for the call for over an hour, and even answered by picking up and asking for General Renzo Clega by name.

In the lead up to receiving the call, his mood had been optimistic. With just one swift, decisive move, they had managed to position themselves against two unwanted nuisances.

The Americans, who had the gall to call one afternoon and extend the notion of camaraderie before trying to sneak four agents into his country without so much as a warning.

And Edgar Belmonte, his opponent that had managed to cut the deficit between them by half with just a couple of quick campaign stunts.

Now, he was flipping the script on everybody. He was using the very same tactics that Belmonte was using to a higher and stronger degree, and the Americans were providing him with the perfect opportunity to do so.

It was the sort of feeling that had been a long time coming. One that he had seen precious few of in the preceding years.

And one that ebbed away bit by bit as he sat in his office, hearing nothing but silence on the opposite end of the line.

"General Clega?"

This time, there was an audible sigh. "Mr. President."

Rising to his feet, Salazar felt his stomach drop. It didn't take an advanced degree in psychology to parse out what was being communicated to him. "What happened?"

"We have had a problem."

Reaching out, Salazar pressed a single button on his phone. The sole one on the console that glowed bright red, it didn't make a sound in response.

Instead, the door opened an instant later, Isabel stepping through and closing it tight behind her.

Waving her his way, Salazar placed the phone receiver on the desk and switched the call to speaker.

"What sort of problem?" Salazar asked. "The plane did not land?"

"No," Clega replied. "The plane is here and accounted for."

"The passengers?"

On the opposite side of the desk, Isabel watched in silence, her face betraying nothing.

"All unloaded and transported to the warehouse."

Feeling his agitation grow, Salazar paused. He did not have the time or the interest in going through this point by point, playing a guessing game.

It wasn't that long until Belmonte took the stage again. At some point, the Americans would start to wonder why they couldn't get a call to or from their men.

And it wasn't like they could keep the signal jammed on the warehouse sitting at the busiest airport in the country indefinitely.

"What happened?" Salazar repeated.

This time, there would be no mistaking the words or the intent behind them.

"Everything went as planned," Clega replied. "The people were offloaded and taken into the office above the warehouse. Using the pictures lifted from the flight manifest, we were able to find and neutralize the four American agents."

Flicking his gaze up to Isabel, Salazar maintained his stance. Leaning forward over the phone, his palms were pressed into the desk.

The back of his linen shirt clung to his skin.

"One of them got a call out?"

Again, there was a pause. "No," Clega eventually said. "It would appear there was a fifth agent involved."

A crease appeared between Salazar's eyes. He shifted his gaze up to Isabel, seeing the same look on her face.

"A fifth? I thought there were only four booked onboard."

"There were," Clega said. "And again, all found and accounted for, no doubt they were working for some agency."

"No doubt, huh?" Salazar said, making no effort to hide his mounting bitterness. Just a day before, he had been informed there was *no doubt* that the four late additions were the agents.

Now, he was less than certain of the general's ability.

"None. All as cookie cutter as it comes," Clega said. "They even dressed the same."

"So how do you know there was a fifth?" Salazar asked.

"Because just a few minutes ago, the two guards assigned to the fourth room didn't report back. When we sent someone to look in on them, both were found dead, their bodies stripped."

Salazar felt his eyes slide shut, a cocktail of emotions to match rising within.

"The body of the fourth agent was also inside the room," Clega added, "meaning there must have been a fifth."

For a moment, Salazar didn't respond. He merely tried to fit the information into place in his mind. Attempted to superimpose it onto everything he knew, both from a local and international standpoint.

In return, he got a litany of red flags and dead ends, none ending well for anybody present.

"Of those left in the room-" he began.

"The man is gone," Clega said. "We found a vent kicked out on the side of the building, our guard on the roof also shot."

Pressing his lips tight, Salazar glared up at Isabel. The operation was supposed to have been simple. It was supposed to have been almost impregnable, Clega so confident it could be done with a minimal team.

Now, it was proving to be anything but.

"The others in the room?"

"Right now, they are saying nothing," Clega said, "and that is why I am calling you. I need permission to start becoming more *persuasive* in my approach."

Bitterness again flared, rising like bile along the back of Salazar's throat. The call had nothing to do with asking permission. It was nothing more than a not-so-subtle reminder that they were in this together.

Shit was going sideways, and they were tied at the hip through it, come what may.

"Do whatever you have to. Just find his ass."

Chapter Thirty-Nine

The fall had managed to tear a strip of skin away from my right forearm. And another from my left elbow. A single jagged branch had even jabbed into my beard, wrenching free a clump of hair from my jawline almost the size of a dime.

All three had managed to draw blood, leaving behind raw flesh. Serving as open invitations for the millions of mosquitos flying around, they all itched uncontrollably.

And stung every time fresh sweat ran into them.

Despite the annoying discomfort, fortunately all three were nothing more than cosmetic damage. They would make it even harder for me to try and flag down a ride on a highway, but the odds of that happening were pretty low anyway.

The more important matter was that no structural damage had befallen me. After the initial jolt of hitting the canopy, I had managed to slide my way down a thick arm of the tree. The rough bark had been the cause of the two abrasions on my arms, but otherwise, it hadn't been as bad as feared.

Just seconds after leaping from the building, I landed on the soft floor of the forest, most of the sound and light from the outside world blotted from view.

Standing by the thick base of the tree that had broken my fall, my first order of business had been to clear the sat phone from its hiding spot. Knowing better than to stay so close just yet, I had held it in my left hand, the gun in my right.

Sweeping the area, I saw nothing of opposition, the air humid and heavy beneath the treetops.

Still acutely aware of how much time I was spending, I took just another moment to gain my bearings before setting a course toward the north.

What I remembered of the area was that Bolivar International was located in the northwest corner of the city. Given my current appearance, that put moving south or east out of the question.

No way a guy looking like I did could slip by unnoticed.

I had no idea what lay to the west, only that it was a long way before finding much worth mentioning.

That left me with the north. On approach, we had been within plain sight of the ocean. Getting there would make it easy for me to call out, would provide a solid place for me to direct any reinforcements I might be able to drum up.

And not the least of which, it had to be a hell of a lot cooler than where I currently was.

Taking off at an easy lope, I worked my way through the trees, going as fast as I dared. Having survived the earlier fall, I was in no hurry to stumble over an exposed root or an errant boulder, knowing my fate and that of a hundred others all rested on my getting out.

With no watch and no map, I ran until sweat was streaming off me. The front of my shirt was saturated, and heavy rivulets followed the veins in my forearms.

Having not had any liquid replenishment since the Atlanta airport, I slowed to a walk, my breathing even. So close to sea level, it was much easier than being at the elevation of Yellowstone, my body responding well.

Though that still didn't mean I should overdo it. Not yet, not without knowing what lay ahead.

Content that I had gone more than a couple miles from the warehouse, I paused. I put my back against the base of a Brazil nut tree and powered the sat phone to life.

Unlike what I had said to Rembert, any wilderness guide worth hiring was intimately familiar with a satellite phone. Modern cell phone coverage only accounted for five percent of the thirty-four hundred square miles of Yellowstone, meaning a sat phone was second only to a sidearm when out in the backcountry.

The model was the newest thing out on the market, the sort of device that looked like it could make calls while simultaneously brewing espresso and rerouting incoming jets. Not even wanting to feign a guess at what it must have cost, I worked my way through a few different touchscreens, eventually getting where I needed to be.

A picture of a keypad staring back at me.

The list of numbers I knew by heart could be counted on one hand. It wasn't that I had become like most Americans, simply entering someone's digits into my phone without thinking about it. It was more to the effect that there were only a couple of people in the world that I talked to with even the whiff of semi-regularity.

Since the murder of my wife and daughter, there just hadn't been much point.

Of those, most were wiped away almost immediately. Calling Kaylan wouldn't do me a bit of good. Nor would hitting up my favorite pizza shop back home in West Yellowstone.

If all else failed, I could call my friend Mia Diaz, Special Agent in Charge for my old DEA office outside of San Diego. It would be long and circuitous, would require the sort of synergy that our government wasn't exactly known for, but there was no doubt that she would eventually figure out a way to get to me.

Never a more capable individual had I known.

The problem therein, again, was time. I didn't have it, and Rembert and the others damned sure didn't.

Fishing down into my left pocket, I pulled out the crumpled piece of paper the man in the warehouse had given me. Only seven digits in total, there was no country code, and no area code attached.

Which either meant he was giving me the number of a wife or

loved one, somebody back at home he wanted me to contact, or he had someone local lined up to provide assistance.

One of the benefits of having been in Venezuela before was that I knew the phone system operated much like America's. Seven numbers, clumped into splits of three and four.

I also knew that for calls within Caracas proper, there was no need for any additional codes.

Taking a deep breath, I used my phone to punch in the digits. Expecting nothing, not completely certain the last scribbled gasps of a dying man were even legit, I hit send and held the device to my ear.

To my surprise, it was answered after only a single ring.

"The mockingbird is flying south."

Jerking the phone away from my ear, I looked down at it, confusion on my face.

The voice was female. It sounded young, otherwise neutral of any inflection.

"Say again?"

"The mockingbird is flying south."

This time, I pushed past any surprise, focusing on the words said.

Nobody answered the phone in such a way. Everywhere I had ever been, people used some form of a greeting. If the person calling was especially well known, they might start with a joke or a nickname, but never something like that.

Unless they were speaking in code.

Feeling my eyes slide shut, I raised my face toward the trees above, sweat streaming down either cheek. I had been completely blind before. Borderline foolish, even.

Not on the plane. That part I had nailed. I knew it would have taken someone with serious juice to force it down in Venezuela of all places.

My mistake had come in the warehouse. I had thought Gold Tooth and Cruz were there to start picking off any able-looking person that might offer opposition.

That didn't entirely make sense, though. The man they had shot was youngish and somewhat fit, but he wouldn't have looked especially imposing. Even given the posture I was using, the man was much smaller than me.

And a far cry from the heft of Rembert.

Gold Tooth hadn't been sweeping the group, looking for any opposition. He'd been looking for a specific person.

The bland clothes. The vanilla haircut. Even the fair complexion of the man that had been shot. It all pointed to one incontrovertible conclusion.

"Your agent is dead." Hearing nothing from the other end, I added quickly, "I didn't do it."

Several moments of silence passed.

"The mockin-" she began anew.

"Yeah, yeah," I snapped, cutting her off. "Listen Mockingbird, this is Hawk, and I'm telling you, your agent is dead. The plane and all its passengers were hijacked.

"The men that did it shot your agent, who just managed to write down this phone number and slip it to me before he died."

Whether he was dead or not, I didn't know. My mood, and the urgency of the situation, both shoved aside a great deal of my caring.

Now was not the time to be playing semantic games with these people.

Damn CIA and all their bullshit.

"My name is Jeremiah Hawkens Tate. Formerly of the U.S. Navy, formerly of the DEA. I am currently headed toward the coast, and I will leave this phone on so you can track it.

"If you can help me, get your ass there now."

Chapter Forty

The meeting to update President Underall was a no-win proposition. Charles Vance had known sitting in the Oval Office the day before that this was going to be one of those situations. The sort of thing where an elected politician smiles and offers them coffee to their face, but instantly hangs them out to dry at the first sign of trouble.

He also had a feeling Director Joon knew that fact even better than he did.

While the closed video conference was by no means a victory, it wasn't an unfettered disaster either.

At least they were given the directive to fix it, rather than being told the whole thing was off.

Perhaps that had more to do with the fact that initial contact had already been made with the Venezuelan president, but Vance was willing to take it as a win either way.

Striding back toward the war room alongside Joon, he wanted nothing more than to turn and ask his assessment of it. He was curious to see if his initial reaction was the same as his boss. If it matched previous encounters with the president.

Knowing better, he held his tongue. The call had been made in an encrypted safe room, meaning it was the highest of confidential. The set of Joon's jaw signaled he was not exactly in the mood for conversation.

Instead, the two men moved forward, making it almost back before spotting one of the young, nameless aides standing outside the door. At the sight of them, the young woman threw a hand in the air.

To match it, she jumped a few inches off the ground, yelling, "Director! Director Joon!"

Making no effort to acknowledge, or even increase his pace, Joon let the glower on his face grow a bit more pronounced. He kept his head down and went straight ahead before pulling up just short of the girl.

"What?"

If the aide picked up on the demeanor, she did nothing to show it.

"Director Joon, we've got Agent Ramirez on the line from Venezuela."

Casting a quick glance to Vance, the director pushed inside. Doing the same, Vance followed in order, barely catching the door long enough for the aide to slide in behind him.

Once they were all in, she disappeared again to the side, her part in the proceedings effectively over.

Around the conference table, each of the people seemed to be leaning forward, their attention focused on the telephone console in the middle of the table.

On the far wall video screen was the naval service record and photo of a man Vance had never seen before.

Ignoring all of it, and whatever prior conversation might have been had, Joon said, "Agent Ramirez? This is Director Horace Joon."

Every person inside the room fell silent. On the line, Ramirez did as well for a moment before saying, "Director. This is Agent Manuela Ramirez."

"Agent, good to hear from you," Joon said. "Please tell me you've heard from our boys?"

"No," Ramirez replied.

"No?"

"No," Ramirez repeated. "In fact, there's no word getting in or out from anybody on that plane."

As if the conversation with Underall had somehow joined them together, Joon glanced to Vance. The look on his face seemed to match exactly with what Vance was thinking.

"Not that it would matter, apparently," Ramirez continued, pulling both their attention back to the phone. "If a call I just received is any indicator, they're dead anyway."

Feeling his brow come together, Vance took a step closer to the table. Once the front of his legs pressed against the edge of it, he leaned forward and said, "Agent, this is Special Director Charles Vance. Can you repeat? *All* of our agents are dead?"

A long exhalation was the first response. Following it, Ramirez relayed the phone call she'd received just moments before.

As she did so, Vance lifted his attention back to the file on display on the far wall, the visual making much more sense than before.

"Jeremiah Hawkens Tate?"

"Flight manifest has him onboard via a ticket change made by Grey Rembert earlier this week," Peter Reiff said.

"He is currently a wilderness guide working out of Yellowstone," Hannah Rowe added. "But his backstory about being with the navy and DEA checks out."

Lifting his gaze back to Joon, Vance fell silent. There was no need to voice the host of questions springing to mind. It was clear the director was having the same ones.

"Any reason to think he's working with somebody?" Joon asked.

"None," one of the men from the opposite side said. "Last year he did a couple of consultant gigs with the Southwest DEA office, but nothing since."

"Financials are clean, too," the woman beside him. "Nothing funny going on."

"Where was he headed?" Vance asked.

"Punta Arenas was his final destination," Rowe said. "He was traveling with Rembert."

"Anything there?" Joon asked.

"No," Dan Andrews said. "Retiree, looks like it was legitimately a fishing trip."

Silence fell for a moment, everybody seeming to try to determine the best way to handle the information.

After a moment, it was Ramirez that broke the silence, asking, "Orders on how to proceed?"

Again, Vance and Joon shared a look. Agents were trained to never give out information. If in fact one had given away the emergency contact info, it meant that the situation was beyond dire.

At the same time, they didn't know a damned thing about this Jeremiah Tate or what he might represent.

"Did Tate say anything else?" Joon asked.

"No, sir," Ramirez replied. "He sounded pretty pissed by the end, told me if I could help, to get my ass up to the coast to fetch him."

Twice over, Vance replayed the final sentence in his mind. As he did so, certain words and phrases caught his attention. Things that he was sure Joon would notice as well.

Most noticeably, those that seemed to indicate ownership in the situation.

"Tate's record," Vance said, turning to glance at Rowe, "was he good?"

"Very. And he's spent time in Venezuela."

The situation was spiraling. He and Joon knew it when they left the call with the president. Became even more aware of it when stepping into the room to find out at least one of their agents was already dead.

At the very least, this guy had some working information that could be shared.

At the most...

"Go pick him up," Joon said, seemingly arriving at the same conclusion Vance had.

Chapter Forty-One

G rey Rembert had been married for more than thirty years. He had been with the same woman for six more than that, their courtship beginning at the tail end of their college career. Save a few rough patches that all couples experience, every bit of it had been quite happy and fulfilling.

Though, to be fair, the travel schedule did help at times.

Over the course of that time, both had developed particular tastes and habits that the other had tried to shift before eventually accepting as the quirky traits of their beloved.

Rembert liked to take fishing trips. His wife enjoyed watching true crime shows.

In total, Rembert must have seen close to a thousand of them. Ranging the full gamut, they included everything from cold case murders to attempted bank robberies.

Of them, not once had he ever even heard about something like the situation he now found himself in. Starting with the mid-air announcement from the captain, everything had seemed like it was scripted from one of the old Jack Ryan movies, Harrison Ford stowed somewhere in cargo, ready to slip off and perform his country's dirty work.

Except this wasn't a movie.

And despite whatever had taken place a little while earlier, he was reasonably certain Hawk Tate wasn't Harrison Ford.

Rembert first encounter with the man had been almost two years prior. Some basic internet research had brought him to Hawk's Eye Views tour company, and a little further digging had shown glowing reviews of both the man and the organization.

His own trip had proven them to be correct.

Tate was a no-nonsense type for sure, especially when out in the elements. At the end of the day though, he had been just as ready as Rembert to relax and open a cold one.

He had laughed and smiled. Never did Rembert have the slightest hesitance around him. So much so that when his guide for Patagonia had backed out, there was no question who he would call to fill the gap.

Sitting now with his bottom on the cool tile and his back against the wall, Rembert had to admit, he didn't actually know a great deal about the man. For all his willingness to enjoy the camp life, rarely did he ever say anything about himself.

If he thought hard about it, Rembert would be forced to concede that everything he knew about Hawk Tate could be counted on one hand.

Up until the part where he saw the man kill two armed guards and disappear through the roof tiles, that is.

There was no way Tate was involved in anything. Up until three days ago, the man had had no reason to be on that plane. If Rembert hadn't called and made the arrangements, he would still be somewhere in Montana, preparing for the upcoming season.

Which meant he likely wasn't actively involved in anything, but he damned sure had been at one point or another.

Nobody had those kinds of skills otherwise.

What that might have been, what organization he may have worked for, how it might even help them now, all floated through Rembert's mind as the sounds of screws being removed from the front door again rang out. On cue, the people around him let out a low murmur of trepidation, many starting to shuffle back tight against the walls.

As if that would do any good. Still piled in a heap at the front of the room were the two guards Tate had killed. Beside them was the passenger that had been shot, his breath lasting just barely long enough for Tate to get the ceiling tile back into place.

There was no way of hiding what had happened, and no point to even trying. Already their captors had been by once and seen the results.

The only question now was how they planned to act on it after having a few minutes to regroup.

Leaning his head back against the wall, Rembert flicked his gaze toward the door. He remained that way, watching, as the last of the barricades were pulled free from the outside and the door cracked open again.

For a moment, there was nothing. Just a pulse of cool air, the puff managing to shove around the scents of blood and death in the room.

An instant later, the fat man with a mustache they had first met when getting off the bus walked into the room. Gone was the saunter and arrogant smile he had before, replaced by a red face and quick strides.

By his side was a second man, much younger with blue-black hair, his mouth set into a scowl.

And a machete in his hands.

"Okay," the lead man said. Moving his gaze slowly, he scanned the room, "We're going to try this again. And this time, I *will* be getting the answers I'm looking for."

Chapter Forty-Two

B est guess, I spent just over an hour in the forest. Based on what I knew my travel time to be when walking through Yellowstone and the break to call out, I'd say that put me at roughly three and a half miles from the airport.

Given that most of it had been at a downward slope, the terrain trending to sea level, maybe as much as four miles.

By the time I reached the edge of the tree line, every bit of clothing I wore was damp with sweat. The open sores on my arms were still slick, unable to even begin scabbing over.

My patience was completely gone.

A busted nose from my DEA days precluded me from being able to smell the ocean, though I was able to see the edge of the tree line long before I arrived there. Slowing my pace, I began to work my way from tree to tree, careful to stay out of direct sight.

There was no way of knowing what I would find there. Odds were, it would be more like I'd encountered in the woods.

Nothing but seclusion and silence, most of the country's population clustered tight in a handful of metropolitan centers. If that wasn't the case, I might stumble across a few wayward fishermen, locals out providing for their families.

Obviously, I would mean them no harm, but it would be difficult to try and make them understand that. Especially given my limited grasp of Spanish.

And the fact that I was armed and bloody, stumbling out of the woods like some sort of hairy beast.

Wanting to avoid that eventuality, I played it slow. I worked my way in a varied pattern, using what cover I could. The phone and the gun I both kept out and ready, hopeful that one or the other might be able to help with whatever I found.

What that might be covered a wide range of possibilities, handfuls of possibilities presenting themselves in my consciousness.

Not one was close to what I actually discovered.

The first thing that caught my eye was the glint of the sun. It refracted off a glass windshield, winking at me through the trees.

Nudging closer, the second was the form of a woman leaning casually against the front hood. A handheld device gripped in her palm, she alternated glances between the screen and the trees, squinting slightly.

If I had time, or better resources, or even the tolerance, I would have gone slow. I would have scouted the area, making sure it wasn't a trap.

At the very least ensured she was a friendly.

I had none of the above.

Plunging straight out of the trees, my sudden emergence seemed to surprise her, her entire body going rigid as she looked my way. Raising her free hand to her chest, she stared at me wide-eyed, saying nothing.

Younger than I would have expected, she looked to be a half-decade my junior. Standing halfway between five and six feet, she had dark hair in a ponytail and wore khaki shorts and hiking boots.

The vehicle she leaned against was a Jeep with the windows zipped out, sand caked in the tires.

"Mockingbird?"

A slow nod was her first response. "Hawk?"

Closing the distance between us, I kept the phone and the gun both out. Making no effort to get too close, I turned my back and took up a position on the opposite end of the Jeep. Matching her pose, we both stared out at the trees I'd just emerged from.

"Do I even want to know what the CIA has going on down here right now?"

In my periphery, I saw her hair flash as she jerked to look my way. Heard as she forced out a laugh.

"The CIA? You watch too many movies."

"Don't," I replied. "I worked for the government for over ten years, too. I know how this works. So let's just skip ahead to the part where we both start sharing information the other one needs."

The girl kept her gaze on me another moment before turning back to the woods.

"There are people that need to debrief you. There's a safehouse nearby we should get to immediately."

"I figured as much."

Using her hips, the girl pushed herself up from the side of the Jeep. "Are our men really gone?"

"At least one is," I said. "They put us all in separate rooms, so I can't vouch for the others."

Again, I played back how it had gone down in the warehouse. "But it's likely."

Looking at me another moment, the girl made no effort to hide her open appraisal. She turned to the Jeep and reached inside, extracting a bottle of water and extending it my way.

"Agent Manuela Ramirez. Call me Ela."

Accepting it with a nod, I said, "Hawk."

Chapter Forty-Three

The office was split into distinct sections. The front half of the space was the same as it had been all day. Still riding on the euphoria of the last two nights, campaign workers bustled about.

They were unequivocally busy, given the third and largest event of the week looming just hours away, but they were happy. Smiles were abundant. Bursts of laughter were the norm.

Things were looking up. The local man that just a week earlier had been a longshot at best was surging fast. Monies would soon start rolling in. A groundswell of support was just starting.

And they were all on the leading cusp of it.

The back end of the suite was different in almost every way. Beginning with the arrival of Hector Ramon earlier in the day, not a single positive thing had been said. No smiles had been cracked.

In their stead was a somber mood that seemed to hang over everything, clinging to them like a thin mist. Having grown to encompass Giselle Ruiz, the three insiders sat tucked away in the rear conference room. On the table in front of each of them were their cell phones, ringers on high, all sitting and waiting for word back from their various contacts.

Thus far, their inquiries had been met with more surprise and curiosity than concrete responses, promises to do some digging and call back later.

The initial burst of looking into things had gone out hours before, all acutely aware of the dwindling time they had.

Seated at the head of the table, Edgar Belmonte had his fingers laced across his lap. Lightly tapping the pads of his thumbs together, he stared toward the table, focused on nothing.

What he knew thus far was that the decision to begin using an anti-American platform had been a risky - albeit necessary - gesture. In a country such as Venezuela, those in command tended to keep it. There was no such thing as equal air time. No true form of a peaceable transition of power.

It had to be wrested away.

For two months, he and his team had paid their dues. They had done as they were supposed to, meeting as many people as possible. They had said all the right things. Stood for pictures. Kissed babies.

Everything that could be asked of a candidate, especially one presenting himself as the common everyman.

It was getting them nowhere.

Something bold had to be done. Whether it had to happen when it did was a matter of debate, as was the route they chose to take, but there was no doubt that it was effective.

And Belmonte would be damned if he was going to apologize for it.

The truth of the matter was, he held no true ill will toward America, or the western world, or much of anybody outside the boundaries of his home country.

The place he had grown up in in his youth was almost idyllic. Whatever change had occurred since wasn't the work of some mysterious outside boogeyman. It was done by those in charge, susceptible to the pitfalls of greed and power.

Men like Miguel Salazar.

Of course, he couldn't go out and just say such a thing. To openly condemn the president would get him locked in prison, or worse.

To criticize his own countrymen with open disdain would disenchant him from the voters in a way that he could never recover from.

In its stead, he had turned to the easiest target he could find. The famed *big bad*, the place that all countries lower in the pecking order liked to blame when things didn't go their way.

Little did many of them realize – his own country included – that by and large, the Americas of the world didn't care for them at all. Unless they had oil or labor or some other easily co-opted commodity, there was no call for the greater powers to turn their attention toward smaller fare.

Not that he could ever say that either.

"Security will be here in two hours," Ramon said.

The sound of his voice ripped Belmonte from his thoughts. His gaze moved upward as he stared across the table. He raised his eyebrows, signaling his Chief of Staff to repeat whatever he'd just said.

"Security will be here in two hours to take us over to the stadium," Ramon repeated. "Apparently, people have already started showing up."

To that, Belmonte nodded. He had expected as much. Early buzz was that it was taking on the same fevered excitement of a music concert or a major football match.

Which was precisely the attitude they were trying to build.

"Any word?" Belmonte asked.

Ramon replied with only a quick shake of the head. Belmonte flicked his gaze to Ruiz to see her do the same.

"Does this change anything regarding this evening?" Ramon asked.

On its face, Belmonte wanted to say no, that things would proceed as planned.

But that would just be foolish.

"I don't see how it doesn't, do you?" he asked.

"But-" Ruiz began, cut off by Belmonte raising a hand toward her.

"I don't want to, and if we don't have to, we won't, but..." he paused for a moment, letting his voice trail off. Again, his gaze glazed over. "The fact that this is happening now, just two days after we burned an American flag, can't be coincidental, right?"

"Doesn't have to mean anything," Ruiz countered. "Lord only knows what Salazar might have done to bring on something like this."

Belmonte again raised his eyebrows, conceding the point. It was possible that Salazar had done something, especially now that he saw their numbers surging.

But they had to be sure before going forward with what they had planned for the evening.

"Security arrives in two hours?" he asked. "That means we have a half hour. If we haven't heard anything by then, start calling everybody you know.

"We need to get to the bottom of this before we go on tonight."

Chapter Forty-Four

The safehouse was actually half of a house. Encompassing the top half of a yellow two-story home on the east end of Caracas, the place was as unassuming as could be.

Yellow paint. Red shutters. A porch along the front. In the backyard was a small fire pit and a chicken coop, a handful of birds scouring the thin grass.

A scene that could have been in any of a hundred cities in a dozen different countries.

Which, I guess, was the point.

A private entry ran up the right side of the building, a reinforced wooden staircase painted red to match the shutters. It was not until the top that what lay inside was even hinted at, beginning with the retinal scanner that Ela accessed for entry.

From there, a voice imprint was required, the second safeguard releasing the enormous metal tumblers in the armored door, granting us entry.

"The place has been in the family for decades," Ela said. "The downstairs tenant has been here that entire time."

She didn't say anything more, but she didn't have to. Whoever was on the first floor was on the payroll as cover.

Stepping inside, the place was essentially one open area segmented into three parts. The front portion was a living room, replete with couch, standard electronic fare, and an aquarium, the sound of bubbling water omnipresent.

Offset by a half-wall, the second part was living quarters, with a bed and dresser built into the wall. Peering through to the back, I could see a kitchen with aged appliances and a small table and chairs.

On the whole, the place was Spartan and quite clean. In a way, it reminded me of my cabin back in Montana.

Given the dimensions, I also knew there was a decent chunk of unaccounted space, the Agency no doubt having a few things stowed away that I would have never thought to bring into my home.

"Bathroom is around the corner," Ela said, motioning with her chin. "John - the other agent here in Venezuela - keeps a few clothes in the bottom drawer for the occasional stopover."

Glancing down at myself, I could see the last couple of hours displayed plainly across me. After riding in the Jeep, my t-shirt was dry, though my jeans were still damp. Blood and mud striped both, clinging to everything.

I could only imagine the same was true for my beard.

Despite that, there would be time to worry about my appearance soon enough. Until then, I was most concerned with the people still stuck inside those rooms in the warehouse.

"It's already been too long since I left," I said. "Let's talk to your people first. I'll shower up after we figure out what's going on."

It was clear that Ela didn't especially like the decision, having wanted the extra time to check in first, but I wasn't terribly concerned with what she wanted. The man that had greeted us as we stepped off the bus earlier made it clear he didn't give a damn about any of the people that came off that plane.

Once he figured out that three of his men were dead, that disregard would grow to open disdain.

Taking a moment, Ela nodded her head. "Follow me."

Moving in the same direction she had motioned earlier, Ela led me into the bathroom. Going to a vertical shelving unit on the back wall, she lifted down a stack of towels before sliding out a small wooden panel.

One at a time she repeated the process she had on the outer door, going through a retinal scan followed by a voice imprint.

Not until the two-part clearance was passed did the entire shelving unit swing inward revealing a hidden compartment.

Much larger than I had envisioned upon first entry to the apartment, the space was almost as large as each of the outer segments. Electronics of various forms lined one wall. A makeshift weapons locker covered another.

In between was a small black table, a pair of matching chairs behind it.

"Have a seat," Ela said, sliding down into one of them. From under the desk she pulled out a small tray, going to work on a keyboard housed there.

As she worked, the screens along the wall came alive, a visual of my service record popping up before being immediately replaced with some form of online calling system.

Seeing it, a tiny flare of animosity rose up, receding as fast as it had arrived. The reason I had given my name on the first call was so that she could check me out and validate what I was saying.

The fact that they had done so and felt at least some bit of comfort with what they found was the only reason I was now standing where I was.

Easing my way down into the seat, I watched the screen. The air inside the room was cool, the faint scent of lavender present.

The only sound was Ela working on the keyboard.

Less than a minute after entering, the image onscreen shifted again. The sound of a phone ringing could be heard.

Just a few seconds after that, the line was picked up, a room full of people in stark business attire staring back at us.

"Good afternoon," a man with silver hair said. "My name is Horace Joon, Director of the CIA. You must be Jeremiah Tate."

Chapter Forty-Five

The name Jeremiah Hawkens was given to me by my father. He was an avid fan of the movie *Jeremiah Johnson* and derived the moniker from the lead character and the beloved Hawkens rifle he always carried with him.

To my knowledge, not one person outside of my mother has ever used the first name when referencing me.

To the world, I had always just been Hawk.

The fact that Joon opened by doing so didn't bother me. It was a common error, the sort of thing many people did before I was able to correct them.

It was his demeanor – from the way he stood to the cadence of his word delivery – that irked me to no end.

The first part of the interaction had gone exactly as I would have thought. Starting at the beginning, I took them through everything that had happened since leaving Atlanta that morning.

Throughout, the handful of people I could see and the untold number sitting beyond the view of the camera sat in silence. Not once did they interject or ask a clarifying question.

More than a few times, I got the impression they already knew what I was telling them. Whether they were listening simply to get a baseline or to fact-check me as a witness, I had no way of knowing.

The entire time, Ela sat beside me, alternating her focus between me and the screen. Not once did she speak, nor did she take a note.

When I was finished, the people on the other end all sat in silence, many casting sideways glances to Joon, allowing him to take the lead.

Standing on the far end of the table, he stood with his arms folded. One hand he had raised, stroking his chin.

"Mr. Tate, do you think you could identify the man that you saw get shot?"

"Without a doubt," I said.

Shifting to the side, Joon nodded to somebody outside the screen. A moment later, ten different pictures appeared before us, blotting the CIA room from view.

All some variation of the same thing, they depicted men in their late-thirties to early-forties. Each one was fit and seemed to have a similar haircut.

Ela had also told me already that there were four agents onboard, meaning most of the men before me were there as nothing more than a test.

Which only made my dislike for Joon grow.

"Second row, third one in," I said.

"Are you sure?" Joon's disembodied voice asked.

"Positive. I'm pretty sure I even have some of his blood still on my jeans if you want to run the DNA."

Either from my passage of the test or from my remark, the grid of pictures evaporated from the screen before us. In their place was the room, the expressions on each of the people a bit more drawn than when we'd last seen them.

"Mr. Tate," a second man asked. This one was standing like Joon, a bit younger, with hair just starting to gray combed straight back. "Charles Vance, Special Director for South American Operations."

To him I only nodded, reserving the caustic comment I had about overcompensation and unnecessarily long titles.

"At any point did you hear the name Edgar Belmonte?"

A few feet away, I saw Joon cast him a harsh glance.

"No."

"You're sure?"

"Positive," I said. "Like I said, Cruz was the only name I heard, and he was just a guard."

The sound dropped out for a moment. On the screen, we could see them discussing something, but couldn't hear a word.

Which, again, made my agitation grow.

When they came back, the same man asked, "Did anybody make mention of tonight? Anything special going on?"

Blowing out a long, slow sigh through my nose, I let them see the acrimony I was starting to harbor. They were still treating this as a fact-finding matter. Not once had there been even the slightest hint of urgency.

"Special? You mean beyond the one-hundred-plus American hostages being held?" I spat, making no effort to hide the venom from my tone. "No. Just the comment in the beginning about everything being wrapped up in twelve hours or so."

For the first time, my words seemed to truly hit home. Faces tightened. Glances were exchanged.

The volume in the room was again cut, this time the various players on the other side becoming a bit more animated. A few waved hands about while others shook their heads.

At the end of the table, Joon did both, directing things like an orchestra conductor.

For more than two minutes, the show played out in pantomime, before finally everyone fell still. Turning their attention back to the camera, the sound returned.

"Mr. Tate," Joon said, his voice stiff and detached. "Thank you. Now, if you'll excuse us, we need to speak with Ms. Ramirez in private."

Chapter Forty-Six

There was no conversation to be had with Ms. Ramirez. As Charles Vance learned the moment the call was disconnected, that was nothing more than a ruse to get off the line.

Once it was cut, Director Joon hooked a finger, motioning for Vance to follow him. To everyone else, he offered only, "We'll be back."

Knowing that the phrase was code for another call to the White House, the others watched in silence as Joon departed. Standing a few feet away, Vance rolled everything he had just witnessed in his mind for a moment before doing the same.

In his wake, he left a slew of faces, all of them falling somewhere between irritated and confused.

Which was not too far off from what he felt.

Prior to getting on the line, he hadn't known what to expect. He'd been prepped with the transcript of the earlier call from Jeremiah Tate. He'd had a look at the man's navy and DEA files. Both told a pretty straightforward story of a man that was a rising star, having done the right things and done them well, before a personal tragedy abruptly ended his government career.

In short, it was the sort of resume that would have likely eventually landed him as an independent contractor for the Agency.

All that hair would have certainly had to go, but he would have gotten an invite.

In the wake of the call, two distinct impressions had popped up. The first was about Tate himself, the man seeming to bear out most of Vance's original suppositions. He had gotten older, was a little rougher around the edges, but he still bore the same hardened visage that his file would indicate.

In short, he was a capable man. An ally, in a place where such things were in desperately short supply.

The second thing he had taken away from the conversation was much less encouraging. It rested much closer to home, and that was the general demeanor of the man now walking beside him.

Everything about the last two days had proven that Joon and President Underall were concerned with political repercussions. Given their respective positions and the two countries involved, that wasn't too much of a surprise.

What was was the line of questioning Joon seemed to be pursuing, his focus still solely on international relations.

In silence, the two men cut a path back to Joon's office. Walking the same route they had just minutes before, they parted through the thin foot traffic, each chewing on what had just taken place.

Five minutes later they were back inside the private lair in the rear of Joon's office, the president up on screen before them. Much like their prior conversation, he did not seem pleased to be having it, a frown tugging both ends of his mouth down toward his jawline.

"Mr. President," Joon opened.

Vance murmured the same, nodding.

"We got a call?" Underall replied, bypassing pleasantries.

"We did," Joon replied, "but not from one of our guys."

In short order, he ran through the conversation with Tate. Careful to leave out nothing, he rattled the information off in rapid fashion.

He also made a point of noting that while one agent was a verified kill, there was nothing definitive on the other three as yet.

Not that it took a great deal of insight to imagine the situation

Tate relayed as having played out three other times inside the secluded warehouse.

Once he was finished, Underall said nothing for a full minute. Chewing on the new data, he wore a look that denoted he might soon be ill. His skin looked pale and sallow.

It was a form Vance himself would likely have if given the option.

"Have we continued trying to reach the other three?" Underall eventually asked.

"We have," Joon replied. "It would appear that the area is still being blanketed, no signal getting in or out."

"And the agent onsite?"

"Agent Ramirez has heard nothing either," Joon replied.

Folding one leg over the other, Underall adjusted himself in his seat. It was a pose similar to the one Vance had seen the day before, intimating he was uncomfortable with the situation.

Even as president, the man's body language left something to seriously be desired.

"So what does this mean?" Underall asked.

"This means Edgar Belmonte is still slated to speak later this evening," Joon replied. "And that our only means of neutralizing him have been removed."

Deep within, Vance felt something tighten. Originating in his core, it squeezed so tight it threatened to take his breath from him.

Like a remembered clip from an old movie, he saw Jeremiah Tate appear before him, the angry scowl he wore on the call just minutes before.

And felt the same thing well within him.

"What about this man, Tate, that you just spoke to?" Underall asked.

Casting a glance over to Joon, Vance saw the man's eyes narrow.

"I don't think so, sir. He's been out of the game for more than five years. To be honest, I think he took advantage of some prior training just to save his own hide."

Nodding, Underall pondered the response. "We do still have two agents in the country, correct?"

Joon let out a long sigh through his nose. "We do. Ramirez is strictly observe-and-report status. Farkus has been in country much longer, would be a loss of a major asset to have him break cover."

The tightening Vance felt grew more pronounced. Prior to the day before, Joon had never heard of either of the agents in Venezuela. They were both under the care of Vance, had been for more than a year.

Both he had met with personally.

The classifications Joon gave on both weren't inaccurate, but the cavalier way he spoke of them rankled him in a way he couldn't quite explain.

"But a loss worth incurring?" Underall asked. He didn't bother finishing the thought, allowing the obvious to be inferred.

"Certainly, sir."

Careful to say nothing, to force himself not to react in any way, Vance glanced between the two men. Each seemed to be debating how to proceed, processing the new information.

"This office has not received any word from President Salazar as yet," Underall said. "Which means as far as they're concerned, everything is as we previously discussed."

"Yes, sir," Joon said.

"And there is no way we can change such a thing without bringing them in. The court of international opinion would crucify us."

"Yes, sir," Joon repeated.

Sighing, Underall went back to thinking for a moment. He stared off, again trying to wrestle the new information into place.

In a move much like the one the previous day, he eventually extended his wrist before him. Folding it back, he checked his watch, noting, "Belmonte goes on in less than four hours. Get on the horn with your man down there, see what you can do."

Chapter Forty-Seven

I t wasn't that the call ended. By that point in the conversation, I was so pissed that I was about to storm out anyway.

It was the way that I was summarily dismissed by Director Joon, just a nuisance that had surpassed any further usefulness and was being cast aside.

The words were no more than out of the man's mouth when I was on my feet and headed for the door. Fifteen seconds later I was stripped naked and stepping into the shower.

Inside with me were the gun I'd lifted from Gold Tooth and the sat phone, both within easy reach should Ela decide to get any ideas.

Turning the water as hot as I could stand it, I used a bar of generic soap to scrub away as much of the blood and dirt caked on me as I could. I ignored the intense burning of the open wounds as I did so, watching until the water swirling the drain ran clear before shutting it off and stepping out.

Taking the time to wash up was not something I would have done otherwise, but I didn't have much choice. I was still acutely aware of the shortened timeframe I was under, but I was also well aware of my appearance.

There were a great many things I needed to do in the coming

hours. Being bloody and filthy might be okay in the backcountry of Yellowstone, but there was no way I would have been able to pull it off in a city such as Caracas.

Stepping out of the shower, I wrapped one of the towels Ela had moved earlier around my waist. Choosing to drip dry, I went to the vanity and rifled through it, using a tube of men's deodorant before glopping some toothpaste onto my index finger and using it as a makeshift toothbrush.

All of it I did with a speed and intensity I hadn't used since my early days in the military, knowing that already I had wasted too much time.

People were depending on me. And I now knew for sure that nobody else gave a damn about trying to help them.

Once the basic cleansing rituals were complete, I dug into the cabinet beneath the sink, grabbing up a can of shave cream and a razor that looked like it had last been used in the late-nineties. The blade was dull and ripped and pulled more than it actually cut, but after five full minutes, I was able to have most of the growth scraped away from my face.

The last thing I did was dig through the drawer a final time, grabbing up a tube of hair gel and a brush.

Ten minutes after exiting the hidden room, I stepped back into the main of the apartment. Towel still wrapped around me, my skin had air dried, my hair twisted into something resembling the latest style.

Standing in the kitchen was Ela, a stack of clothes on the table beside her. In one quick movement, she looked the length of me, her eyes widening slightly.

"The men at the warehouse have already seen me," I said, "whether they realize it or not. I can't go back over there looking the way I did."

Nodding slightly in acceptance of the explanation, Ela said, "You're going back over there?"

Animosity still pulsed through me. Right now there were a hundred people, folks that had done nothing wrong, that had done nothing at all besides trying to take a dream vacation.

Men like Grey Rembert, that just wanted to go catch some fish while he was still able to do so.

Through no fault of their own, they had been pulled into a power struggle, and nobody seemed to give a damn about what happened to them.

I didn't know how much I could help them.

But I damned sure knew I was going to try.

"Somebody has to."

For a moment, Ela looked at my exposed torso. She saw the cluster of scars I had collected, from the furrowed skin of a gunshot trench on my arm to the pink filet of seared flesh on my stomach.

"These are some of John's clothes," she said. "You're quite a bit taller than him, but the shorts should work."

I hadn't put on a pair of shorts in years. They weren't a very practical clothing item, especially in a place like Montana.

I guess at the very least they might help me blend a bit better.

"Do you have any water? PowerBars or something I can eat on the fly?"

Flicking a gaze to the kitchen, Ela nodded. "Where are you headed?"

"I'll figure it out."

Again, her only response was a nod. "If you need anything, you have my number."

Chapter Forty-Eight

It was impossible not to be angry as I strode away from the safehouse.

Not that I had called Ela. The agent in the warehouse had used what I presumed to be his dying breath to get me that phone number. She had taken the time and employed the electronic wizardry of tracking me down. Had even provided me with a place to clean up, change, and replenish my body.

My animosity existed in the fact that despite all that, it was impossible not to feel like I had just wasted a couple of hours. Time that Rembert and the others did not have. Precious moments that I could have been using to help.

Sitting bitter on my tongue was the fact that for all the time I'd spent that afternoon, all I had gained was a healthy distaste for the CIA director and a few precious bits of information.

Namely, that a warehouse full of hostages wasn't the highest-ranking thing on his to-do list.

Which, in turn, amped my hostility even higher.

And round and round it went.

Striding away from the place, I let the anger seethe, burning just beneath the surface for five blocks. In that time, I put on blinders, moving straight ahead. With teeth gritted, I clenched my fists into tight balls, allowing my adrenaline to spike.

Not once did I even look at my surroundings, unaware of where I was or who was around me.

And at the end of those five blocks, I pulled up abruptly. I took one deep breath and used it to lift my face toward the sky. For as long as I could, I held it, feeling the sun on my skin, before slowly pushing it out.

And did the best I could to shove aside the vitriol I felt with it.

Simple science dictated that nobody functioned at their best when they were angry. Synapses didn't fire as they should, thinking became cloudier than necessary.

And it wasn't like I was anywhere near a state of just being *angry*.

Expelling every bit of air I could, I stood on the corner. For the first time, I took in my surroundings. Saw the Caracas neighborhood for what it was. Forced myself to focus on the problem at hand.

Right now, I was in a foreign country, a place that was only above being the third world in the strictest of definitions. Historical relations between them and the country that had employed me for a long time were considered tense at best.

I also was the only person on the ground there that could help a plane full of hostages, people that were being held by armed guards trying very hard not to be identified.

Adrenaline continued to seep into my system as I stood and thought. I allowed my vision to glaze over. Already, enough time had been wasted. No longer could I simply keep moving just for the sake of it.

My next steps had to be with purpose.

Receding deep into thought, I didn't see the Jeep come speeding up the street toward me. I didn't notice the whining of the engine as it accelerated my way. Barely even heard the moan of tires as it began to slow.

Not until the front end pulled up abruptly just inches from my exposed knees did I snap myself to attention. My right hand instinctively went for the small of my back, my left rising to block, as the Jeep idled along the curb.

A plume of dark smoke engulfed me, bringing with it the acrid scent of charred rubber.

"Get in," Ela spat.

Keeping my right hand on the grip of the gun, I scanned each of her hands. Both were empty.

"Joon send you?"

Seeing my stance, Ela showed me both her palms before lowering her right hand to the middle console. From it, she snatched up a cell phone and held it my direction.

"Vance."

Again, I checked her over. Not once had I gotten a whiff of aggression from her at the safehouse, but that didn't mean she hadn't been given an explicit order the moment I'd stepped away.

It wasn't like it was unheard of for the CIA to extract what they could and then cast something aside once its usefulness was complete.

Maintaining my grip on the gun, I nudged forward, accepting the phone with my left hand. Pressing it to my cheek, I receded a few steps.

"Yeah?"

"Tate?" It was the same voice I'd heard onscreen a little while earlier.

"Vance?"

"Yes, and I don't have much time. We need to talk."

My gaze never left Ela, who sat alternating glances between me and the road ahead.

"We're talking now."

"No, I mean we need to talk about how we're going to get those hostages out of there."

This time, I did the same as Ela, checking our surroundings. To either side there were scads of people, many of them glancing our way.

And possibly listening to every word that was being uttered.

"Call us back in ten minutes."

Chapter Forty-Nine

The list of things President Miguel Salazar should have been attending to was lengthy. While he had managed to streamline his schedule into aligning his meetings and public sightings on particular days, that didn't mean there wasn't plenty else to keep him busy.

What started each day as a trip through the global news and a few sips of Cafecito often ended with dinner at his desk. Sometimes it included lugging things home with him in the evening.

By his count, the number of post-midnight phone calls he received from Isabel sometimes numbered in the double digits. Per week.

He was not a man that could afford to push an entire day's agenda aside. Whatever he didn't get to would just pile up, seemingly with interest. And it would no doubt still be waiting for him the next morning.

Along with the rest of an already packed slate of things to get through.

The morning visit from Isabel the day before alerting him to what was going on had already begun to shift his week. The call with the United States President Mitchell Underall had added to that.

The meeting with General Renzo Clega the night before had ensured that the next couple of days would be sprints.

But all of that paled in comparison to what his day had now become.

In the wake of his conversation with Underall, he had expected a move to be made. The Americans were rarely ones to ask permission or give a preemptive warning about their intentions, meaning even the perfunctory exercise of having the phone call had been a giant warning sign.

Even at that, never would he have expected the move to be so sudden, or so brazen.

Any chance of conducting usual business was shattered the moment he received word that a plane was being rerouted for an emergency landing.

The first call from Clega telling him there had been a problem pushed it far past anything he could have imagined.

In the time since, he had moved Isabel permanently into the chair on the opposite side of the desk. Rising from his own seat, he had pushed it in tight, using the extra space to begin pacing.

Eight steps in one direction, turn, then eight steps back the opposite way.

For hours he had kept up a steady rhythm. When the heels of his leather shoes started to rub blisters, he cast them aside, going barefoot over the cool tile.

The second call from Clega came in a full two hours after the first. Arriving on his direct line, the ring sounded like a foghorn within the office. It snapped Isabel's head toward the sound as Salazar leaped for it, tossing the receiver onto the desk and flipping the call onto the speaker.

"Salazar."

"Mr. President," Clega replied.

Already, Salazar could hear a hint of trepidation in the man's voice. "You didn't find him?"

"No," Clega said. "As best we can tell, he found a path into the woods beyond the property and made his way out through the forest."

His eyes sliding shut, Salazar pressed his lips tight, his entire upper body clenching. "Out? To where?"

"We don't know," Clega said. "The trail went north to the coast, disappearing along the shore."

Lifting his gaze to Isabel, Salazar let her see the anger he felt.

"Mr. President, there were tracks."

Keeping his focus locked on his cousin, Salazar asked, "Tracks? As in footprints?"

"No," the general replied. "As in tire treads. It looks like somebody picked him up."

A string of expletives floated through Salazar's mind. As did the urge to lift the phone from his desk and hurl it at the Plexiglas covering the window behind him.

This was the sort of thing he was assured the night before would not happen. This entire thing was supposed to have been simple, a chance to reclaim his commanding lead over Belmonte, stamping out the threat for good, ensuring them another six years in office.

From there, he could simply walk away. There would be nothing left to prove, a decade-plus more than ample time to leave his mark on Venezuela forever.

"So you think this man had help?"

"We do," Clega confirmed. "We're looking into any cameras that might have caught a glimpse of them, but you know how remote some parts of the shore are up there."

Salazar nodded. He was aware, just as he was sure that whoever had made it out was as well.

"How are you coming with finding a name?" Salazar asked.

"Nothing yet," Clega said. "And we have tried everything short of executing more hostages. Threat, intimidation, even some physical violence.

"Whoever it is, nobody knew the man. The most we got was a physical description, a few people claiming he had a scruffy beard and shaggy hair."

"Sound familiar?" Salazar asked.

"No," Clega replied, "but there were more than a hundred people, and I didn't see them all personally. The only two guards that did..."

His voice fell away, not needing to state the obvious.

The only men that could positively ID anybody were both now dead.

Shoving back from the desk, Salazar resumed his pacing. He shoved his hands into his pockets, trying to think of the best way to handle the situation.

Things were spiraling badly. That much was certain.

The only question now was how to best stem the damage that would be done moving forward.

"Tell me, how long would it take to load every person there up and make them disappear?"

Chapter Fifty

Grey Rembert's jaw throbbed. Each breath he pulled in sent a spasm the length of his neck, electric surges pulsating down his body.

There was no doubt that it was broken. He had felt it the moment the butt of the guard's rifle connected with his face, sending a plume of bloody spittle across the floor. A fair bit of it had also ended up on the front of his shirt, the cotton fabric just drying, dark blotches stretched in a haphazard pattern.

Though, to be fair, at least it wasn't the blade end of the weapon.

The sound of the bone snapping still settled in his mind, playing on loop one time after another as he sat in the corner. With his vision glazed, he looked over every few moments to the young woman beside him.

Curled into a ball, her legs were tucked up tight to her chest. Somewhere in her mid-twenties, Rembert would guess her to be somewhere around five-ten, though at the moment her entire body was tucked no larger than his golden retriever at home.

With her eyes pressed shut tight, she could be heard murmuring softly. Dried salt was present around her eyes from crying herself to sleep.

The red handprint of the man with the mustache was just starting to fade from her face.

Rembert had known the moment they entered what the man was after. There was no way they wouldn't be angry about what Hawk had done. Bringing along a man with a machete might have been a bit over the top, but that didn't mean the thought process behind it was incorrect.

The man wanted answers. He had a room full of people that he was going to extort them from.

A to B. As simple as that.

When the first round of questioning had yielded no results, the man had turned to his friend. Seeming uncertain exactly what to do, the young man had thrashed about some, had even made some believe he might act, but to everyone's relief, the blade did not touch flesh.

The same could not be said for the assorted fists, clubs, and in Rembert's case, the butts of rifles that followed.

From where he was seated, Rembert could see nearly half of the room lying in various states, all on the receiving end of some attack. Many wore the same telltale features as he and the young girl, some combination of tears or blood drying on their person.

"It was a good thing you did."

The voice was low and female. Coming from the right, Rembert rolled his head in that direction, his gaze landing on a woman that looked to be a decade or more older than him.

With short gray hair, she wore a matching cardigan over a plain t-shirt. Pearl earrings were visible on either side.

"Helping the girl," the woman said, nodding with her chin toward the sleeping young woman. "I noticed when we got off the bus he had his eye on her."

Rembert rolled his gaze in the opposite direction to again look at the girl. Less than half his age, she reminded him of his granddaughter, which was the reason he had done what he did to begin with.

It wasn't a hero thing for him any more than he imagined whatever Hawk was now doing was to him.

He'd just like to believe that if somebody had put their hands on his granddaughter, someone nearby would have done the same. Broken jaw or not.

Not trusting himself to speak, or even wanting to risk moving his jaw, Rembert looked back to the woman, giving only a nod. For a moment, she seemed to be waiting for a response before her gaze drifted down to his misshapen face and she nodded.

Just as Rembert trusted she might. Every person in the room had seen what had happened. Even if not, they had certainly heard the snap of his mandible.

Turning her focus out to the room, the woman leaned over a couple of inches. "The man that killed those guards and escaped, he's a friend of yours, right?"

Warmth crept to Rembert's face. He'd been so certain that someone would give him up to the guards after seeing the way he had hoisted Hawk into the rafters.

To their credit, nobody had, though that didn't mean it came without consequence.

Flicking a look her direction, Rembert nodded.

"Yeah, I saw you guys talking earlier," she whispered. She paused a moment, seeming to debate her next question, before asking, "You think he's got a shot?"

If not for everything else that had happened since Hawk's departure, that one thing would have dominated Rembert's thoughts. As it stood, he didn't know the answer, though seeing the way he'd handled the guards did at least provide some modicum of hope.

However small it might be.

The reality was, they were in a country that was known to be on the brink of civil war. The man had already killed two guards and if he did manage to get out of the building, would be alone and on foot, trying to match up with some form of armed opposition.

Making a fist, Rembert extended his thumb and pinkie, making the universal signal for a phone. Raising it only as far as he dared, he mimed it next to his cheek for a moment before dropping it back into place.

It took the woman a moment to place the reference, her brows coming together for an instant before receding.

"He has a phone."

Again, Rembert nodded.

How much good it might do them, if Hawk knew anybody worth reaching out to in such a situation, he had no way of knowing.

All that was certain was if anybody in that room had any hope of seeing the next day – let alone ever making it home – it rested on whatever Hawk was doing at that very moment.

"Well, that's something, I guess," the woman said.

Recognizing the weariness in the woman's tone, already starting to feel a bit of the same himself, Rembert was for the first time glad his jaw was broken.

At least that way, he had an excuse for not voicing any of the things he was feeling.

Chapter Fifty-One

The ride back to the safehouse was short. Moving slow, obeying all posted traffic signs, Ela somehow managed to stretch it out to a full five minutes.

Twice she tried opening up a dialogue, each time cut off by my upraised palm.

Getting the point, she didn't attempt again, not even after she used the dual scanners to get us back into the apartment and away from anybody that might be lurking nearby.

Not that I actually thought that was an issue.

The moment the door was open, I went into the kitchen, leaving her by the front. Doing a quick scan of the place, I went for the first drawers I saw, pulling them open. Finding nothing but silverware and random utensils, I pushed them closed, going in order for the next.

"Need something?" Ela asked. This time, there was a bit of annoyance present.

Most likely, it stemmed from a combination of my earlier stifling the conversation and my now borderline frenetic movements.

Not that I particularly cared either way. The red digits of the clock in my mind had been sitting in my frontal lobe since climbing through the ceiling tiles in the warehouse. Now, each second passing seemed to be accompanied by a siren, making sure it had my attention.

"Paper, pen."

Staring at me a moment, Ela went to a small table tucked away in the corner. She drew out a tablet and a blue gel pen, putting both down on the table, before glaring up at me.

Ignoring the look completely, I bent over the table. One hand I rested flush on the smooth wood. The other I used to flip open the tablet and go to work.

"Okay, this here is the airport."

I began by drawing a single rectangle at the bottom of the page. Around it, I sketched a dotted line, outlining the various pieces of the grounds.

"From what I could tell, this was the basic layout of the runway, and this was the route the bus used to pick us up and take us to the warehouse."

Another square in the back corner. "Which was here."

As I worked, Ela came up alongside me, peering down over my shoulder.

"Now, around the outside here is a fence that's about ten feet in height, with razor wire along the top of it."

I drew a curlicue along the dotted line, denoting the feature.

"And all this out here was heavy woods, clear to the coast. Maybe as far as four miles or so in total."

When I finished, I ran everything back through my mind, making sure it all played out the way I remembered. Content that it was right, I glanced up to Ela.

"You know anything about the grounds?" I asked. "Is there another entrance? A way of accessing the warehouse or even the terminal?"

Narrowing her eyes, Ela stared down at the page. "We know someone that works in baggage there. He might be able to slip us inside, but there's no way we could get a hundred people out like that."

I made a notation of the info in the bottom corner of the page. "I never intended to."

What I was thinking I didn't bother sharing yet, the sketch as much to align my ideas as to provide her with a basic schematic.

If I had a few more hours, and knew that the people inside would be safe, I could probably come up with something sleek and elegant. It would have a dozen moving parts, all synchronized beautifully, and result in a successful operation without injury or even a single casualty.

Hell, if we had a few days with the same assurances, I wouldn't need to do anything. I could just wait for the CIA to slip in another crew, and we'd be on our way.

Neither was the case, which meant I was going to have to be creative. And maybe a little risky.

The lives of Rembert and a great many others were resting on it.

Not bothering to push it further, Ela checked her watch. "It's been ten minutes. We should duck inside for Vance's call."

Grunting in agreement, I took up the drawing I'd just made and followed her back into the bathroom. The steam from my earlier shower had dissipated, though the smell of cheap soap and shaving cream still hung in the air.

Passing through the built-in shelves, we both took the same seats as earlier.

"Tell me," I said, "is Joon as big an ass as he seems?"

Ela raised one shoulder in a shrug. "Truth? That was the first time I've even seen the man since training."

There was something in her tone that told me there was more she wanted to say. Deciding to wait her out, I merely sat and stared, knowing she would get there eventually.

Which turned out to be less than a minute.

"But yes, in my few encounters, he's been a consummate prick."

One corner of my mouth twitched upward, the closest I could manage to a smile given the situation. *Consummate prick* was a phrase I hadn't heard in ages, a favorite of Martin Diggs, one of the guys on my FAST team years ago.

Never was it meant as a compliment in the slightest.

"And Vance?"

"Vance I know a little better. Seems like a pretty straight shooter, all things considered."

Generally, when people threw a qualifier like those final words on the end of something, it wasn't necessarily a good thing.

"Meaning?"

"Meaning, he's in a tough spot. Venezuela isn't real high in the South American pecking order yet, and he does still have to pretend to play the political game."

Nodding, I accepted the information in silence. Whether she knew it or not, Ela had just answered exactly what I was looking for.

The call from Vance alone was a curious one, especially in the wake of everything Joon had just said. On some level, they must have sensed my frustration, might have even inferred from my file that I likely wasn't leaving this alone.

The question was whether or not his reaching out was meant to keep me in check, out of their way and on the sidelines, or if it was an actual olive branch seeking aid.

As yet, it was still a touch too early to tell.

Not that I had a great many options, the plan I was concocting depending entirely on the man's help.

Two minutes after we stepped into the office, the sound of ringing piped in through the speakers. Just barely loud enough to be heard, it pulled both our attention toward it, Ela scrambling to work the keyboard before her.

After the second ring, she had it up and connected.

"Special Director," she said.

"Ramirez, Tate."

Unlike the previous discussion, there was no video for this one. Nothing but a black screen before us.

"I don't have much time," he said. "I'm in my office now, had to excuse myself for a second time to get away when I did."

Based on his lowered voice and quick cadence, if he was trying to do a sell job, he was off to a good start.

"Vance," I said, bypassing any greeting or even his opening line, "what did you have in mind?"

"I was hoping you could tell me," Vance said without pause.

"Right now, Joon and the president are still wanting to push forward on the original plan."

Beside me, Ela's brows pulled in tight. "The original plan? How?"

"Farkus."

I had no idea what the original plan was or who Farkus was, but based on Ela's reaction, neither was a good idea.

"Original plan?" I asked. "Farkus?"

For a moment there was no reply. Ela avoided my gaze, deferring to the Special Director. Vance remained silent, seemingly weighing how much to share.

"We don't have time for all that right now," Vance eventually answered. "Agent Ramirez can brief you on it as soon as we're done here."

Not overly fond of the response, I shoved aside any incredulity. If the man was acting out of turn, as he was at least trying to give the impression of, then he likely didn't have the time to get into everything.

"But it's bad?" I asked.

"It was bad to begin with," Vance responded, "and that was before everything went to hell."

Picking up exactly what he was getting at, I didn't push any further. Joon was attempting to salvage something that for all intents and purposes was over.

In my history with multiple government positions, never did that end well.

"Okay," I said. "Who is Edgar Belmonte?"

Again, a pause. "That's part of the original plan. Agent Ramirez will fill you in."

This time, I couldn't help but feel a tiny spark of animosity rise. If they were going to need help, they had to start extending the same my direction.

"So where does that leave us right now?" I asked. This time, I didn't attempt to hide the edge in my voice.

For his part, Vance skipped right by it. "Exactly where we were when I called the first time. Right now, everybody else seems convinced those hostages are window dressing. They're being held, but now that the agents are gone, nobody will be harmed.

"I'm not so sure."

Having been inside the warehouse, having seen the way Gold Tooth took down their agent, I was positive they weren't. Those people were nothing more than protection, ready to be cast aside at a moment's notice.

If they weren't already.

"So we need to help them," Vance said. "And we need to be quick, and we need to be quiet. Is that doable?"

It was too early to say definitively. The plan I was working on still needed some shaping. And a shitload of luck.

"I guess we'll find out."

Chapter Fifty-Two

Charles Vance had ascended to the post he was in by playing the game. Not the political one – for that he'd never had the appetite – but the internal one.

The only one that truly mattered at the Agency unless somebody rose to the highest seat in the building.

He had started out as an analyst, someone even lower than the aides that now lined the back of the conference room he was returning to. Assigned to New Zealand, he had endured eighteen months of the most mind-numbing work possible, the country quite possibly one of the least concerning on the planet.

Why the Agency still felt a need to have a presence there was a question he didn't feign to have any understanding of.

From there, he had worked his way up bit by bit. His resume sported undergrad at Berkeley, graduate studies at the University of Virginia, and for more than a decade he had done things that other people of his background wouldn't even consider.

Had been paid on a level commensurate with it as well.

Not until his thirties had things finally started to take shape. He had passed whatever internal vetting process the Agency put new recruits through, proving to them that he was in it for the haul.

At which point they had started to reward him in kind, the most recent example being his ascension to the post of Special Director of South American Operations.

In sum total, his career with the Agency had spanned twenty-five years. Long enough that if he wanted, he might even be able to walk off into retirement soon.

Not once in all those years had he ever gone against the system. He had not so much as disagreed with a superior, had done his best to always follow orders, even when he questioned their legitimacy.

Which was what made what he was doing now so curious.

Taking his time, Vance walked down the middle of the hallway. He kept his gaze up, making eye contact with each person he passed, even going as far as nodding to those that did the same.

In short, making sure that nobody noticed a thing out of the ordinary.

Even if just beneath the surface, a tempest of thought and emotion was occurring.

He didn't regret sitting in on the first campaign event for Edgar Belmonte. Such decisions were made with the point of sniffing things out early, the burning of an American flag certainly rising to that level.

Neither did he regret reporting it up the line, the director and the president both getting involved because that was their job and that was how the hierarchy of things worked.

What he was fast coming to regret, though, was how naïve he had been. Much the way that Tate had reacted, his own response to hearing Joon was one of shock.

A lifetime in this role had shown him that politics were never far from thought, but never would he have believed they would supersede the lives of more than a hundred Americans.

There were a great many things that this job had imprinted on him. Some were things he wasn't proud of, actions he would have to carry to his grave.

This would not be one of them.

If given his choice, this would not have been the point where he drew a line in the sand. Not with so little working intel, and with his only assets being a pair of non-combative agents and a former DEA agent that he still didn't know much about.

But that was all he had.

His first impression of Hawk Tate was very similar to many men with military backgrounds that had passed through at one point or another. They were often quite committed, adhering to a code of honor that many others could only guess at.

Having picked up on some of that in their brief interaction, that alone wasn't what had made him inclined to trust him, though.

It was more the fact that his agent had passed along the number to the safehouse.

Rarely, if ever, were such actions taken. If done under the circumstances, the man must have read the situation as catastrophic. He must have also read Tate as an ally.

And that together would have to be enough for Vance right now.

Pushing his way back into the conference room, the conversation with Tate and the plan he had outlined sat at the front of his mind. The logistics of pulling off what the man had in mind was going to be difficult.

Doing it on a truncated timetable, even more so.

Moving in a constant swirl through his mind, Vance only barely registered that the lights in the room had again been dimmed. Not until he heard the automated pulse of a ringtone did he draw his attention back to the room, noticing that Rowe and Andrews were both staring at him, as was Joon at the head of the table.

"Everything alright?" Joon asked.

"Yes, sir," Vance replied. "My apologies, sir."

Grunting, Joon gave a nod. "Glad you're back. Just in time."

Before Vance had a chance to respond, he was cut off by the line being answered. On screen, the visual of a man he knew to be John Farkus appeared, nothing but a plain white background behind him.

Meaning he had abandoned his post at the Belmonte campaign event and had worked his way back to the other safehouse in Caracas.

Which also meant that Joon was barreling straight ahead with the improvised plan.

"Good evening, John," Joon opened.

"Good evening," Farkus said, giving a slight smile.

The director didn't respond to the gesture. "Thank you for meeting with us. I know it was a difficult request."

Farkus brushed the comment aside with his hand. "No worries, Director. It was a large crowd, easy to slip in and out of."

Hearing that, knowing the reason behind the call in the first place, Vance felt his core contract tight.

Such a statement would only play right into the misguided plan that was being put together on the fly.

"Excellent," Joon replied. "That's actually why we're calling you now."

Chapter Fifty-Three

E la chose to remain seated at the desk. I opted to stand, nervous energy starting to roil through me, making it almost impossible to sit in one position.

Especially in the tiny metal chairs that were provided.

As much as I wanted to get out into the main of the apartment, someplace where I could begin moving about, I didn't press her on it. I suspected the decision was because there was sensitive information that we were about to discuss, meaning we needed to stay somewhere with soundproofing.

Even if I wasn't pleased with it, I understood it.

I just hoped it went quick.

"What was the original plan?" I asked. "And who are Farkus and Belmonte?"

Without glancing my way, Ela continued to work on the keyboard in front of her. With a few keystrokes, she managed to shove aside the calling program we had used a moment before to talk with Vance. In its place, she brought up a series of windows, the first one showing a picture of a man with dark hair. Latino, he appeared to be in his late-forties.

"This is John Farkus," she began. "The other agent on the ground here in Venezuela."

Giving the man a quick look, I deduced that like the agent that had been shot in the warehouse, his appearance was the definition of average. "Looks like a professor."

"Close," she said. "He is a history teacher at a local high school."

"How long has he been here?" I asked.

"Eighteen years," Ela said. "Completely integrated into the community. Dual citizenship, votes every election, the works."

There was no file associated with the image. No background data for me to read, not even a summary of his hometown or education.

All I had was Ela's report.

Damn CIA.

"So he's the brains, you're the muscle?" I asked. The question might have seemed a bit indelicate, though it wasn't intended as such.

I'd just been around these sorts of pairings enough times to know how they generally worked.

"Actually, we're both the brains, so to speak. My cover is as a graduate student here."

Nodding, I considered the information for a moment. "Which is why they sent in a team. You guys did the scouting, and somebody was about to be eliminated."

To that, Ela neither confirmed nor denied, simply staring my way. Matching her gaze, I continued to let the information work itself into place in my mind.

"Edgar Belmonte," I said, eventually coming around to the second piece Vance instructed her to tell me about.

"Mhm," she replied, nodding slightly.

"The original plan was to take him out, but that got cut off at the airport," I said.

"Yes."

"And now it sounds like they're forcing Farkus to become the executioner."

"Sounds that way," Ela replied. It was clear she didn't like the idea any more than Vance had.

If the picture on the wall was any indicator, I couldn't say I blamed them, though appearances had proved me wrong before.

Pausing, I allowed all of that to resonate, bringing with it a host of other questions. I had assumed the plane was forced down by the CIA, but somehow somebody on this end must have figured things out and cut the attempt off before it could occur.

Definitely explained the short timeframe the man in the warehouse had alluded to.

"When was the attempt on Belmonte to be?"

"Tonight," Ela said. "He's giving a speech at the football stadium here in town. Tens of thousands of people all expected to show up."

Turning to the left, I wanted nothing more than to be free to pace. To start moving back and forth, roaming as I let my mind wander.

Unable to go more than a foot or two, I leaned against the wall. My eyes glazed as I parsed through everything I knew.

And kept coming back to one enormous hole in the narrative.

"And who is he, exactly? Why does everybody suddenly need this guy to disappear?"

As if waiting for me to get there, Ela smiled slightly. "He's the presidential opponent in the upcoming election."

I felt my eyebrows rise slightly. "And we're backing the incumbent?"

"Up until a few days ago, I don't think we had a favorite at all," Ela replied. "But, that was before Belmonte started burning flags and spouting anti-American hatred."

Chapter Fifty-Four

Most campaign events followed a pretty standard script.

They began two hours out with a pick up from the security team. If the engagement was to be held in Caracas, personnel would report straight to headquarters. If the event was on the road, the crew would go on to the hotel.

Upon arrival, there would be a few minutes as Edgar Belmonte and his team finished up any last-second items. Then, as a group, everybody would pile into a vehicle and head out to the site.

Once there, Belmonte and his inner circle would retire to a side room while the crowd assembled.

In the very beginning, there hadn't been much point in arriving early. Few people were familiar with Belmonte, even fewer were taking the time to show up to his events.

Wasting time and energy on unnecessary security measures wasn't a step anybody was really excited about.

Over time, they had become a bit tighter. The arrival time had been pushed back some, as much to accommodate traffic and commotion as anything else.

Even at that, never had there been the need for a pickup three hours prior to start time.

Before tonight.

The same group that had been assembled in the underbelly of the stadium two nights prior was clustered inside the conference room of headquarters when the call came in. Already the bulk of staff had headed out, going early to pass out programs and pamphlets, there to take advantage of the enormous momentum the last few days had generated.

Leaving behind just a half-dozen or so people, all were seated around the table. All dressed and prepped, the group sat largely in silence.

A quiet that was shattered by Hector Ramon's cell phone going off, the Venezuelan presidential march sounding out as the ringtone. Eliciting a couple of smiles around the table, he snatched it up, pressing it to his face.

"Yes?"

He waited a moment, saying nothing else, before setting the phone down.

"Security here?" Belmonte asked.

"They are," Ramon replied.

Just an instant later, there was a knock on the door, a shadow appearing behind the frosted glass. Stepping to it, Ramon pulled it open to reveal a man in dark tactical dress, sunglasses on his face. On either hip was a sidearm, a trio of men in similar attire standing behind him.

"Is the candidate ready?" the man asked.

Standing on the far end of the room, Belmonte felt his brows come together. He looked at the man in the doorway – every indicator being that he was prepared to go into battle – a far cry in every way from those that usually arrived to pick him up.

"Excuse me?" Belmonte asked. "Is all this necessary?"

"Sir," the man replied, offering nothing more.

Shifting his attention to Ramon, Belmonte repeated, "Is all this necessary?"

It was no secret what was happening at the airport across town. All six people in the room had been brought up to speed, the details still somewhat fuzzy. Beyond the initial report of a grounded plane, nobody knew who was traveling or where they now were.

At last check, it was still impossible to get a line in or out to anybody onboard.

The general consensus among the team was that it had to have been related to their recent surge, the burning of the American flag and the origin of the flight too much to be ignored as coincidence.

Still, Belmonte refused to believe he was in any real danger.

Venezuela or not, people with his level of visibility didn't merely just disappear.

"Sir," Ramon replied. "Until we know what is happening, we can't be too cautious."

Belmonte knew the call to bring in extra security would have been made by Ramon. He also knew his Chief of Staff was in favor of canceling the event altogether, waiting until things were a bit clearer before putting themselves out there again.

Time and again, Belmonte and Giselle Ruiz had both refused, arguing that backing down now would show weakness, undermining everything they'd been able to build the last couple of days.

Sighing, Belmonte gave Ramon a look that intimated he didn't agree with what was taking place, but that he would go along with it.

For the time being, anyway.

Sliding around the table, he made it as far as the door before pulling up short. There, the man that had addressed him ordered the other three into position, the trio peeling off to the side.

Taking a single step back, the man motioned for Belmonte to come forward. Once he had done so, creating just a bit of separation from the door behind him, the three grouped in tight, creating a diamond formation around him.

None more than six inches away, they served to form a wall of human flesh, insulating him from every direction.

"You all know I can't go onstage like this later, right?"

Not bothering to respond, the guard turned on a heel, leading the procession to the front door. Once there he stopped, turning his chin to his shoulder and speaking into a microphone.

"The package is ready."

On cue the doors parted, more guards standing outside, all heavily armed. Each stared out in a different direction, searching for an enemy Belmonte was positive didn't exist.

Feeling his cheeks burn, he clamped his jaw shut, following the procession to the oversized SUV sitting on the curb. Much larger than the vehicles they usually employed, it was clear at a glance that the enormous tanks were armored, virtually impenetrable.

Arriving first, the lead guard snatched the door open, practically shoving Belmonte inside. His bottom barely hit the seat before the door was shut, the vehicle speeding off into the distance.

Chapter Fifty-Five

The food was brought at six o'clock sharp, just as it was every evening that President Miguel Salazar wasn't going to be making it home for dinner. Early in his term, those nights were few and infrequent, the meal being whatever could be thrown together at a moment's notice.

Now, the kitchen staff knew to just assume he would be eating at his desk, the dinners an exercise in decadence.

To the point that some nights he stayed merely for the food, the chefs on hand infinitely better than anything his wife could concoct.

Even if he would never dream of uttering such a thing.

Tonight was no exception, the smells of grilled steak, rice and beans, fried plantains, and homemade tortillas wafting up from the corner of his desk. A ramequin of fresh salsa sat to the side. The promise of flan for dessert had been made.

None of it appealed to Salazar in the slightest. His stomach tied into a knot, he had pushed the tray to the side the instant the staff person delivering it had left the room.

Across from him, Isabel sat wearing a similar expression, not so much as glancing to the food.

"Dare I ask," she opened, "what was meant earlier by you asking

General Clega how long it would take him to round everybody up and make them disappear?"

Knowing the question had been coming for some time, Salazar gave no reaction to it. Coming from anybody else, he might have been frustrated, or even angry.

From Isabel, he knew it was at least partially based on needing to know how to react moving forward.

"Just what I said," Salazar whispered.

He hadn't liked asking the question. The mere notion of doing such a thing made him sick. But he had to remind himself that this was all started by somebody else, he had just become an unwitting party in things.

And it wasn't like they were Venezuelans in that warehouse.

"And by disappear, you mean take them into the woods somewhere and keep them quiet, or..."

The thought of that had never crossed Salazar's mind. The point would be to ensure that there were no witnesses left, nobody that could finger any of the men holding them hostage.

And to paint an especially condemning visual on Belmonte.

Leaving behind a hundred people that would eventually be found would serve neither purpose.

"The latter," he said.

"Hmm," Isabel said. She gave a slight nod, shifting her gaze to think about that for a moment.

Moving his focus to her, Salazar waited, watching for any outward sign. Given everything the two had been through – both to ascend to and since taking over the presidency – he was far beyond worrying over any judgment she might levy.

They had both quit keeping score a long time ago on that front.

"So what are you thinking?"

It was the question he knew she would get to eventually. Staring back at her, it was hard not to feel a tiny flicker of pride at how far they'd come together, even despite the atrocity of the current situation.

"Clega says he can activate an evacuation inside an hour," Salazar said. "Meaning he can have transport lined up and the people out and away from Bolivar."

"Whatever travel time is needed on top of that," Isabel said. She paused, and added, "Not that it would really matter, I guess."

"Right," Salazar agreed.

"Okay. And I assume the best hour would be..."

"Exactly," Salazar said, already knowing where she was going. "The last two nights, Belmonte has spoken for almost forty minutes each. I figure if we call Clega a half hour before he is scheduled to start-"

"The hostages are loaded up while he is speaking, further adding to the narrative that he is the one behind it."

Wincing slightly at the use of the term *hostages*, Salazar nodded.

Hostages were usually seen as bargaining chips. Points of leverage. These were nothing more than unfortunate souls who would accomplish more in death than they likely ever would have in life.

Checking her watch, Isabel said, "So that gives us about an hour and a half."

"It does."

Nodding in agreement, Isabel fell silent. She leaned back in her chair, her body losing just a bit of its standard rigidness.

"Anything else between now and then?" she asked.

"Yes," Salazar replied. "Call the White House and ask them for a phone conference in exactly two hours."

Chapter Fifty-Six

Coming from Montana, I had seen weapons bunkers. Not the official kind, housed by the National Guard or the military bases over in Helena or Great Falls.

I mean the sort of private, individualized collections that the state was famous for. The type hoarded away by people that were certain the End of Days was coming. Whether brought on by government interference or the zombie apocalypse, they were going to be prepared.

Freeze dried food. Tactical clothing for every weather pattern. First aid supplies.

And enough concentrated weaponry to take on the collective armies of the entire Baltic region.

By comparison, the collection on the back wall in the hidden bunker of the safehouse was woefully lacking. Given that we were on foreign soil, and that both in-country agents were considered non-combatant, it made sense.

But it damned sure didn't make me feel much better.

"You sure this is everything we've got?" I asked. I didn't bother turning around as I asked it, working my way through what was present.

"Positive." Her voice let me know she didn't quite appreciate the question or the underlying supposition.

In total, there were four Glocks, split between the 17 and 19. Essentially the same weapon, both were standard government issue, the only difference being one was a bit smaller than the other, designed for a woman's grip.

Having carried a 19 myself for years, I was familiar with it. Lifting the closest one from the wire rack it hung on, I pulled the slide. It had been oiled recently, in good condition.

It would be a decent enough start.

Hanging beneath the Glocks were a couple of smaller handguns, snub nose models meant to be easily concealed.

Again, very sensible choices given the circumstances, but nothing like what I had in mind.

"Allow me to rephrase," I said. "Do you have anything with some range?"

An audible smirk was the first response. "Sorry. We keep the missile launchers over at John's place."

Not appreciating the comment or the tone, I turned over a shoulder, glaring her way. Leaving the look in place long enough to make my point, I said, "What I meant was, is there a rifle here? Something that could be fired from a distance?"

The plan that had taken shape in my head could theoretically work with only handguns, but it would be much more difficult.

And infinitely more dangerous.

"Oh," Ela said. Her features fell flat for a moment as she thought about it. "No, not that I know of."

Turning back to the collection of small arms, I nodded. Right now in Montana, there was a gleaming Winchester 30.06 stowed in the gun safe in my office. Beside it was a Remington 7600 with a four-round magazine that I could shoot from two hundred and fifty yards into a clump the size of a quarter.

Either would serve magnificently in the terrain I had tramped out of hours before.

"Okay," I said. "Going to have to do this the hard way."

Everything about the situation was starting to get beneath my skin. Never had I been accused of being a man that was overly patient. And that was under the best of circumstances.

This was far from that.

"What time does the sun go down?" I asked.

"This time of year? Maybe an hour."

Giving the cluster of weapons before me one more look, I nodded. "How much ammunition do you have here?"

"Four boxes for each," she replied. "In the drawer at the bottom."

Four boxes tracked with what I'd expected. It would be enough to finish a job, while at the same time forcing the weapon to be cast away within a reasonable amount of time.

Having twenty boxes of ammunition left behind a lot of chances for forensics. It could allow a smart investigator to match firing pins and ballistics. Keeping it around that long would be inviting trouble.

Four boxes ensured it was destroyed by the time anybody knew to look for it. And it wasn't like it was hard to cycle new Glocks into a country.

"You have any experience with these things?" I asked.

"Enough."

There was just a trace of defiance in the tone. I knew it stemmed from the fact that my question probably sounded misogynist, but that wasn't how I intended it.

I just needed to know what I could rely on.

"Meaning that you haven't fired since the Academy?" I asked.

This time, there was a small sigh, air pushed out in a huff. "No, I have."

But not a lot. And definitely not at anybody with the ability to fire back.

The plan I was working on was choppy as hell. It would be messy, as most things like it tended to be, and it would work better if I wasn't the only person on our side holding a gun.

Though right now, it appeared that's the best that we could hope for.

Not that it greatly mattered. All that did was those people in the warehouse and the simple fact that if we didn't act soon, they likely wouldn't make it until morning.

That's just how things like this tended to play out.

Shifting away from the weapons, I turned to face Ela and folded my arms across my chest. "We need to get Vance on the phone again."

Chapter Fifty-Seven

I didn't know how Charles Vance kept managing to slip away from Joon and the others. I could tell he was agitated as he came back on the line, his hushed whisper having more than a little edge to it.

I also knew I didn't give a shit how irritated he was. I had spent most of the afternoon in his damn safehouse, getting no closer to helping any of the people in that warehouse.

Evening was fast approaching. Dawn, not far beyond that. If any of us were going to get where we needed to be, things had to start happening.

And sitting around waiting on some bureaucratic bullshit was not going to make that happen.

"Yeah?" he asked, coming back on the line.

"What's the plan over there?" I asked.

This time, I didn't feign to let Ela take the lead. She might have been the local agent, but right now I had all the working knowledge of what we were up against.

And I had a lot more experience with the type of work we were about to be undertaking.

Vance let out a sigh. "Joon is pushing forward on the plan with Farkus."

My eyes narrowed slightly. "The thing kicks off in less than two hours. Can that even be called a plan at this point?"

"Probably not, but that's what we're running with."

Hearing him be so candid, the tension the man was feeling was palpable.

Which was good. At least I knew where he fell on things, that I wasn't the only one appreciating the urgency of the situation.

"And the goal is to somehow get a man that is not trained with this sort of thing to what? Sneak a high-powered rifle inside and pick off a presidential candidate onstage in a stadium full of people?"

I didn't bother hiding the derision in my voice. It was a ridiculous plan, and he needed to realize that.

"I agree," Vance said, "but right now the only other option on the table would be a drone strike, and that would be infinitely worse for a variety of reasons."

Chief among them being the lack of plausible deniability. Again, my hands curled into tight fists. My rear molars ground down tight.

Even as the man was trying to do the right thing, he was still staring through the prism of political ramifications.

"Tell me, what is the goal in all this?"

Beside me, Ela's eyebrows rose. Possibly attributed to either my question or the tone, I figured it was probably equal parts both.

"The goal?" Vance asked.

"Yeah, what is the take home for tonight? That the man is dead, or that he doesn't give his speech and stir up any more anti-American venom in the world."

It seemed a simple question to me. In my mind, the most urgent issue should have been the hostages. For some reason, the people on the other end of the line seemed to think it was the speech.

"I mean, I guess," Vance stammered, "it's the speech. Ultimately we need to put an end to the way he's doing things-"

"But we don't necessarily need to end him," I inserted. "At least not tonight."

Again, there was a pause.

"No, not tonight."

I wouldn't say I was happy with the admission, but it damned sure went a long way to improving the odds of the plan I was putting together.

"But what does that have to do with anything?"

"Right now," I said, "you, and damned near everybody else, is going to be staring at that stadium to see what happens."

I paused, hoping he could infer where I was going with things.

"Meaning, we won't get a better chance at getting into that warehouse," he finished.

"Nope," I agreed. "Which again, means we need to be moving. Fast."

There was a pause, this time Vance seeming to be considering what that would entail. "What do you need from this end?"

Already I had a care package in mind, the list lengthy, the sort of thing that would be tough to pull off.

I guess we were about to find out just how good the CIA really was.

"We need a boat," I said. "Large enough for a hundred or more people, and we need it right off the coast where Ela picked me up this morning. She can give you the coordinates."

At the desk beside me, her head was down, taking notes.

"We need a plane. Doesn't matter the size or shape, it doesn't even have to land here. We just need it to pass through the area and make some people believe it is coming from the States."

"In less than two hours?" Vance asked, skepticism clear.

I skipped right past it.

"Like I said, it only has to be airborne. We're going to hit these guys with so many different things at once, they're not going to know which way to look."

From the desk, I heard Ela murmur something that sounded vaguely like *divide and conquer*.

She was right, though I didn't bother saying as much. I was on a roll, and I wanted to get the list out before I forgot anything.

"I need a rifle. Something with decent range and a scope, bolt cutters, and a pair of night vision goggles."

Having been over the terrain once already, I would have a slight advantage over the kidnappers. Being properly armed and with the ability to see through the darkened woods would take that to the next level.

Ela continued scribbling down what I said. Over the line, Vance muttered, "Jesus, anything else?"

"Yeah. Have whoever drops off the weapons bring me a damn pair of jeans."

Part Four

Chapter Fifty-Eight

"President Salazar's office called a few minutes ago and asked for a meeting in one hour," President Mitchell Underall said. Peering intently into the video camera in his office, the angle was pulled in tight on his face.

So tight that it was clear the strain he felt. Bags hung under each eye. His mouth was drawn back into a tight line, the ends curled downward.

"I assume this has to do with something that has occurred on your end in the last two hours."

Back inside the small room in the recesses of Director Joon's office, Charles Vance glanced over, ceding the floor.

As a longtime employee of the CIA, he had heard all the stories. He was familiar with the Cold War legends, things like exploding cigars and video cameras hidden in ink pens. He had heard every story about their possible involvement with the JFK assassination. Every errant attempt they had made to take out Castro in Cuba over the years.

But it was the first time he himself had ever felt like a spy.

Three times already he had managed to steal away for quick calls to Venezuela. Each one had been met with a skeptical look from Joon, all growing in intensity.

By the third, his return had been punctuated by, "Feeling okay, Special Director?" a not-so-subtle jab at his repeated disappearances.

The first had been made under the guise of requiring something from his office. The next with the pretense of needing to get to the restroom.

There was no way he would be able to get away again. Even less that he would find the time to put together everything that Tate had asked for.

Which meant he was about to do something that he would never have thought possible. The sort of thing that would either launch him into the upper echelon for the foreseeable future, making him untouchable, or it would bring his career to a fiery finale long before intended.

When he had gotten out of bed a couple days before, he would have never dreamed this would all come to pass. Monitoring the Belmonte campaign was no big deal, a perfunctory exercise on par with the sort of thing he had done scads of times before.

Somehow, in just forty-eight hours, it had consumed his every waking thought.

And now it had him on a potential collision course with the sitting director, one of the most powerful people in the country, and damned sure not the sort of man one crossed without making sure they were completely insulated before doing so.

Vance had no such assurance.

But he had no choice but to move forward anyway.

"That I can't speak to, Mr. President," Joon said. "We have had no contact with Salazar's office. That is a role we would never deign to enter into."

The polite way of saying that if any international relations were going to be severed, it was going to be at the hand of Underall.

With each passing word, Vance sensed that the moment he would need to speak up grew closer. His stomach drew in tight. Sweat began to line the small of his back.

"I see," Underall replied. "And what is our plan on this end?"

"The plan has evolved into a variation of what we previously discussed," Joon said. "Agent Farkus is on the ground and is currently devising a scheme to complete the original task."

Everything was said in code, nobody wanting to blatantly state what was already known to the group.

That the country was looking to perform an execution on foreign soil with an audience of tens of thousands.

A small grunt was Underall's immediate response. "Anything else?"

Knowing this was the moment, that if ever he was going to put things out there, to even give the pretense of being above board, this had to be it, Vance drew in a sharp breath.

His heart pounded. His pulse raced through his temples.

"No, sir," Joon said. "Belmonte goes on in-"

"Well, actually," Vance said, cutting him off. Extending a hand to his boss, he registered surprise and incredulity on the man's features.

Pushed past both.

"I got a phone call a few moments ago," Vance said, "which I think might warrant at least a minute of discussion."

In his periphery, he could see Joon look his way. The man's stare was so intense, it practically burned his skin.

"It came in so recently that I haven't even had a chance to share it with the director yet."

An angry exhalation was Joon's immediate response, a quick sign to let it be known that going off script was not appreciated. Not that he could say as much in front of the president.

Wearing the same grim demeanor, Underall motioned for him to continue.

Drawing in a sharp breath, feeling his every bodily function move into hyperdrive, Vance said, "Jeremiah Tate just called me."

It was a slight inversion of the truth, but the most Vance was willing to admit to. And the only chance he had at keeping his job.

The veracity of his claim could of course later be checked by phone records or a host of other things. His only hope was by then, things had progressed well enough that he was secure in his position.

"Tate?" Underall asked.

"The man that first contacted us," Vance said. "The one that broke out of the holding warehouse and told us our agent was dead."

"The cowboy," Joon said.

"The former sailor and DEA agent," Vance corrected.

Glancing over, he could see growing vitriol on Joon's face. If this conversation was taking place between just the two of them, it would have ended already.

His only hope was to use the audience he had to state his case.

Or any hope of getting those hostages out was gone.

"With a record of going outside the lines whenever he sees fit," Joon countered.

"And a man that has made it very clear he isn't going anywhere," Vance said, "not with more than a hundred people still being held as hostages."

"I don't think-" Joon shot back.

Just as fast, he was cut off by Underall. "Made it clear how?"

"He called and told me as much," Vance replied.

All the air seemed to be sucked from the room. On one side, Vance had a seething director. On the screen before him, a world leader that just wanted it all to go away.

"He also laid out his plan for me," Vance said. "And called because he needs our help to pull it off."

This time, there was no immediate response from Underall. He cupped a hand under his chin, mulling things over.

"What about Belmonte?" Joon asked. A final gasp at trying to save his original intentions.

"It even sort of solves that," Vance answered. "At least, for the time being."

For more than a full minute, there was no further discussion. No probing questions. No biting comments.

Just three men sitting and thinking, trying to make sense of what was being presented to them.

"What does he propose?" Underall eventually asked.

Chapter Fifty-Nine

G eneral Renzo Clega was back in the second-floor office that he had first stood in and watched the LATAM Airlines flight arrive from earlier in the day.

His position was about the sole similarity between the two.

The initial moment he had been inside the office, he was in an optimistic mood. The decision to move on the flight and its passengers was the first time President Salazar had made a decisive stance in quite some time.

A marked contrast from the man Clega was fast coming to loathe, it showed that at least the president understood what Edgar Belmonte was doing and was willing to make some sort of fight before being ousted.

Feeding off of that knowledge, Clega had stood at the window. Dressed in jeans and a polo, he had felt the warm sun on his skin. A hundred different ways the day could play out had all floated through his mind.

None of them were even close to what they were now dealing with.

Now, the world outside was fast darkening. Given the spring

month, it would be just another half hour before the sun was completely blotted from view.

The air was cooling fast. If not for being back in the tactical attire he was used to, he was certain he could have felt it creeping through the bank of windows behind him.

Whatever hope he had felt that morning was gone. Getting the president to act in such a manner was the culmination of years of effort on his part. Constant prodding, trying to convince the man that a more proactive approach was necessary.

Incessant needling that Clega and his men could handle whatever needed doing.

In less than an hour, any trust that he had managed to build was completely destroyed.

How the CIA had managed to sneak a fifth person onto the plane, he hadn't a clue. An entire afternoon of threats and beatings had produced nothing. Same for relentlessly scouring through the passenger list and flight logs.

To even consider that whoever had killed three of his men and stolen away wasn't affiliated with the Agency was something he refused to believe. The men chosen for this operation were hand-picked for their skill and their loyalty.

In no way could they have been bested by anyone that wasn't equally trained or better. And probably had a large amount of help.

However it had happened didn't much matter now. It had, taking with it any hope he had for an active ongoing partnership with Salazar for the remainder of the campaign.

The best he could hope for now was to hold on into the new term. Potentially then his role could in time regrow.

The thought of such a thing, of again having to act subordinate to such a weak and ineffective leader, grated on his nerves. It brought a sour taste to his mouth. Caused him to clench his hand into a fist, tight enough that tendons stood out on the underside of his wrist.

Holding it flexed for more than a minute, he managed to eventually release, a tiny bit of the venom he felt going with it.

There would be time for all that later. In the interim, he had to make sure and complete every task to the fullest, starting with the one just handed to him.

One that was on the worst end of the things his position required. A task that seemed set to begin, announced by a simple two-note knock on the door.

Pulled from his thoughts, Clega said, "Come in."

Through it strode his aide, the same young man that had been by his side throughout the day. Like Clega, he had swapped out his clothing, returning to the standard tactical dress.

"General."

There was no salute. Despite their clothing, there could be no other formal recognition of their respective posts. Not even a single shred of military insignia was present on either.

To anybody with a working knowledge of such things, they would be recognized instantly as military. But that didn't mean there was any point in stating the obvious.

"Staff Sergeant."

The young man stepped inside and closed the door behind him. The overhead light shined from his blue-black hair.

"Sir, we just received word that the three transport trucks you requested are on their way. They should be arriving within the half-hour."

Clega nodded. Taking the prisoners away wouldn't have been his first choice, but it wasn't far down the list.

Salazar might have been pulling the plug a bit early, but at least he was seeing things through.

"And our men?"

"They have been instructed to begin moving their people into order in exactly twenty minutes."

"Good," Clega replied. "When the trucks arrive, we won't have time to waste."

The goal was to get the trucks in and then back out in as short a window as possible. The sooner they were gone, the less likely they were to be spotted.

"Also," the staff sergeant said, "we heard back from the disposal team. They are moving now, will be on the ground and waiting when the trucks arrive."

Chapter Sixty

After a few hours being pent up in the safehouse, it was nice to be out and moving. Just being free of the small interior space did wonders for my psyche, giving the illusion of progress again.

Whether any of it was bringing me closer to fulfilling my promise to Rembert and the others, I had no way of knowing. What I was certain of was that I was actually doing *something*, and that in itself helped tremendously.

Now I just needed to make sure whatever that was, it was worthwhile. The shortened timeframe and the frequent conversations were making it abundantly clear that we were only going to have one shot at this.

I had built in some wiggle room. Every plan had to have some to survive first contact with the enemy.

But what I had on this one was preciously thin.

Our first stop was a meeting set up with us and two different men. Back in the front seat of the Jeep, Ela and I drove through the evening air. Despite the sun slipping beneath the horizon, most of the warmth had lingered behind, aided considerably by the heavy humidity in the air.

Without the windows zipped into the Jeep, wind whipped around us. It tugged at both of our hair, keeping conversation to a minimum.

After leaving the safehouse, we drove due east out of the city. In the distance, I could see the faint domed glow of stadium lights, where I presumed the Belmonte event would soon be taking place.

For several miles I focused on the pale illumination, watching it work along the outer rim of my periphery. By the time it passed from our field of vision, most of the lights of Caracas had faded as well.

Pushing fast, we made it a few miles outside of town before turning onto a smaller road. From there we took two more turns, each successive street smaller than the one before it.

By the time we arrived, we were bouncing over potholes. Dust from the dirt road rose around us, causing us both to lift our shirts over our noses and mouths.

A mile after making the final shift, the road ended abruptly in a turnabout. Like a closed fist on the end of an arm, it gave just enough room for a vehicle to curl back and return the opposite direction.

Pushed in tight on both sides was sugar cane, growing thick and dense.

Pulling to a stop, we could see a pair of vehicles waiting for us. Parked nose-to-tail, dark silhouettes sat behind either steering wheel.

Once we arrived, each waited until our dust had cleared before all four of us stepped out at the same time.

The two men that exited bore a faint semblance to one another, the kind that hinted it wouldn't be out of the question to think they were related. Each had thick hair that was dark, grey just setting in around the edges. Both had leathered skin from years of sun exposure.

A few extra pounds graced both their frames, giving them the soft appearance of desk workers.

The only difference I saw between them was that one wore wire-rimmed glasses. Recognizing him as the man from the images Ela had shown me in the safehouse, I approached him first, extending a hand.

"Agent Farkus."

He returned the shake. Thick calluses lined his palms. Clearly, he was more physical than I gave him credit for.

"You must be Tate."

I nodded.

"Thanks for what you did back at the airport."

"Sorry about your fellow agent."

Bobbing his head, he turned toward the third man. "Which means you must be..."

"Call me Santa Clause," the man said. His accent much heavier than Farkus's, it was obvious that he was a local.

How Vance had managed to line him up as the care package provider, I didn't feign to know.

Turning a shoulder, he walked around to the rear of his truck and dropped the tailgate. Grabbing at the edge of a black tarpaulin, he dragged it forward until it was flush against his thighs.

"Were you able to get everything?" I asked.

"Everything he ordered," the man replied. Using his chin, he gestured toward the far end of the truck bed. "Mind giving me a hand with this?"

Glancing to Farkus, I circled around, waiting as the man slowly dragged the package his way. Once it was within reach, I grasped the end, finding it much heavier than anticipated, and the two of us lowered it to the ground.

The instant it hit the dirt, he pushed his tailgate back into position and nodded. "Pleasure doing business with you."

A moment after that, he fired up the engine and was gone, nothing but twin red lights peeking back at us through a plume of dust.

Chapter Sixty-One

I didn't bother saying anything in the wake of the man's departure. Instead, I merely smirked, waiting until the cloud of dust had passed before turning back to my two new cohorts.

"Welcome to the CIA," Farkus said.

This time, my lips parted wide enough to flash some teeth. Beside me, Ela's smile was even larger.

Bending at the waist, I grabbed the corner of the tarp and peeled it back, an odd assortment of items spread out on the ground around us. Under the glow of our headlights, each one stood out plainly, practically beckoning us toward them.

Starting on the end closest to me were two rifles. Both oiled and polished, they looked to be exact copies of one another, both standard Army-issue M-24s.

And not the Venezuelan army. The United States edition, this being the preferred firearm of Chris Kyle, the most well-known shooter in recent history.

Based on the Remington 700, both looked to be pristine, boxes of ammunition lined up beside either.

How these two mint items had found their way here, and in such a short time, was truly amazing.

Beside them sat a pair of bolt cutters, the handles elongated so they resembled garden shears.

A few inches away was a pair of night vision goggles. Essentially one large plastic and rubber piece made to fit down over the eyes, an elastic strap was tied to the back end for securing them in place.

Not the most up-to-date model on the planet, but more than sufficient for what I needed.

Leaving each of those where they lay, I shifted my attention to the far end of the spread. Taking up most of the space - and comprising the bulk of the weight - were the items we had requested for Farkus.

Enough fireworks to put the July 4th shows of most midwestern cities to shame.

"Think that'll do it?" I asked.

I didn't bother going into further detail. Already I had shared my idea with Vance, who in turn had shared it with Farkus, leading to his standing before us now.

At the time, I'd had little more to go on than the man's file portrait.

Now, having met him in person, I felt completely at ease that my decision was correct. This man was not a killer. He wouldn't be able to even get the rifle inside the stadium, let alone execute someone with it.

I had no doubt he was a capable agent, but that was a far cry from what Director Joon was wanting him to do.

"Damned sure ought to," Farkus said.

If he had any misgivings about the plan, he didn't say them. Likely because - like me - he knew that voicing the obvious wouldn't do much good.

It was ugly, but it was the best we could do.

"Just remember," I said, "get as close to the stadium as you can, and be sure they go off before he goes on."

Raising a hand, Farkus nodded. "Yeah, I got it. Otherwise, it just looks like part of his show."

"Which would defeat the whole purpose," Ela added.

"Exactly," I added.

For a moment, none of us said anything. We merely scanned the items again, fitting each piece into the plan we had devised for the evening.

Every single one had a clear purpose. No extraneous evidence to be left around. Nothing that couldn't be easily cast aside at a moment's notice.

Farkus was the first to break. Taking up the closest few items, he began to load them into his rig.

I went next, grabbing up an armload as well. Ela brought up the rear, cleaning up the last few fireworks.

Once everything was stowed, Farkus opened the driver's side door, intent to be moving again. Sensing the countdown in my own head continuing to run, I made no effort to stop him.

As soon as he was off, we were loading up and doing the same.

"Thank you," he said, extending his hand a second time.

He didn't bother detailing exactly what for as I returned the gesture, but he didn't need to. We both knew this scheme was a bit crazy, but it was a hell of a lot better conceived than whatever Joon wanted to pull.

And in this one, I was the only one that was likely to end up a martyr.

Leaning in, he took up something from the passenger seat. Pulling back, he thrust it my way. "Good luck."

Looking down, I saw a pair of dark jeans rolled up in his hand. A smile came to my lips as I accepted the gift. "You too."

Much like the man before him, he closed the door and was gone, nothing but a cloud of dust in his wake.

Three minutes later, we did the same.

Chapter Sixty-Two

J ust six words had passed between Charles Vance and Director Joon in the wake of the meeting with President Underall. The moment the video feed had cut out and the screen shifted to black, Joon had set his jaw. He didn't even bother to look at Vance, anger pulsating through him.

"Go. Do what you have to."

Every syllable was muttered with dripping bitterness, a clear signal that he did not appreciate what had just taken place.

And that Vance would likely later be crucified for it.

Vance didn't have the time or the inclination to sit and dwell on such things. Rising from his seat, he bolted from the enclosed office, swallowing deep pulls of fresh oxygen as he made his way back.

In short order, he had returned to the conference room and briefed everybody, sending them in a handful of different directions, all with explicit orders.

Now that the better part of an hour had passed, every one of them had been completed, the energy having shifted from organized chaos to more of a wait-and-see vibe.

Standing at the front of the room, Vance had his jacket off. With his shirtsleeves rolled to the elbows and his arms folded, all he needed was an oversized headpiece to be an image from central casting of some beleaguered NASA mission control engineer. Maybe even a New York Stock Exchange broker.

On the table in front of him was the remaining dregs of his third cup of coffee since leaving Joon's office. Armed with the renewed jolt of liquid caffeine and a steady natural drip of adrenaline, every nerve was running high.

"Okay, let's count it off. Starting in a half hour, all hell breaks loose, and we need to be ready for it.

"Step one, John Farkus creates a diversion at the stadium."

"Correct," Hannah Rowe said without waiting to be prompted. "His supplies arrived with the care package."

"Sufficient to make a scene?" Vance asked.

"Sufficient to make it look and sound like a war zone," Rowe replied.

Nodding, Vance asked, "Range?"

"Best part," Rowe confirmed. "He won't have to be closer than a quarter mile to achieve his objective."

Again, Vance nodded. Farkus was a quality agent, a man with many talents, but murder was not one of them. Pushing forward with Joon's plan would have almost certainly gotten him killed, a waste in every sense of the word.

"Excellent," Vance said. "Simultaneously, we will have a plane signal to Bolivar International requesting an emergency landing."

"Yes," Peter Reiff said, jumping right in. "We were able to reroute a cargo liner bound from Miami to Rio. Nothing on board but fruit and assorted produce, the captain has been ordered to claim mechanical problems before buzzing the airport and continuing on his journey."

Vance knew it was probably not exactly what Tate had in mind when making the request, but given the circumstances, it was the best they could hope for.

The show from Farkus was, after all, going to be the bigger of the two. This was nothing more than a bit of sleight of hand at the point of contact.

"On the ground at the airport?" Vance asked.

This time, Rowe moved back into the fray. "Agent Ramirez's contact – Manny, the baggage handler – has agreed to help us. It isn't yet known exactly what he'll do, but it has been assured that a scene of some sort will be waiting when Tate arrives."

Vance didn't particularly care for phrases such as *isn't yet known* and *a scene of some sort*, but again, this was all being done on the fly.

If they had more time, they would have put together a proper operation from the beginning, and none of this would be occurring.

"Good," Vance said. "And extraction? How we looking there?"

"Currently working up the coast as we speak," Dan Andrews said. As he spoke, the people on the other side of the table scribbled furiously. For many, this was their first time hearing these aspects of the story.

Which was exactly as Vance intended it to be. If this was going to be the Viking funeral for his career, it was going to happen while working with the people he trusted.

"Will be in position in exactly one hour," Andrews added. "Disguised as a fishing boat, it will send two rubber inflatables to shore to ferry people back and forth once they arrive."

Of everything, the evacuation was the part that Vance was the least comfortable with. Some of the hostages were no doubt children or far along in years. A few might have even been tortured or physically harmed.

Getting through thick woods and onto a boat was far from ideal.

It was also the fastest way to get them to safety.

Fighting through whoever was holding them at the airport would be a nightmare with so many civilians on hand. As would trying to get them across the Venezuelan countryside.

A quick hike through the forest would be tough, but the instant they were onboard, the boat would push into international waters.

He just had to trust that Tate, and to a lesser degree Ramirez, were as good as he hoped.

"And how about our team?" Vance asked.

"Care package was picked up fifteen minutes ago," Rowe finished. "Everybody is moving into position."

Chapter Sixty-Three

More than an hour had passed since the doors were last opened. Over half of that had slid by since the older woman had come over to speak with Grey Rembert, the one-sided conversation ending with nothing more than a nod between the two.

Not that there wasn't plenty Rembert would have liked to have said. His mind was packed to capacity with thoughts and concerns, things about their situation that he wanted to get out.

Since the woman had made the effort to come and speak to him, she was the closest he had in the room to an ally, or even an acquaintance.

As it stood, though, he was unable to do anything more than some very basic pantomiming. Gestures that suffered the double indignity of not only failing to get across what he wanted, but also opening up his motions to interpretation by everybody in the room.

Already, most of them had seen him aid Hawk. The fact that they hadn't already turned on him wasn't something he could continue to bank on moving forward.

So in the meantime, he sat as still as possible, the entire lower half of his face throbbing.

More than once he had fought the urge to touch it. To let his fingers explore the skin tightening and the swelling growing, the combination making his face feel as if it was on fire.

Of those that had been on the receiving end of the guard's brutality, his wasn't the worst, but it was easily in the top three.

Inside the room with the windows covered and the door shut, the environment had become timeless. The lights overhead kept it in a perpetual state of day, though if he were to guess, he would venture that it was slipping fast into the evening.

Mercifully, the temperature was dipping just slightly, as sure a sign as any that the relentless sun outside was finally abating.

However little that might have been, it was still a reprieve.

Glancing down at the young girl beside him, Rembert saw she was still in the throes of a fitful rest. Every few moments her body would spasm slightly, a small sound escaping her lips.

Wishing so badly that he had a blanket, or a jacket, or anything to cover her with, he stared down at her a moment, trying in vain to push the image of his granddaughter from his mind.

Her name was Clementine. Most would assume that the shortened version was Clem, but to them, she had always been Emmy. Now a senior at Georgia Tech, she lived less than ten miles from Rembert and his wife, was planning to pursue a master's in engineering in the fall.

He could not be more proud of her.

Nor could he imagine how he would feel if she was the one now curled onto the floor in a room far from home.

Or even worse, if he never made it back to see her.

The thought threatened to bring hot moisture to the underside of his eyes. With it came the involuntary act of slightly gritting his teeth, a move that sent a searing pain through his jaw, drawing the air from his lungs.

Clamping his eyes down tight, he leaned forward at the waist, lowering his face between his knees. Slowly pulling in air through his nose, he forced it back out again, not yet trusting himself to so much as open his eyes.

Not until he heard the dreaded sounds of the screws on the door being removed again, signaling that the guards were near, did he so much as move.

Chapter Sixty-Four

The Jeep was parked in the same spot it had been when I first encountered it earlier in the day. Facing the opposite direction, I was standing closest to the sea, the body of the vehicle between me and Ela as I tugged on the jeans Farkus had given me.

In my nostrils I could faintly smell the briny scent of the ocean, the close proximity still just barely penetrating. A few feet away, the engine ticked softly. Humidity was heavy in the air.

"How they fit?" Ela asked.

Farkus was at least a couple inches shorter than me, meaning they barely came down to the tops of the ankle socks I was wearing.

On the plus side, he was a bit heavier, giving me plenty of room.

"Perfect," I replied. Cinching my belt into place, I transferred over the knife and sat phone I'd been carrying since leaving the warehouse that morning.

Having opted against the gun I swiped from Gold Tooth, I now carried the pair of Glock 19's from the safehouse, one stowed above either haunch. With noise suppressors screwed onto either end, they were a little longer than usual.

A trade-off I was more than willing to make, given what I was about to embark on.

"You're sure you don't want to go in through the service entrance?" Ela asked. "Manny can have you inside in minutes."

Manny was her contact at the airport. How she knew him or what she had promised in exchange for his help, I didn't know.

I just knew it was worth it.

Together, we both moved to the rear of the Jeep. Getting there first, I took down the tailgate and peeled back the tarp, each of us staring down at what Santa Clause had brought us.

"I can hit him up again," Ela said. "He can get us into coveralls and have us inside in no time."

Of that, I had no doubt. And if only trying to get in was the goal, that wouldn't be a problem.

"Can't," I said. "Earlier I thought maybe we'd have more people, but with just the two of us, we can't take the risk."

Reaching down, I took up the closest M-24. Sliding my hand along the stock, I fitted my palm into the grip, the base in the crook of my elbow. Pointing the barrel toward the sky, I checked the slide and chamber for the third time, finding it just as smooth as before.

Where this beauty had come from on a moment's notice, I would have to make a point of asking Vance later.

Assuming I ever got that chance.

Checking to make sure the first magazine was loaded and ready, I set the rifle back down.

"By now, whoever is there knows I got out through the forest, meaning they have people patrolling it as we speak."

If we went in through the front, we would have to fight our way out, a hundred civilians in tow.

If I started on this end, presumably I could clear a path before we ever got there.

"You bring the bag?" I asked.

The look on Ela's face told me she didn't like what was occurring. She didn't appreciate that I had parachuted in and seemed to be taking over. She sure as hell didn't like that I was the one going in first.

But, again, all things considered, it was the best we could do.

Digging into the backseat, Ela extracted a black nylon bag with a drawstring closure. Handing it over, I accepted it with a nod.

Into the bag went the bolt cutters and three spare magazines for the rifle. At five rounds each, I likely wouldn't get any more chances than that, the weapon too large and cumbersome to be effective once I got into close quarters.

Along with them also went spare magazines for the Glocks, everything weighing in at a total of maybe five pounds. Slinging the strings around either shoulder, I bounced a few times, settling the load on my back.

Watching me, Ela stood with her arms folded, her lips pursed. Dressed in black, she cut a harsh silhouette against the white sand we stood on.

"You sure about this?" she asked.

Not even a little bit. But I didn't have a choice.

And we both knew it.

"The other rifle is loaded," I replied. "Five rounds, semi-automatic feed. Just point and shoot."

Sensing that I had bypassed her question, Ela arched an eyebrow, but didn't comment on it.

"You're not going to ask a second time if the girl knows how to shoot it?"

Taking up the night vision goggles from the tarp, I placed them against my brow. Resting on my forehead, I tightened the elastic cord on either side, making sure it would fit snug.

"Since my wife and daughter died," I said, "I can count on one hand the number of people I would consider friends. Of those, one is my business partner, and I trust her with my livelihood. Another is the Agent in Charge for the DEA Southwest office, and I trust her with my life."

"Me asking you that had nothing to do with your gender."

Sliding the goggles down into place, I flipped them on, the world instantly shifting to shades of green. In the corner of my vision, Ela stood out red and white, glowing bright.

"It had to do with getting those hundred people up there out alive."

Chapter Sixty-Five

I left Ela standing by the Jeep. I'm sure there was plenty more we could have said, enough to keep us chatting far into the night, but there was no point.

This was weak. We both knew it. Thanks to Vance it had come further than it had any business doing, but that didn't really change things.

For this to work would take a confluence of luck and timing that no sane person would believe in.

And so I took off without another word. No wishes of luck, no false prophesies of seeing each other soon.

My last trip through the woods had been during the heat of the day. It was while fighting thirst and dehydration, spurned onward by fear of what lay behind me and the uncertainty of whatever was ahead.

This time, I had no such compunctions.

I'd had all afternoon to replenish my body. Armed with the M-24 and the Glocks, I had nothing to fear. With the goggles down over my face, I had a clear view of the world around me.

Once upon a time - when tramping through South America with a gun in hand was a common thing - I had been criticized for being a bit too aggressive. My team members more than once had to pull me back. My supervisors had to caution me time and again not to go diving headlong into something.

Never once did I think of it that way. I wasn't foolish. I had a family at home that I cared about, and I always intended to make it back to them.

It was just that for whatever reason, there was something inside of me always hurtling me forward. Some inner thing that fed off adrenaline and refused to let me go at anything less than a breakneck pace.

After their death and my resignation from the DEA, that went dormant in me. It didn't die, but was starved from the inside out.

I refused to acknowledge it. Made myself tuck it away.

Not until a year prior, finally given the opportunity to avenge their deaths, did that aspect of me have a chance to re-engage.

And just as I had always feared, it did so without a moment's pause.

In the time since, there have been a few instances that caused a similar reaction. Unlike earlier in life, I had learned better to harness it, to make sure I was the one in control, but that didn't mean that it didn't exist.

Or that I couldn't now feel it pulsating through me.

Driven on by that electromagnetic charge in my system, I pounded forward. What had before been covered in measured steps was now being gobbled in long strides.

For more than a mile I kept that pace, knowing that any patrol wouldn't be that far away from the warehouse. Not given the limited manpower that I had witnessed earlier.

Certainly not with the amount of time that had passed.

If forced to guess, I would venture that whoever was in charge had assumed I was in the wind. I had eventually made it to the coast, or back into the city, and had melted into being just another face on the streets.

A face there was no way they'd recognize, not without the beard and hair I'd been carrying just hours before.

After ten minutes, I slowed my pace slightly. If my timing was right, I still had twenty more before Farkus started with the fireworks. Twenty-five before the plane was scheduled to fly over the warehouse.

Knowing there was just shy of two miles left, I leveled off at a jog. Curling my hand around the base of the rifle, I used the other to support the barrel.

Swiveling my head from side to side, I kept a careful watch for any smudges of bright color.

They were out there. It was just a matter of time before I found them.

Chapter Sixty-Six

Even though he had been the one to set up the call, President Miguel Salazar was still dreading having to make it. The sort of thing that no leader ever wanted to do, it felt like a lead brick in his stomach, threatening to force out everything he had consumed in the previous two days.

Sitting at his desk, he leaned forward with his elbows resting on the front edge of it. His fingers were laced before him. Thick furrows were carved through his hair from running his hands through it.

The plan in the beginning hadn't been simple, but it had made sense. There was no way they could let the Americans simply come into their country and eliminate Edgar Belmonte, especially not after they had all but called and announced it.

As much as he wanted Belmonte gone, he couldn't just let that happen. Doing so would only strengthen the narrative that Belmonte was now riding to inexplicable approval. It would prove that outside influences were having a far greater effect in Venezuela than anybody realized.

Instead, they would take the hostages and pin it on Belmonte. They would tie it to the vitriol he had already been spitting, and say this was just an extension of that.

Nobody would think to look at the president. Especially not the Americans, not in the wake of the first realistic discussions they'd had since he took office.

Politically, it would be a giant victory, the sort of thing he could ride to an easy second term. His upstart competitor had been so desperate to seek power, he had conjured an international incident, and then almost brought it to fruition.

And the best part would be in the wake of the election, once everybody had moved forward, it could almost be assured that the Americans would quietly dispatch Belmonte for what he did to their agents.

It's not like they were one to take such things lightly.

The previous night, it had seemed like a solid plan. General Clega had made it sound so simple. There was virtually no downside.

But that was before they let someone slip away.

Where that man was now or what he knew, there was no way to be sure, which made the call he was about to make all the more daunting.

All he could do was stay the course. Continue to assign blame and hope for the best.

And the minute everything was finished, deal with Clega.

Sitting on the desk in front of him was a single scrap of paper. No more than a few inches square, it had a string of digits scrawled out in blue ink.

The penmanship he recognized as Isabel's, his cousin now seated across from him. The look on her face matched his own.

"It's time," she whispered.

Knowing it already, Salazar sighed. Releasing his laced fingers, he reached out and placed the phone receiver on the desktop before beginning to dial.

The future relations of Venezuela and the United States depended on how the impending conversation went. On how well he was able to sell the fact that he was just now being made aware of what was going down and that Edgar Belmonte was behind it.

Over the speakerphone, there were three rings before the call was picked up.

"Mitchell Underall."

"President Underall, this is Miguel Salazar. Thank you for agreeing to speak like this."

In his voice was the din of false camaraderie, a tone that was instantly matched by his American counterpart.

"Of course, President Salazar. My hope in reaching out yesterday was to establish an open line of communication."

Setting his jaw, Salazar looked to Isabel. The point of the previous call was nothing more than a ruse to allow Underall to sneak agents into the country.

"And in that spirit, I am now doing the same," Salazar said. "Earlier this afternoon, it was brought to my attention that an airliner called into Bolivar International Airport here in Caracas and requested an emergency landing due to mechanical trouble.

"Rare, but not unheard of, nobody thought a thing of it. Not until many hours later was I made aware that the flight was bound from Atlanta to Punta Arenas and that the passengers onboard never made it as far as the terminal."

There was a pause on the other end. An audible gasp that sounded forced.

"They never made it? I don't understand."

"I did not either," Salazar replied, "which is why I called your office and asked to schedule a meeting for this time. In the interim, I had my men look into the report."

He paused, glancing up at Isabel.

"Sadly, it would appear that the early reports were not only true, but may have even been an understatement."

"Meaning?" Underall asked.

"Meaning, we have reason to believe that everybody onboard – more than a hundred people in total – are currently being detained against their will."

The story was sterile, and required a brief suspension of belief, but it was a version of the truth. Salazar just hoped that the suddenness of it, and the faux collegiality they were both constrained by, would be enough to get it through.

"Detained?" Underall asked. "Where? Are they alive?"

Salazar let out a lengthy sigh. "My apologies, Mr. President, but right now I do not know the answer to either question. My top officials are currently out scouring the countryside, and the moment I know something, you will know something."

Despite not being able to see Underall, Salazar could hear a series of sounds. Huffs and groans, the sorts of things that tended to denote outrage.

"Does this have anything to do with what we discussed yesterday?" Underall asked.

Looking up to Isabel, Salazar again felt his stomach draw tight. "We believe it does, sir. And like I mentioned, his third major campaign event of the week is occurring later tonight."

"You don't think he's going to try something there, do you?" Underall snapped, his voice rising.

Salazar hadn't considered such a thing before, but now that it was presenting itself, he was not about to cast it aside.

"We don't know, but we're not discounting anything at this point," Salazar said. "First, it was a burning flag. Last night was a spectacle with clothes and goods."

Nobody would do such a thing. Not with full knowledge that the eyes of the world were staring at them.

But that didn't mean Salazar was above shoving Edgar Belmonte into the fray if he could.

"Tonight, it wouldn't be too much of a stretch to think he wouldn't march a bunch of Americans on stage and try something. What that could be, I shudder to even think about."

Chapter Sixty-Seven

Peering through the double lens of the night vision goggles and the Leupold scope atop the M-24, the guard glowed brightly. Deep crimson and flaming orange, it was as if the man were built in Technicolor, the saturation density amplified to the highest degree.

Making him even brighter was the burning tip of a cigarette he held, the small circle moving to and from his face in even intervals.

Lying prone on the forest floor, I could feel the cool of the earth passing through my clothes. It permeated my body, leveling my breathing as I exhaled.

Pulling air back in slowly, I tugged on the trigger, the sound suppressor on the end and the heavy canopy above swallowing most of the sound.

One moment, the man was leaning against a tree, taking a smoke break.

The next, his body was a crumpled mass at the foot of it. A haphazard pattern of blood spatter decorated the bark where he had been standing, the color already fading through the night vision goggles.

Maintaining my post, I swiveled the rifle a foot to either side, scouring the grounds.

It was only a matter of time before somebody came to check on him.

If Ela would have asked, I would have told her I would encounter the first roaming patrol within ten minutes. I would have assumed that even though hours had passed, they would still have teams out scouring the area around the warehouse, awaiting a return visit.

There was, after all, still more than a hundred hostages they had to be concerned with.

And that worry had to be even higher knowing that somebody with insider information on the situation had slipped away.

To my surprise, it had taken almost twice that. The first glimpse of human life hadn't come until I was just a mile out from the warehouse, the faint glow of the airport managing to penetrate the forest.

With each step closer, trepidation had risen, my heart rate pounding.

Ela's contact at the airport had assured us that nothing large enough to handle even a fraction of that many people had departed. I couldn't imagine them trying to get them out through the woods, even if that was what we were about to attempt.

The people had to still be inside. Whether or not they were alive was a question best answered by how many guards were assigned to secure the area.

Not encountering a single one on the first two miles of my journey had drawn my core into a ball. It had settled there, pressing on everything, making me almost sick as I had pounded forward.

Only once the first flare of opposition had been spotted did I release the tension, thankful for the first time ever to see an armed man standing opposite me.

A man that now had a friend coming to look for him.

Probably responding to an unanswered check-in, the man circled in from the west. With his weapon held at an angle across his torso, he moved slow and easy, obvious that he wasn't expecting anything out of the ordinary.

Tracking his movement, I eased the front tip of the rifle along with him, matching his timing as he worked forward.

I couldn't let him get close enough to see the remains of his cohort. Doing so would put him on alert, would cause him to shift his movements in an erratic pattern.

Instead, I followed him for more than twenty yards, synching with his pace perfectly before drawing back on the trigger a second time.

The heavy weight of the round slammed into him just beneath the left armpit. Cleaving a hole directly through his chest cavity, it tossed his body laterally for several feet before depositing him on his side.

Blinking away the momentary blindness from my own muzzle flash, I focused in on the man, waiting for signs of movement I knew weren't coming.

Nobody could survive a match grade NATO round working straight through their heart.

Still lying prone, I ejected the magazine light two rounds and inserted a new one. After it was locked in place, I slid the sat phone out from my rear pocket and flipped it open, pressing a single button to connect to Ela.

"Yeah?" she whispered.

"Two down. Call Farkus. Twelve minutes. Put Manny on standby."

I didn't wait for a reply. Flipping the phone shut, I was on my feet and moving again, my destination just under a mile away.

Chapter Sixty-Eight

The bolt cutters were never a way of getting in. They would take far too long and leave me overly exposed along the base of the fence.

Not to mention they would be loud as hell, each tendril of metal cleaved apart with an audible snap.

The plan was for me to go inside and work my way to the hostages. To perhaps recruit an ally or two from the ranks of the passengers to help lead the others downstairs and out through the back.

Only then would I hand over the tool, telling them to cut as big an opening as necessary and to be on their way. Ela would come and find them halfway, guiding them on to the coast.

I would stay behind, clearing any strays from trailing them before working my way back.

That plan also meant I had to go up the very same tree I had used to aid my descent earlier in the day. To climb as high as I could, use the vantage to pick off any visible opposition, and then try to get myself across.

If my footholds were strong and my memory accurate, I could

probably make the leap and even reach the bottom ledge of the vent I'd climbed out of earlier in the day.

If not, I would at least be able to clear the barbed wire on the fence. I could use the side of the building to ease my momentum, sliding down it to the ground level.

Doing so would make things more difficult, meaning I had to work my way up and back down again, but it would be doable.

Of course, that was the plan before I'd arrived and gotten eyes on the situation at hand.

Scattered throughout the area surrounding the warehouse were five bodies. All shot from distance, none had even sensed I was there. More importantly, none had drawn any gunfire in their wake.

Far less than I would have expected, I suspected that whoever was behind this was working with a much smaller team than they would like, in the rare position of being unable to call for reinforcements.

Counting the three I had put down earlier in the day, that meant eight were already out of action. Assuming they were able to get in at least a few more bodies, I had to assume there were no more than the same still inside, plus the man in charge.

A total of nine.

At least three of which I could plainly see patrolling the top of the warehouse. Weapons in hand, they walked in overlapping circles, no more than two ever coming into sight at a given time.

Tucked away at the base of the tree I had shimmied down earlier, I could peer up at them, using the very hole I had cleaved as a vantage point.

The thick foliage covering most of the area was what had saved me thus far. It had kept my muzzle flashes hidden, had prohibited them from seeing their comrades get picked off one at a time.

I had been lucky, but trying to continue with my original plan of going up and over would put an end to that. It would be a suicide mission, the type of thing I could ill afford with so much left to do.

Perhaps on the extraction, if there was absolutely no other way, but definitely not with those people still trapped inside.

Which meant my original supposition was going to have to be scrapped. I would be the one snipping through the fence.

Resisting the urge to pull out the sat phone and check the time, I instead sighted in with the rifle. Aiming directly into the heart of the small opening, I waited, knowing the diversion I needed would be arriving at any moment.

Chapter Sixty-Nine

Any hope of meeting in the home locker room had been jettisoned in favor of security protocols. Unlike the previous evenings, where Edgar Belmonte and his team were free to take over the spacious player confines, they were now sequestered in a series of small offices deep in the recesses of the stadium.

Reserved for what he could only assume was the officiating crew, the space was no more than eight feet on either end. A series of folding chairs lined both sides.

A folding table with some light refreshments sat along the back wall.

Also unlike the previous two nights was the mood inside. What had once been loose and upbeat, bordering on optimistic, had now been shoved aside. In its place was palpable tension, terse faces and glances to watches the standard posture.

Seated in the corner of the room, Belmonte held a copy of the speech he was about to give. Already he'd been through it a handful of times, the words just barely sticking in his distracted trance. Never did he make it more than a few paragraphs in when his mind started to wander, a state that had gotten worse since leaving the head-quarters.

The drill with loading him into the armored SUV had been beyond ridiculous. The sort of thing he would have thought was more a training run than an actual event, he had let it pass because he didn't want to make a scene in front of his staff.

And because the sheer gall of it had caught him by surprise.

Tucked in the rear of the SUV, though, he had had plenty of time to think about the absurdity of things. He might have burned a flag, may have torn off a suit coat and tie, but it was a far cry from some of the things going on in the world.

The Taliban was lining American journalists up and broadcasting their executions to the world. ISIS was bombing sporting events and train stations.

Every disaster that hit a first world country these days was immediately examined for ties to terror.

What he was doing was not on that level. It was merely tapping into the angst that his countrymen felt. Nothing more than trying to put a face to their unhappiness simply so they could collectively shove it aside and focus on themselves moving forward.

Arriving at the stadium, it seemed clear that such a hope wasn't without merit. People lined the streets outside, trying to peer into the darkened windows to see who was inside. Many held signs voicing their support for him. Others waved the Venezuelan flag, something he hadn't seen in ages.

Even from the spot they now occupied deep in the underbelly, the cacophony of their support was omnipresent. Coordinated into chants and cheers, it could be heard rising and falling in even sequences, a mass of people ready for him to take his place.

Which was exactly what he intended to do.

The thin stack of papers was damp in his hand as Belmonte cast them aside. Snapping to his feet, he used a cloth napkin to wipe the sweat from his face before taking up his suit coat.

"Sir?" Hector Ramon asked. "We don't go on for ten more minutes."

Aware that every person in the room was watching him, Belmonte shook his head. "You hear that crowd? This is happening now."

As if apparated there, Giselle Ruiz appeared by Ramon's side. "But sir, your introduction hasn't even begun yet."

"We don't need it," Belmonte countered. "Everybody is ready, myself included."

He didn't bother adding what else he felt. That he was sick of being penned up. That he hated the notion that they were doing something wrong, something that warranted the need for protection.

"Well, at least let us alert security we're on the move," Ramon said.

Even more, Belmonte hated the idea that he was a man that needed security personnel to make a simple walk through the empty bowels of a stadium.

"No," Belmonte snapped. His voice rising, every other sound in the room fell away. "No! This sort of thing is exactly what whoever is doing this wants. They *want* us to be scared. They *want* us slinking around.

"Well, you know what? I don't give a damn what they want. This is about what the people in this room, and the people in this stadium, and the people in this country, want!"

Leaving Ramon and Ruiz both standing with jaws open, Belmonte pushed through the door and out into the hallway. At the sight of him, the same contingent of guards that had escorted him from the headquarters looked on in surprise for a moment.

Using the opening, Belmonte pushed right by them. Striding fast, he made his way through the hallway, not bothering to look to either side as the sounds of heavy footsteps found their way to him.

The first to arrive was the man that had done the speaking for the crew back at headquarters. Appearing on Belmonte's shoulder, he held up a hand, trying to get him to stop. "Sir-"

"No," Belmonte shot back. His pace did not falter in the slightest. "I will not stop, and I will not wait for your team."

Again, he held back on the rest of what he was feeling. He knew that these men had been hired to do a job. That Ramon and Ruiz had done so for the purpose of protecting him.

He appreciated everybody's efforts, but the time had come to push past it.

They all had a bigger goal in mind, and tonight was their chance to seize it.

Only someone else got there first.

Assorted thoughts were still in Belmonte's head, spurring him forward, when the first explosion hit. Somewhere high above, it sounded like a percussion bomb, an enormous boom so close it slammed his molars against each other.

The instant it hit, a second followed in order, followed immediately by a third.

A moment after that, he was blasted from behind, a two-legged takedown by one of the guards. Quick and fierce, it lifted him from the ground, depositing him flat on the concrete floor.

Unable to so much as raise his hands to break his fall, his face took the brunt of the landing. Stars erupted before his eyes. The warmth of fresh blood flowed over his chin.

And the heavy weight of three men pinning him to the floor was the last thing he registered before his world cut to black.

Chapter Seventy

I didn't see the fireworks go off. Not from my spot at the base of the tree, with such a narrow view of the night sky. Definitely not while peering through the end of the scope on top of the M-24.

But I damned sure heard them, the sound like a thunderclap from a mountain cloudburst.

And more importantly, I saw that the two guards standing in plain sight on top of the roof heard them, both jerking their attention to the east.

In the wake of the first boom, I paused a moment. I waited to make sure their positions were fixed, their attention focused in the distance.

Starting on the right, I went for the guard furthest west in order. Knowing that the other two wouldn't immediately see him, I counted to three in my head.

Timing the shot with the second firework, I eased back on the trigger. Firing from such a short distance, the power of the shot tossed him out of view, no human body able to stand up to that amount of damage.

Shifting the front end of the gun to the side, I sighted in on the second guard. Still standing with his back to me, I fired into his center mass, his body crumpling on impact, a thin mist just visible through the goggles in his wake.

In the distance, the second cluster of percussive beats began. Not knowing where the third guard was, or even if he had spotted his two comrades yet, I had a choice. I could either wait and hope to catch a glimpse of him, knowing that if I didn't he would either figure out a way to spot me or call in for reinforcements.

Both would give them the high ground, and eliminate my element of surprise.

Conversely, I could hope that the fireworks show would give me the few seconds I needed to get inside.

As anybody that had ever been in a gunfight before knew, that wasn't a decision that even needed pondering.

Always, *always* err on the side of aggression. Leaving the rifle where it lay, I jumped to my feet, sliding the nylon bag from my shoulders. One hand I used to extract the bolt cutters.

The other drew one of the Glocks from my back. Holding it at arm's length, I sprinted straight ahead, hidden beneath the cover of the tree for most of my run.

Not until the last few yards did I step out from beneath the heavy overhang, the night sky opening wide.

Without the added veil of the treetops, the sound of the fireworks was much stronger. Mixed with them was the faint whine of an aircraft coming in on descent, part two of our diversionary scheme.

Knowing I had to move fast, I held the gun up high for just an instant, sweeping it the length of the rooftop, before stowing it back above my right haunch.

The bolt cutters were a two-handed model, the sort that resembled pruning shears with much smaller blades. Starting at waist height, I snipped a random link, the razor-sharp tips making quick work of the aging metal.

Dropping down a few inches, I went through the next as well, the adrenaline I was feeling so strong I might have been able to rip through without the aid of the cutters.

Chancing only a couple of quick glances to the roof above, I cut down in a straight line, bits of metal shrapnel collecting in a random pile at my feet. My breathing grew short as I fought through one after another, the line somewhat jagged but doing exactly what I needed it to.

Once the final link was cut I dropped the cutters in the dirt. Using both hands, I peeled one side away, the flap swinging back slowly, carving trenches through the dirt and sediment that had settled at the base of it.

Veins stood out along my forearms and biceps as I leaned away, swinging the fence open into an impromptu gate.

And apparently making a hell of a lot of noise in the process.

The first round hit less than six inches from my boot. Slamming into the ground with an audible thud, it sent a plume of dust up, my body seeing and registering the shot within a split second.

The next round struck against the fence two feet above it, a spark flashing as it scraped the metal.

Knowing I couldn't count on a third miss, I tucked my body through the narrow gap, feeling the sharp edges of the freshly cut metal against my skin. Fueled by adrenaline, I shoved my body through, the jagged links scratching my exposed arms. Fresh cuts opened the length of both, blood sliding along my skin as I hurtled myself forward, pressing my back tight against the base of the warehouse.

Reaching to the small of my back, I pulled both Glocks free, holding them high above me, every focus on the straight line of the roof. There I stayed, waiting, until the first red glow of the guard's head appeared through the goggles, peering out over the side to check my position.

Firing in tandem, I squeezed off a pair of shots from each hand, the man disappearing as fast as he had arrived, not to be seen again.

Chapter Seventy-One

Director Horace Joon quite literally slid into the back of the room. Opening the door no more than just wide enough to push his shoulders through, he took a lateral step in before shutting it behind him.

In his wake, there was a slight hiccup in the cadence of the conversation, each person looking over. Unsure how to respond, they fell silent for an instant, glancing from him to Charles Vance.

Sensing what was going on, Vance looked to see what was the source of concern, his core seizing tight as he saw Joon standing there.

"Director."

"Special Director," Joon replied. "How are things progressing?"

If given the choice, Vance wasn't sure which would be preferable. Having the Director stand in the corner watching over his shoulder, or remaining in his office, steaming, leaving Vance to wonder where things stood.

Forced to answer in an instant, he would give the edge to this option, but only by the thinnest of margins.

"Everything is going according to schedule," Vance replied. "Agent Farkus has ignited the fireworks and our cargo plane just made a pass by the airport."

On the screen across from them were maps and schematics, a detailed itinerary for how the night should progress. Planned down to the minute, everything was done with as much precision as could be mustered from a different continent.

The rest would have to ride on a man that they had never even met in person.

"The final piece – the activity from the baggage handler on the ground – is set to begin any moment."

Leaving it vague, Vance was not about to mention that as yet, nobody knew exactly what that would entail.

"Any word from Tate?" Joon asked, bypassing the last statement.

"Only the preliminary report telling Agent Ramirez he was in position and to alert the others," Vance replied. "Two more confirmed kills at that point."

The last bit wasn't necessary, but it did lend a bit of credence to the sequence of events.

The man might not be one of their agents, but thus far he had put down five enemy combatants. That would have to count for something in earning the director's trust.

Accepting the information, Joon gave the slightest nod. Not quite one of approval, it at least ceded the floor to Vance.

It was his operation to sink or swim.

Returning the gesture, Vance turned back to the room, the faces of everybody present looking to feel exactly the way he did.

Chapter Seventy-Two

The chair General Renzo Clega had been seated in was on its side at the base of the far wall. On his feet at the first thundering boom moments before, Clega had cast it aside, pressing himself as close to the windows as he could.

With his heart pounding, he had raised the binoculars, not drawing in a single breath until he saw the colorful explosions occurring across town.

Keeping the optical device in place, he allowed a small smile to form, his enormous mustache shifting under the movement.

"Belmonte," he muttered, lowering the binoculars back into place.

He should have known the man would pull some such stunt. Everything he had done in the previous days was nothing more than for show, a lot of unnecessary glitz to try and cover his shortcomings in other areas.

"Enjoy it now, because in an hour or two..." Clega added, letting his voice tail away.

What had potentially been an ugly day was starting to look up. He had lost a couple of able men earlier on, but it appeared whoever it was that got away had managed to do that and nothing more.

Slip away and disappear, never to be heard from again.

Which still left their original plan of blaming it on Belmonte and submarining the only real opposition they had in place.

If forced to think about it, things did make sense. All four of the men that had boarded at the last moment were accounted for, their bodies soon to be in shallow graves that would never be found.

All some variation of the same look and dress, they were as clearly American agents as if they had been wearing signs around their necks saying as much.

Beyond them, there might have been one or two rogue people in the bunch, former military types or such, but nothing that warranted any real consideration.

The fact that so many hours had now passed in the meantime only served to prove that.

America was not known for subtlety. If they knew their agents were dead, or had contingency plans in place, they would have already made an effort to launch them.

That he was now staring out at a firework display in honor of the man that was believed to be the cause of all this proved that no disparate word had gotten out yet.

Given the sound of the rockets exploding across town, Clega didn't hear the knock at the door behind him. He barely even noticed as it cracked open.

Not until his aide slid inside did Clega see the young man's reflection in the window beside him, the smile falling from his face as he shifted his focus to the side.

"Nothing to worry about, Staff Sergeant. Just some fireworks over at the Belmonte rally."

Standing ramrod straight, the young man gave a terse shake of his head. "Sir, there have been some developments."

Continuing to use the reflection for another moment, Clega slowly turned. The smile slid from his face as he lowered his hands to his side.

"Developments?"

"Yes, sir. Just a moment ago, a request came in for a plane to make an emergency landing."

Feeling a tiny flash of recognition in the back of his mind, Clega asked, "Reason being?"

"Reported mechanical problem."

The same exact reason the LATAM flight he was now holding hostage had touched down earlier in the day.

Maybe the Americans weren't being quite as passive as he suspected.

"When do they arrive?"

"They just went by," the sergeant said.

Clega's eyes narrowed. "They just went by?"

"Yes, sir. Without stopping."

Feeling tiny pricks in his chest, Clega glanced back through the window. He saw the fireworks exploding, coupling it with the plane that requested entry and flew right past.

"Diversions," he muttered, turning back to his aide. "They're making a move on us. This is all just misdirection."

If the young man was surprised, he gave no indication of it. Instead, he merely stood and stared, as if he'd been waiting on Clega to come to that same conclusion.

"Developments," Clega said. "Plural."

"Yes, sir."

Not wanting to know the answer, Clega asked, "What else has happened?"

"We haven't received word from any of our forest patrols in the last ten minutes."

Chapter Seventy-Three

I f the team of abductors had brought in help, I had to assume I would have already seen them. They would have been roaming the surrounding woods like rabid dogs, moving in packs, firing at anything that moved. Or they would have been scouring the top of the warehouse, using night vision and heavy machine guns, and anything else available to keep me from getting within a mile of the place.

At the very least, they would have mowed me down at the first sign of shooting. Teams of thugs should have been standing inside the fence, smirking as I cut through the metal links, just waiting for me to look up so they could finish me off.

None of that happened.

Which meant those men didn't exist.

I had known the possibility was always there. The way passengers were rerouted off the airplane and siphoned away into the corner warehouse showed there was definitely some inside collusion, but it still wasn't the sort of thing they could take right out into the open.

Not with so many international hostages onboard, many of them from a media-driven first world country.

That meant they had to at least abide by some level of decorum, keeping their head down and being careful not to raise too much commotion.

They had likely thought the dozen men they started with was plenty, the presumed handful they brought in as help more than sufficient.

Yet again, arrogance being a decent plan's undoing.

I had killed three men before getting away from the warehouse earlier in the day. Five more now littered the area behind me. Three were up on the roof, at least two of them dead, the third at bare minimum wounded.

That left seven, maybe eight, including the leader.

The Glock 19 I had in either hand was equipped with a fifteen round magazine. Having fired just two from both, I had twenty-six bullets at the ready. Thirty more in total were stowed in the nylon bag, the item now light the bolt cutters splayed out in the dirt by the fence.

Fifty-six rounds to go after eight men.

I didn't need to be a math whiz to do the numbers on that, knowing that if I couldn't finish things off with that ratio, I had no business being where I was anyway.

Seated with my back braced against the outer wall, I nudged myself forward a few inches. Checking either side and the roof in a quick three-point sequence, I returned the nylon bag to my shoulders.

With the adrenaline and heightened state my body was in, I barely even registered the weight, the slim bag sliding down between my shoulder blades.

Already, I had a pretty decent schematic of the warehouse in my head. My best bet for getting inside was going to be the open end where the bus had pulled through earlier in the day. Designed for the purpose of loading and unloading quickly, the entire southern exposure was left open.

While there might be regular sized doorways on the other walls, they would be locked tight or, even worse, guarded by armed men or explosives.

Getting through them would be an unnecessary risk.

There would be no way to seal off the far end. My opponent would know that, and they would do what they needed to to protect it.

Which meant it was time for my final act of subterfuge.

Stowing the gun in my right hand, I fished the sat phone from my pocket. Without worrying about who might see the light, I flipped it open and hit redial.

"Ela, tell Manny to go in thirty."

Chapter Seventy-Four

My first move was getting my ass away from that spot at the base of the warehouse. If I hadn't managed to finish off the guard above, or if any additional guards had come looking for him, I would be an easy target with no hope of cover.

Unacceptable.

Stowing the phone, I took up a Glock in either hand and sprinted hard to the west. Having entered on the north side, I had to travel the same distance to get around to the front regardless which direction I went.

But at least moving to the west allowed me to stay along the fence line, out of sight for as long as possible.

Charging hard for twenty yards, I stopped for an instant at the corner. Dropping to a knee, I peered out around the base, seeing nothing.

Shifting my focus up to the roof line above, I looked for the outline of anybody on patrol, hoping to catch the telltale feature of a gun barrel extended over the edge.

To my relief, I saw nothing, the trio of men appearing to be the extent of the rooftop watch.

Further proof that additional arms likely wouldn't be arriving anytime soon.

From a crouched position, I buried the toe of my shoe into the dirt and gravel along the base of the building. Using it as leverage, I exploded forward, hurtling myself along the darkened path.

Clutched in either hand were the Glocks, their elongated noses passing above my shoulders with each pump of my arms. The drawstring bag bounced against my back, the metal clips inside pelting my spine and kidneys.

Sweat streamed over my brow and smooth cheeks, burning my eyes.

In the distance, I could still hear the last few bits of Farkus's fireworks display. The drone of an airplane could faintly be heard filling the short spells in between.

My gaze I kept aimed at the front corner of the building. Each second I counted in my head, willing myself forward, knowing the last bit of assistance I was going to be getting was growing ever closer.

Stride by stride I went, ready to slide myself to a stop and watch it happen, waiting for the opportune moment to slip inside the warehouse.

A moment that I would never realize.

A moment that came and went while I was still tucked up along the side of the warehouse, sprinting forward with everything I had.

Chapter Seventy-Five

The man standing at the front of the room was a near copy of the two that Hawk had dispatched earlier in the day. And equally similar to every other person that had passed through the door in the time since.

Smaller, with a wiry build, and clear Latin features.

If forced to guess earlier, Grey Rembert would have pegged them as former soldiers. Men that had been trained up by some government in the region and then turned their skills over to the highest bidder.

Which would make sense, considering that they were now in the act of taking hostages, an incident that would certainly have international repercussions if performed by an actual head of state.

In its stead, there was no way of knowing who these men worked for or what the motivation behind their actions might have been.

All Rembert knew was that there was clear malevolence in all of it.

And that with each passing moment, the likelihood of survival for every person in the room dwindled.

Unlike earlier in the day, when the guards had operated in pairs, this time there was only a single man before them. Not to be caught unawares the way Cruz had been before, his weapon was raised into a loose firing position.

Every word he spat out was laced with agitation, as if he might begin firing at any moment.

The first few commands he had issued had taken some time to sink in. In the wake of hearing him scratching at the door outside, many had recoiled back into fear.

Seeing him standing with a rifle at the ready had only solidified that stance.

Not until he stepped forward and began kicking at those closest did the demands he was issuing sink in.

The people were to get on their feet. They were to form back into a line. They were to be ready to move as soon as he said so.

Where they were going, nobody knew. The looks of terror on the faces around Rembert suggested that speculation was quite rampant. He himself was doing the same, locked behind a swollen mask of a broken jaw.

Doing as told, not needing to see any more blood for one day, the group inside moved as instructed. Through much grunting and forcing air in and out through his nose, Rembert managed to make it to his feet.

Once he was up, he helped the girl beside him upright as well, both of them standing near the rear of the pack.

A stance they maintained even as the thunderous sounds of booming began in the near distance. Sounds that echoed through the small space, like bombs exploding nearby.

Sounds that were interspliced a moment later by a plane buzzing close overhead.

And again a moment later by another form of explosion, this one sounding much closer still.

Chapter Seventy-Six

The length of the warehouse was about eighty yards, which meant either I was much slower than I thought, or Manny had jumped the gun on me.

Twenty yards still separated me from the corner as the signal went up, a fiery explosion much larger and more intense than I would have imagined. Thinking that it would be a small fire, maybe a crash of a loading truck, it sounded like Manny had opted to go with a combination of the two.

In short order, the sounds of squealing tires found their way to me. After that was the clear impact of metal crashing into a solid structure, shearing away in an angry wail.

And finally, there was the angry blast of detonation, heat finding its way even to me, tucked along the back of the warehouse.

Optimally, I would have liked to have had a look at the front of the warehouse first. To have reacquainted myself with the design. Seen what I was working with free of the tight confines of being crammed into the bus earlier.

But we all had known from the moment we left the safehouse that this was a long way from optimal. Everything about it was done on the fly, trying to coordinate a handful of different aspects, working with people on different continents.

All things considered, the fact that it had gone so well for so long was a miracle.

No point in sitting around and bitching about things now.

As I covered the last few strides to the corner, I cast aside the full-throttle sprint. Instead, I extended the Glocks at shoulder height before me, slowing my pace just enough to take the corner tight.

Underfoot, the ground changed from dirt to concrete, my first solid footing in more than an hour.

To my right, whatever Manny had put together was visible a few hundred yards away, the acrid scents of smoke and fuel distinct in the air.

Giving nothing more than a quick glance in that direction, I kept my focus on the front end of the building. I slowed to a walk, both guns extended.

Manny might have gone earlier than I'd asked for, but that didn't mean it still wouldn't do the job. Human nature being what it was, there was no way whoever was inside wouldn't react in some way.

They would stop to stare. They would be momentarily startled. Their senses would momentarily freeze.

Or, in the best possible eventuality I could have hoped for, they would wander out of the front of the building to gawk at what they saw.

The two men were both young and fit, near copies of Gold Tooth and Cruz earlier. Dressed in exactly the same manner, both stood with Kalashnikovs held across their laps, taking a few lazy steps out of the front to get a closer look.

Neither even knew I was there. Never so much as glanced over as I hit them both with a pair of rounds each, striking them center mass.

On contact, both bodies melted to the ground. Slowing just slightly, I took a moment to put a third into their heads, ensuring there would be no chance of them stringing together just enough strength to shoot me in the back later on.

This was not some Hollywood movie. I'd be damned if I was foolish enough to make the same kinds of mistakes.

Two more down. Six to go.

Chapter Seventy-Seven

The last of the fireworks still left bright orbs behind President Miguel Salazar's eyelids each time he blinked his eyes. With his hands clasped behind him, he stood with his nose just inches from the Plexiglas lining his office and watched the last of their smoke fade.

In their wake, the sky seemed a shade paler than the hour would dictate, city lights reflecting off the haze. The lack of amplified booming made the world seem especially quiet.

"Leave it to Belmonte to put on such a gaudy show," he whispered.

Turning, he saw Isabel was on her feet as well, standing behind her usual seat. In her arms was a stack of papers, her posture making it appear she was ready to be off again.

In the wake of the call with President Underall, there were things to be done. There were press releases to be drafted and various departments to be notified.

In today's age, nobody was taken at their word. If Salazar wanted the world to believe he was innocent, his administration needed to carry out the actions that would reflect as much.

"Fool doesn't even realize he's playing right into our hands."

Again, Isabel remained silent. She merely watched as he walked forward and gripped the back of his chair.

The first time he had ever thought of his office as a cell was when the thick panels had been screwed down over his windows. Put in place overnight, he had arrived one morning to find his beloved veranda off limits forevermore.

Since then, not a day had passed that he hadn't sat and stared out with longing.

The feeling he now had was even more pronounced. Since the first call from Underall, he had been unable to leave the space, trying to balance a handful of different people and events, all with the goal of managing something that a week ago wasn't even a concern.

He was ready for it to be over. He wanted to go home and eat his wife's bad cooking. Put his feet up and watch television, something completely independent of politics or the world today.

More than anything, he just wanted to show up in the morning and sit out in the sun, drinking his coffee and preparing for the day.

But, like so many things in his life, he knew none of it would come to pass.

Not for a while longer, anyway.

"Think the Americans bought it?"

The right side of Isabel's face scrunched slightly. Just as fast, it relaxed, returning to normal.

"Possibly, but they won't just take our word for things."

Salazar nodded in agreement. "We'll have to move fast now to make sure everything we told them is true."

"We will."

One item at a time, Salazar ran the list through his mind. Right now, Belmonte was still off preening to the crowds, which meant that aspect could wait.

But there was still plenty else to get moving.

"You'll take care of-" he began.

"Of course."

"And the other-"

"Already done."

Anybody else, and Salazar would have taken it as a sign of disrespect. At the very least, he would have been supremely annoyed.

Coming from Isabel, he could only offer a thin smile. "Thank you, that will be all. I need to call the general."

Chapter Seventy-Eight

There was no joy in this for me. No moments to be relished of myself strutting along in front of a fiery backdrop. No future sessions in front of the mirror, counting scars or flexing my muscles.

This was not an assertion of manhood. Not a way of measuring myself against others the world over.

If things had played out the way they were supposed to, Rembert and I would probably be sitting down to dinner on the southern end of the continent right about now. We'd both be sore after an interminable day of travel.

He'd be easing away the pain through libations, yelling "Hellfire! Damnation!" to anybody that would listen.

I would smile and continue mapping out our path for the next day.

That's not how any of this had gone. The day we thought was on tap hadn't come to pass. The trip we'd put together likely never would.

None of that mattered a damn bit now. Even if we didn't make it to Patagonia, we were getting our asses back home.

Us, and every other person left inside this warehouse.

The pair of bodies was sprawled on the concrete in front of the open end of the building, their limbs contorted in various positions. Blood leaked steadily from them as I strode past, still feeling the warmth of Manny's explosion to the south.

I resisted the urge to pick up one of the Kalashnikovs, casting it aside for the same reason I'd left the M-24 behind earlier. Moving into the tighter confines of the place, I wanted something that could be operated quicker and easier.

And with only a single hand.

Keeping that in mind, both Glocks were extended at arm's length as I stepped past their bodies, finally making my way back into the warehouse several hours after first entering.

Without the enormous extended bus and the light of day, the warehouse seemed much larger. Almost cavernous, the only light on the first floor came from the faint flicker of fire behind me, casting elongated shadows over everything.

Along the back wall sat a pair of small all-terrain vehicles, presumably how the backup I had suspected had arrived. Small and inconspicuous, they had probably pushed right through the service entrance, making their way to the warehouse without a second glance.

Sweat continued to flow down from my scalp. It ran along the tips of my hair and over my clean chin, dripping from my jaw. Inside the enclosed space, the temperature and humidity seemed to rise exponentially, both helped greatly by the fire burning nearby.

Even more so by the adrenaline surging through my system.

Staying close to the wall, I made three hard steps, practically diving from the flickering light of the fire into the shadows. Sliding to my knees, I kept one Glock aimed outward, placing the other on the ground. With a quick twitch of the shoulders, I slid the bag down and dug inside, fishing out the night vision goggles.

I didn't bother to put them on, instead just holding them up and doing a quick scan of the first floor.

Counting the two I'd just put down, there were at most six people remaining. One was still on the roof. Another was the leader, who would be less likely to engage, and probably have someone serving as personal protection.

That meant four guards upstairs.

The first thing they would have likely done was bring the hostages together. After I'd slipped away, they wouldn't want to take the risk of losing anybody else.

And fewer groups made for easier guarding.

The rooms I saw weren't big enough to hold all hundred-plus passengers, but two rooms would be more than enough space. They also wouldn't want to barricade the doors any longer, not after so many had seen how I'd gotten out.

Which meant two people each for groups of fifty to sixty, one inside, one out in the hallway.

At least, that's how I would have handled it.

Scanning the first floor confirmed what I'd suspected. Aside from the occasional flash of color in response to the fire and the two bright orbs of the men lying outside, there were no signs of life in the main body of the warehouse.

Even the engines of the ATV's had cooled enough to keep them from showing up hot.

Dropping the goggles into the bag, I shifted the sack back around my shoulders. Taking up my second Glock, I rose to a standing position and began to move, my back just inches from the wall as I made my way toward the staircase.

Pausing at the base of it, I glanced at the main floor once more before shifting my attention upward toward the door I'd passed through once already on the day.

If I was running this operation from that end, I would recognize that the door was the only point of entry. I would rig it to blow, or at least warn me if somebody tried to breach.

Cameras would be mandatory. Explosives would be better.

Both Gold Tooth and Cruz had been inked with the insignia of the Venezuelan military and the man that had spoken to us carried himself with sort of relaxed authority that would certainly denote he was used to giving orders.

They would be trained. They would have thought exactly what I was.

And they would have also noticed that they had backed themselves into a poor position, there being no other way in or out of the second-floor spread.

Built clearly as an add-on, the space was not part of the original design. There was no secondary exit, not even the required ventilation for such a space.

Poor configuration was what had allowed me to get out in the first place.

And it was the same exact thing that was going to get me back in.

They couldn't rig the door to explode because doing so meant they would be stuck. I might have been able to jump into the surrounding vegetation, but I had also torn away chunks of flesh and been damn lucky. Such an escape was a crapshoot, not the sort of thing anybody would consider a contingency.

Their only route in or out was at the top of the staircase.

And while it wasn't optimal, it was going to be the same for me.

Chapter Seventy-Nine

General Renzo Clega had made it as far as the door when his phone erupted from the desk in the center of the makeshift office. Under most any other circumstance he would have ignored it, the urgency in what his aide was telling him taking precedent.

They had not received any word from their outer patrols. The guards on the roof had gone silent as well.

Whatever thoughts Clega had been having just moments before were gone. However much he might have hoped that whoever had slipped away had evaporated into the ether, nothing more than wishful thinking.

Either they had returned - or more likely - they had provided somebody else with the information they needed to do so.

Knowing that, Clega was heading out fast. Transport was still too far out to be of assistance. Equipped with a very light detachment that was growing smaller by the moment, he needed to make some instantaneous decisions.

What to do with the hostages. How to best defend the warehouse.

How to get himself away should things get really ugly.

All of that was pushed to the side by the ringtone of the phone. Instantly recognizable as the one reserved for the president, he knew there was no way he could ignore it. That doing so meant Salazar was aware of the shitstorm occurring around them.

Not answering would only add to the growing maelstrom.

"Keep a watch. One minute."

The aide accepted the information with a nod. He slid his sidearm from his hip and stood just outside the doorway, his feet wide and braced like he was expecting a linebacker to come charging ahead at any moment.

A crease appeared between Clega's brows as he saw the posture taken.

Just as fast, he shoved it away, swinging the door closed behind him.

The phone had been ringing for close to half a minute by the time Clega got to it. Snatching it up, he pressed it to his face.

"Mr. President."

"General," Salazar replied. "I trust you are seeing what is going on?"

Not sure if the president was aware of what was occurring around the warehouse, Clega felt his chest draw tight. Losing his men was bad enough. Having the leader of the country already calling him on it made things much worse.

"Sir?"

"The fireworks," Salazar said. His voice was almost a hiss, the cadence used when trying to sound tough. "Belmonte is making a mockery of us."

Pushing out a breath, Clega felt his body relax slightly. Salazar was still in the dark. He just had to finish the conversation and fix things before they got any worse.

"Belmonte is making it easy for us," Clega corrected. "By drawing so much attention to himself, the list of people he's pissing off is endless."

Whether that was true or not hardly mattered. Clega knew the president would grab for the easiest explanation, this being the justification for their actions he was looking for.

"Yes, well, that's why I'm calling," Salazar said. "I just spoke to the American president. They don't suspect a thing."

Clega hadn't expected them to. They had a very small presence in Venezuela for a reason. The place had little to offer.

Just like with Salazar, they would snatch up the easiest result and be on their way.

And spoon-feeding them Belmonte was just that.

"And coupled with whatever Belmonte is about to do tonight..." Salazar added, letting his voice trail.

"Precisely."

Pausing, Clega turned back over his shoulder. He looked at the door, seeing it stand closed. At the foot of it, he could still see twin shadows where the staff sergeant was posted up.

He needed to be on his way. This was starting to drag on too long.

"Which is why I'm calling," Salazar said. "I think it's almost time."

Snapping his attention back to face forward, Clega's features crinkled. "Now? Already?"

"Yes," Salazar replied. "The U.S. is on board. Everybody is looking at Belmonte. We can't afford to have anybody later come back at us."

Clega's mouth opened to respond. His mind worked through a handful of answers, all lined up to be fired back.

None ever got as far as his lips. Instead, his jaw went slack at the sight of the orange plume of an explosion rising before him. An instant later came the thudding wail of it, the reflection of fire climbing into the night sky across the glass he was staring through.

"I'm going to have to call you back."

Chapter Eighty

M y first thought was to go back to the ATV's. I would try to find a gas tank, or siphon off a bit of fuel, or do something to create my own form of improvised explosive.

From there, I would steal up the steps and plant it along the handle, then retreat and fire on it from below. Once the door was open and whoever was on the opposite side was scrambling, I would burst through.

As fast as the plan arrived, it was dismissed. Doing all that would require a great deal of time I didn't have. It would need even more luck, to ensure I didn't maim myself or some of the passengers.

It would also minimize whatever lead the conglomerated efforts of Farkus and Vance and Manny had given me.

For the last forty-five minutes, I'd had someone running interference for me. Some form of diversion to make my opponent look the opposite direction as I stole my way inside.

The rest was on me. They had all put themselves on a limb to ensure I had the greatest chance of success.

Now it was time to do just that.

Turning sideways, I kept my back flat against the wall. With knees bent, I ascended one step a time. My left arm was pointed upward at an angle, finger practically twitching, ready to fire at the first sign of movement. The right was aimed in the opposite direction, the tips of both weapons extended from my torso in a straight line.

Every two seconds my head shifted sides, checking one front and then the other, each glance in time with rising another stair.

At the halfway point I stopped on the small landing. Crouching low, I contemplated going to the goggles again before deciding against it, not wanting to expend the extra time, before pushing on again.

With each step, my body rose a little higher into the air, an easy target should anybody slip inside.

Even easier if they happened to be outside peering through a scope.

Tension rose in my body, sweat seeping from my pores, knowing that I was so exposed.

Resolve climbed in direct correlation, realizing there was nothing I could do about it.

"Twelve more," I whispered, the words so faint I barely heard them, instantly swallowed by the vast expanse around me. Spoken more to calm my nerves than anything, I increased my speed just slightly, the top landing coming ever closer.

From this point on, there would be no slowing. No stopping to check my rear. Not even a quick moment to assess the door when I reached it.

All I could do now was hurtle myself forward. Hope that any mistakes made would be covered by being the aggressor. That my sudden appearance and perpetual motion would be enough to get me through.

One by one, the last of the steps disappeared underfoot. By the time I reached the top landing, I was more than twenty feet in the air. Nothing but a single metal bar separated me from the ground below.

My shirt clung to my body with sweat. The open wounds on my arms glistening under the flickering light of the fire outside.

The combined tastes of brine and bitterness passed over my tongue.

To an outside observer, there was no reason why I was doing what I was doing. Besides Rembert, I didn't know a single person on the plane. I wasn't involved with law enforcement any longer. Aside from Ela, I didn't even know a single person in the entire country I was standing in.

I didn't have to do what I did to Gold Tooth. Didn't have to jump from a building and run through the woods to track down help.

Damned sure didn't have to put together a rescue mission and come back.

But what those observers wouldn't realize was, sometimes we do things just because there's nobody else to do them.

I had no idea what was waiting for me on the other side of that door. I didn't know if there was a hundred armed men or a hundred murdered passengers.

All I knew was, somebody had to go through there and find out.

The door was a simple affair. It was a solid metal structure with a horizontal push bar across the middle of it, silver standing bright against a dark green background.

Sliding away from the wall, I put my back against the metal rail. If anybody was out there, this was their perfect shot, the full width of my back on plain display.

For a moment, I stood still, listening, waiting, as I raised the Glocks to shoulder height. Elongated tips extended before me, they were trained to explode at anything that moved.

Ten seconds passed, not a single sound or movement coming back to me.

It was time.

Chapter Eighty-One

I expected the door to be locked. Given the position of it and the fact that the offices were on the other side, I figured that there would be some way of securing it from that side.

And I was right.

It just didn't matter.

Using the rail for leverage, I hurtled my body across the short expanse of the landing. Raising my leg parallel to the floor, my heel smashed into the push bar, a move that was a combination of martial arts and professional wrestling.

For just an instant, the door pressed back, the metal hasp on the end holding tight, before the intensity of the kick was too much.

Driven by pure animosity, my leg drove straight through the metal bindings, the door swinging open wide. Arcing away, it crashed into the wall beside me, bright halogen light flooding out.

Just as I remembered, the door entered on the side at the far end of a long hallway. To my right, it extended out for thirty yards or so, eight feet wide and the same in height.

To my left was an oversized door, presumably opening into the presidential suite that looked out over the airport and accommodated the other half of the width of the warehouse.

All of that, my subconscious managed to register and file in a split second. Already having been inside the space, none of it came as a surprise. Like seeing a picture again, familiarity kicked in, everything clicking into place.

What occupied my conscious mind was the young man standing no more than five feet in front of me. Dressed in black military attire, his eyes and mouth all went wide for a split second at the sight of me.

Just as my foot landed back onto the white tile underfoot, the rest of his senses seemed to catch up, the front tip of the Kalashnikov he was holding rising slightly.

Using the momentum of my kick, I dropped to my knees. The denim moved smoothly against the polished floor, both weapons rising at an angle as I slid forward, unloading a pair of shots from each weapon into his chest.

Entry wounds spat bright red stripes across the floor, random spatter fanning out in a wide arc. With each shot, his body jerked in a spastic movement, the gun sliding from his hands.

An instant later it landed in a clatter at his feet, his body teetering unevenly before drifting backward. His shoulder blades were the first to hit the door, his weight remaining propped upright until gravity won out and he slowly slid downward.

By the time he made it all the way to his ass, his eyes were already fixed and dilated. Bloody spittle ran down over his chin.

Five to go.

Chapter Eighty-Two

The journey for Grey Rembert and the other passengers huddled in the fourth room lasted all of fifteen feet. Nothing more than a quick scuttle from one holding cell into the one beside it, no sooner had the group went inside than the doors were closed tight behind them.

Crowding into the space that was much too small for a mass so large, more than fifty people – half of those that boarded the plane in Atlanta that morning – were wedged in tight.

Watching over them were a pair of guards, the two so close in appearance they might have been related. Each standing with assault rifles before them, their foreheads glistened beneath the bright overhead lights. Every few seconds they exchanged hushed comments, neither taking their gaze from the room.

With their backs to the wall, they were careful to keep a wide swath of space between them and those they were watching over.

"What do you think's going on?"

It was the first time Rembert had heard the girl's voice. Jerking his head to the side, he stared at her for a moment, surprised to see her awake and alert. Any residual sign of what had taken place seemed to have bled away, the heightened stress of switching rooms having brought her senses alive.

Parting his lips to respond, Rembert felt a searing pain travel the length of his jaw and down into his neck. A sheen of tears came to his eyes as his hand shot up, his body's natural reaction to massage the area.

Stopping just short of doing so, he looked down at the girl, saying nothing. Pressing his lips together, he gestured to his face and shook his head slightly.

A silent move meant to relay he wanted to respond, but physically couldn't.

Gathering as much, the girl's eyes traveled down to his jaw, settling on the unnatural swelling that had left the lower half of his face twisted to the side.

For an instant, a look of sorrow passed over her features as her gaze shifted back up to match his.

"I'm so sorry," she whispered. "Thank you for doing that. I can't imagine what would have happened if that creep..."

Her voice drifting away, the same veneer of moisture rose to her eyes that had gotten Rembert a moment before.

Tucked into the corner of the room, they were just two more people in a sea of many. From where they were, Rembert would have been nominally evident by virtue of his size, the girl invisible as she stood tucked behind him.

Throughout, both were acutely aware of the guards at the front of the room and the weapons they carried.

The last twenty minutes had been a whirlwind. It had started with the heavy thudding sounds from outside, thunderous wailing that could have been anything from fireworks to bombs.

After that had come the quick relocation, being yelled at and prodded forward, the group practically sprinting from one room into the next.

Third in line had come a secondary explosion, this one undeniable, the sounds quick and angry.

Something was certainly happening. Deep in the recesses of his brain, the place where things like hope still resided, Rembert wanted to believe that this was the work of Hawk. That he had found his way out, was making good on his promise to return.

As much as he wanted to believe that, the much larger portion of his mind forced him to remain more realistic. Capable as he may be, Hawk was just a single man in a foreign country. The odds of him having survived a heavily guarded warehouse were slim enough.

To bring down this kind of chaos just hours later would be asking the impossible.

The more realistic option was that whatever they were hearing now was an outcropping of the very reason they had been abducted in the first place. They had been part of a much larger scheme, an act that was just now coming to fruition.

The fact that they had been consolidated, left under the watch of just a few guards, certainly lent itself to that.

"They look nervous," the girl said. She didn't have to clarify who she was referring to, her focus locked on the front of the room.

Grunting softly, Rembert couldn't help but agree, an admission that brought about the same feelings within him.

Nervous people, he had found, tended to make rash decisions.

Given that these two were holding high-powered weapons and standing guard over a room full of hostages didn't exactly put him at ease.

"What do you think's going on?" the girl asked again.

Rembert knew the question was more rhetorical than anything. The girl was simply trying to work through whatever emotions she had.

He didn't take it personally. Didn't bother pointing out a second time that he couldn't speak.

Not that it would have mattered, any thoughts he had ripped away by the sounds of gunfire in the hallway right outside.

Chapter Eighty-Three

The guard's features had barely even settled from his fall to the floor when the door above him erupted. A series of bullets ripped into it, sending shards of wood cascading down over his head and across the floor.

Moving in a diagonal stripe, they passed from right to left.

Directly toward where I was still sitting, tucked up tight on my knees along the wall.

There was no doubt the shots were coming from the hallway behind me. They gouged chunks from the exterior of the door, not ripping out from within.

Inside the confined space, the sound was nothing short of deafening.

Whoever was behind me had the jump. Bullets were already flying, being fed in by an automatic rifle with a large clip.

There was no way I could turn and get off a decent shot, not before he was able to put a handful of bullets into my back.

An even worse option would be trying to retreat and use the door for cover, the smooth tile slick beneath my feet, fresh blood droplets striping everything around me.

Driving forward off my right leg, I dropped the Glock from the same hand. Reaching out, I grabbed the front torso of the man I'd just killed, jerking him away from the door.

Bullets continued pelting the door and wall, plaster and sawdust both hanging in the air, as I dove hard for the narrow stretch of space I'd just opened up behind the man's body.

For what felt like an eternity, I hung in the air, suspended as I made my way at my target. From the far end of the hall, I heard a man scream, a blood-curdling yell that reminded me of the southwest Native Americans I'd read about in history books.

Hitting the ground hard, I ignored the stab of pain that shot through my arm, the wound on my elbow opening up again. Fresh warmth dripped down over my forearm as I tugged the lifeless body back over me, curling my legs in as tight as I could.

I was a good bit larger than the guard. His body did little more than cover my torso, my shoulders and head exposed. Extending my left arm out straight before me, I felt the man jerk twice against me, more blood bursting forth as rounds found his flesh.

Under the makeshift shield, I got my first glimpse of my attacker. Not much different than Cruz, he had black hair shorn tight and sunglasses on, despite the hour. In his hands was an assault rifle, a steady pattern of muzzle flashes sprouting from the tip.

Holding the gun like some sort of modern-day Rambo, he stood in the middle of the hallway, a snarl on his features. Twisting from side to side, he sprayed the wall a few inches above me, oblivious where he was aiming or what he might be hitting.

I had no such luxury.

Taking just long enough to get a bead on his position, I squeezed off two quick rounds. The first drew nothing, whistling straight past him. The second hit him in the shoulder, jerking his upper body to the side, the front end of his weapon twisting with it.

A terrible marksman with my left hand under the best of conditions, I adjusted my aim a few inches and squeezed off two more rounds.

The first hit in the center of his throat, shredding his Adam's apple.

The second was two inches higher, passing through his open mouth as he continued to scream. On contact, it jerked his head backward, hitting hard enough to lift him off his feet.

Just as I had a moment before, he seemed to levitate there, hanging in the air, before landing in a heap on the ground.

Chapter Eighty-Four

F our more to go.

Two directions to pursue them.

Stretched out in front of me was a large hallway. One man was sprawled through the center of it, a puddle of blood working steadily away from him. The remains of another were lying in a choppy mess, most of it smeared across the front of me.

Behind me was a heavy door. Considering it was closed and somebody was standing guard outside it, I had to assume that's where the important people were based.

The heavy guy with the dark mustache from earlier. Whoever else might have been brought in.

If I was still with the DEA, there was no question that's the direction I would have gone. Taking the leader would have been the most important objective, without question. All effort would have been expended to get inside and make sure they were neutralized.

Only then could I move on any remaining guards.

The problem with that now was, I didn't care who was in charge. Not really, anyway. My goal was to preserve those hostages, to find the people that had been brought in against their will and make sure they made it out alright.

And that meant I had to go in the opposite direction, even if it meant someone else might slip away.

Keeping the Glock in my left hand extended before me, I managed to wriggle my way out from beneath the remains of the guard. With so many heavy rounds having entered his body, most of his connective tissue was shredded. Limbs moved almost of their own will, bodily fluid leaking from every possible source.

By the time I managed to extricate myself, the remains were nothing more than a twisted mass. The front of my shirt clung to me, the dark material stained almost black with blood. The jeans I wore felt much heavier than I knew them to be.

The stench of death clung to me, practically hanging like a fog in the confines of the hallway.

Which was fine. It wasn't the first time I'd been around it, and my busted nose masked the majority of the aroma.

What it did let through managed only to heighten that long-dormant part of me. The part that still remembered doing this for a living, running all over places like the one I was now standing in.

Shifting out to the right, I put my back toward the door I'd just entered through. Knowing that the entrances to where the hostages were hidden were on the far side of the hallway, I wanted to be sure to be facing that direction on approach.

And I damned sure wanted to make sure I didn't leave myself exposed to whoever was behind those double doors.

Inching away from the twisted remains of the guard, I could feel the viscous remains of bodily fluid sluicing off me. In tiny droplets it hit the floor, demarcating my path as I eased down the hall.

In either hand were the Glocks, my gaze rotating between the two sides.

Best guess, there was at least one person behind the double doors. There would be no call for a guard otherwise. And regardless if the guard from the roof survived or not, he likely hadn't made it back down to lend a hand.

So at most, there were two guards remaining. Two guards spread between four doors.

Two of which were still boarded up tight.

And two of which had support slats sprawled on the floor outside of them.

Including the very one I had first stepped through just hours before.

Chapter Eighty-Five

Every part of me wanted to go straight after that fourth door. I wanted to burst through and make sure Rembert and the others I might have endangered earlier were okay. Of everybody that had been on that plane, they were the ones I had the closest resemblance to a personal connection with.

The more prudent part of me knew that wasn't the wisest of decisions just yet.

At the moment, I still didn't know if a single hostage was alive. Or if they had been moved yet. Or any of a hundred other things.

What I did know was that the guards likely wouldn't have taken the time to lock the doors on empty rooms, or even rooms full of dead bodies.

They also wouldn't have barricaded themselves in after the fact. If anywhere I was going to find the people from that plane alive and needing help, it was going to be behind those two doors standing locked.

Which still had to be my primary focus.

With the Glocks still held at shoulder height, their barrels extended wide in either direction, I sidestepped down the hallway. Every few seconds I alternated my glances, looking in either direction.

From where I stood, I couldn't see any obvious cameras placed high along the walls. That didn't mean they weren't there, today's technology enabling them to be smaller than a pencil eraser.

I was acutely aware that somebody could be watching every move I made. Coupling with the clock that continued to race forward in my mind, I moved as quickly as prudence would allow.

By the time I reached the first door in order, sweat was pouring from my skin. Lactic acid burned in my deltoids from holding the weapons at attention.

Every nerve ending in my body seemed to be pulled taut.

Once this was over, I had no doubt my entire system would crash hard and long. In direct reaction to the stress I was under, I would succumb to a comatose state, not to be moved for the better part of a day or more.

I just had to make sure I made it that far.

Pulling up even with the first door, I pushed my way across the hallway. Without the wall behind me, I had the same sensation of being exposed that I'd felt on the stairway outside, shoving myself across the open expanse as fast as possible.

Not until I was safely across, my rear pressed tight against the wall again, did I take another breath, again checking my surroundings in either direction.

Content that everything was clear, that the two guards now lying dead were the only cover for the area, I shifted my gaze to the door beside me.

The barricade was so basic, it could barely even be considered as such. Nothing more than a pair of two-by-fours, one was stretched across the top half of the door, a second around knee level.

On either end were a trio of wood screws securing them tight.

It was the kind of thing that would take me less than two minutes back home in Montana. I could stick a screwdriver bit into a power drill and have every last one out in no time at all.

At the moment, it seemed far more daunting. I didn't have a drill, or even a basic screwdriver. Didn't see either lying close by.

There might have been one on the guard I had just killed, though

I didn't have the time or the inclination to go digging through his pockets.

Especially to gain entry to a room that might not have a single living person inside.

Checking either direction once more, I returned my attention to the door.

The item looked to be the sort often used for the front doors of homes. Unlike the standard office issue that was generally nothing more than two thin panels with a lot of spacers and air between them, this was a solid chunk of hardwood.

Which made just kicking my way through impossible.

Muttering softly, I ran the possibilities through my mind, not coming up with many good options.

I needed to see what was on the other side, and I needed to do it fast. Going back through the ceiling wouldn't work, nor would trying to fashion a screwdriver and working at a dozen wood screws that were two inches long or more.

Leaving me with only a single choice.

Pressing my chin to my shoulder, I raised my voice just slightly and said, "Stand away from the door."

Pausing a full three seconds thereafter to make sure anybody inside had heard me and done as instructed, I twisted my body away from the wall. Both guns I pointed down at an angle, aiming just beneath the crosspiece serving to hold the door in place.

Hoping I wasn't about to do something insanely stupid, I fired both more than a half-dozen times, completely chewing away at the bottom portion of the door.

Chapter Eighty-Six

None of the dozen or so holes cleaved into the bottom portion of the door went clear through. Not on hardwood almost two inches thick, which was exactly the point.

I didn't want to risk injuring anybody inside, either through a direct shot or a ricochet. What I wanted to do was make the structure weak enough that I could tear right through it in the aftermath.

Standing in the middle of the hallway, I didn't bother checking my surroundings. If anybody was close, they already knew I was there from the earlier encounter with the two guards.

My own shots might have the aid of a noise suppressor, but the Kalashnikov had sounded like a cannon within the narrow confines of the hallway.

Holding the guns out as counterweights to either side, I rocked back. Pressing my weight against the ball of my right foot, I balanced for just a moment before exploding forward. Halfway there, I twisted my weight to the side, lifting my foot and driving my heel at the pattern of bullet holes across the bottom of the door.

On contact, the splintering sound of wood sheering away could be heard.

Not quite enough to punch clear through, I retreated a foot and repeated the move, this time my momentum sufficient to rip away a chunk of wood almost eight inches in width.

More than enough to do what I needed it to, I dropped to a knee, debating whether to lead with a Glock before deciding against it.

Just like before, there would be no point. No way had a guard locked themselves inside, and if they did, they would have already opened fire the instant the chunk of wood broke free.

Lowering my chest toward the ground, I peered inside.

The room was an exact replica of the one I had been in before, right down to the size and the lights blazing bright above.

And including the more than two dozen people crowded tight against the back wall, all staring back at me, looks ranging from disgust to open fear splashed across their faces.

For an instant, relief surged through my system. It forced a sigh out, the smallest modicum of tension releasing from my body.

Just as fast, the feeling evaporated. I might have found a quarter of the people in need, but there were still plenty more to go.

Not once in the ensuing hours had I thought of what I might say in this moment. A product of never thinking I would make it this far or simply not wanting to invite a jinx, I had no way of knowing, but the execution of it I hadn't spent a second dwelling on.

Which was why I had no planned remarks lined up. No words of encouragement or empathy.

Just the extreme need to impart the urgency of the situation into the room.

"We need to move fast," I said. "I've weakened the bottom of this door. If you kick at it, the rest will come free and you can all crawl your way out."

The first response was nothing at all, just twenty-some remaining rooted in place, staring back at me.

"Now!" I snapped. "I've got more people to find. If you want out of here, get your asses out through this hole and get outside."

My directive out, I pushed myself back to my feet. I didn't have much time, knowing there were still guards nearby.

And that they were likely holed up behind the double doors at the end of the hall or one of the two doors without braces on the opposite side.

Moving away from the door, I left the people inside to do what they could. Already I had cleared a path for them, had opened up the bottom part of the door.

The remainder would have to be on them. I could only do so much, especially with so many in need of help.

I had only promised that I would return. I couldn't make them want to live, too.

The Glocks both still in hand, I walked to the next door in order. Finding the exterior of it to be much the same – the only differences being a few less screws and the wooden slats being put on crooked – I knocked twice at the door.

"Stand back."

To my left, I could hear the muted thumps of people inside beginning to lash at the bottom part of the door, enlarging the hole I had started.

Giving them nothing more than a cursory glance, I pushed back out into the center of the hallway and brought the Glocks to shoulder height again. Firing both in unison, I unloaded the remainder of the magazines before springing forward.

This time, there was enough concentrated adrenaline pushing through my system to send my foot through on the first kick, wood splinters and sawdust sprawling across the floor.

Chapter Eighty-Seven

Charles Vance could almost feel the latitude he'd been granted from Director Joon shrinking by the moment. With each passing second that brought no word from Tate, the tension in the air seemed to grow noticeably.

Standing at the head of the conference table, he paced back and forth, aware of both the director behind him and the assorted stares of those before him.

In the last hour, it felt like the temperature inside the room had risen by more than ten degrees. Every drop of coffee seemed to be rushing back to the surface, doing little more than making his nerves jump at the slightest twitch of stimulation.

One thing at a time he pushed through his mind, analyzing and discarded them as fast as they'd arrived.

The plan with the agents had been ugly. They'd known it when they'd thrown things together, intent on heading off Edgar Belmonte's campaign before it really gained steam and they needed to fear a new wave of terrorists flooding into the country.

Trying to employ the military would have been a disaster in the international arena. Ditto for using a drone of any sort.

In retrospect, Vance couldn't help but wonder how much alerting

President Miguel Salazar had contributed to the situation they were now in. Never had they told him what was planned, but they could have put him on alert enough to keep an ear out for anything unusual.

Like a plane requesting an emergency landing.

How or why Salazar might have acted, Vance hadn't yet worked through, putting it on his mental to-do list for once the operation at hand was over.

An operation that was far, far messier than even the attempt by the agents had been.

It wasn't that Vance had a problem with the man running point. While not an agency employee, the file on Tate showed he was about as trusted an ally as could be asked for.

All things considered, they were quite fortunate he had even been on that plane.

It was more for the twisted jumble of moving parts that comprised it. Cumulatively, they had forced Vance to call in several favors and issue a couple of markers, all without the slightest assurance of success.

A situation the agency generally made a point of staying far away from.

Swirling the various thoughts and ideas through his mind, Vance was positioned just behind the high-backed leather chair at the head of the table when the intercom system in the center of it erupted. With the volume turned up extra loud so as to not be missed, the shrill chirping echoed through the room.

And likely down the hall outside as well.

Every head snapped toward it as Vance stepped forward, squeezing the back of the chair in both hands.

A few feet away, Hannah Rowe reached forward, accepting the call.

"Charles Vance."

There was nothing more added. No use of a code term. Certainly no mention of where they were or who he worked for.

"Ela Ramirez."

Recognizing the voice instantly, Vance felt his lungs draw tight. This was either good news or extremely bad news.

No middle ground whatsoever.

"Go ahead, Agent."

The line crackled slightly, the connection over a sat phone on a stretch of beach a few miles outside Caracas.

"Just received word from Hawk," Ramirez said. "Two groups of hostages have been cleared and are headed this way. Some minor injuries, fifty-three people in total."

Vance felt his body sag slightly. Fifty-three was a long way from the full manifest, but it was a hell of a start.

And a solid sign that the plan thus far was successful.

"And the others?" he asked.

"He's working on it."

Shifting his gaze over to Rowe, Vance narrowed his eyes slightly. "Meaning?"

"I don't know," Ramirez said. "My guess is they were separated at some point, but he didn't say as much."

The backs of Vance's fingernails flashed white as he squeezed the chairback tight. "What *did* he say exactly?"

"Just that the first half of the rooms had been cleared and were on their way. In total, a dozen enemy casualties, though he suspected more on the premises."

Rotating at the waist, Vance looked back to Joon. The director met his gaze, the two men locked in the stance for an instant before Joon nodded slightly.

Original estimates had been that the opposition had a limited number of men at their disposal. A dozen gone had to mean there were extremely few remaining.

"Excellent work, Agent," Vance said.

Ignoring the compliment, Ramirez added, "And he also told me to get my ass into the woods and help get them out. I'm on my way now, will report back once they're on the boat."

Chapter Eighty-Eight

I waited until the last of the hostages were out of the first two rooms before going any further. Not wanting one of them to be caught in inadvertent gunfire, I stood impatiently in the hallway. One by one I willed them forward, even employing some of the younger and more able to help pull others through the narrow openings at the bottom.

As every last person was extracted and moved off to the stairwell, I could feel the clock in my head continuing to push forward.

There were still over fifty people unaccounted for. Not to mention at least a few guards hidden with them.

I had made a dent in their total numbers, that much was certain. If these guys had had a full slate of men at their disposal, there's no way they would have ever let me get within a mile of the place.

The woods would have been littered with roaming patrols. The roof would have been covered. The main floor of the warehouse and the hallway I was standing in would have both been lined.

That still didn't mean that there weren't more available. Certainly not that I could just go busting through the last doors with guns blazing, hoping for the best.

Little by little, I let what I knew about the situation percolate in my mind, watching the people slither out from the holding rooms. On their faces was every possible emotion, many whispering silent thanks to me, others already giving in and letting tears stream down their cheeks.

Some of the men looked like they were ready for a fight, suddenly swollen with toughness and anger.

Saying as little as possible, I waited until just a handful remained before stopping a middle-aged woman with graying hair as she slid through on her back. Helping her to her feet, I asked, "How many left inside?"

Matching my whisper, she replied, "Three."

"Men?"

"Two of them," she replied.

Nodding, I stepped aside as she straightened her clothes and set off. Behind her, a young girl in her late teens or early twenties went through, making the move look effortless.

Behind her was a man with a ring of white hair around his head, all-too-happy to accept a hand as he made his way through. Once he was just past the threshold, I dropped to my knees, blocking the exit, and peered through.

On the opposite side was a man just a bit older than me. Like an athlete gone to seed, he had thick arms and chest, with the stomach to match.

"Give me a hand for a second?"

His brow came together slightly as he stared at me. His lips parted, about to lob some objection, before he flicked a hand back, waving me in.

First through the hole went the drawstring bag. Still carrying a few items, it would soon be vital to my plan.

Next went my feet. Dropping to my butt, I kept a Glock in either hand, one ready to fire on both sides, before inching the rest of my body through.

The interior of the room looked exactly as ours had earlier in the day. The sole difference was the enormous stench in the air, a product of body odor and the assorted urine and fecal droppings of so many people all piled in the corner.

Mixed together in a gelatinous sludge, small rivulets of liquid extended outward like rays from a drawing of the sun, the smooth tile allowing it to flow unimpeded.

A foul sight to behold, it was still better than the alternative, the floor clear of any of Vance's agents.

Maybe some had survived after all.

The man on the other side was a couple of inches shorter than me and maybe twenty pounds heavier. Extending a hand down my way, he tugged me to my feet with a strength I hadn't quite expected.

He would work perfectly.

"Thanks," I said. Retrieving the bag, I cinched it into place before stowing the Glocks. "Hawk Tate."

"Eric Kolb," the man replied. "FBI?"

Feeling one nostril rise in a snort, I bit back the reaction.

Just because other agencies didn't think too highly of the more famous division didn't mean it wasn't a natural assumption by the common civilian.

"Fellow passenger," I said.

"No shit?"

"No shit," I replied. Making sure my gear was all exactly where I wanted it, I added, "But for the time being, working with the help of the CIA."

"No shit?" he repeated, this time a bit of disbelief clear in his tone.

"Crazy, huh?"

Kolb's eyebrows rose slightly. "This whole damn thing has been crazy."

To that, I couldn't argue. I had been through some of the worst shit the world had to offer, and I even I was a little taken aback by the events of the last day.

I couldn't imagine what these people must be thinking.

"Can you give me a lift up into the rafters?" I asked, flicking my gaze to the ceiling, for the first time noticing twin trails of bullet holes through the thin material.

Following my glance, Kolb said, "That was you, huh?"

"That was me."

"I'll be damned. And you're going back for a repeat performance?"

In no way would I term what was about to happen as a repeat performance, though I didn't see how I had a choice. Not with so many passengers still left.

Not with armed guards still about.

"Something like that."

My tone was such that I hoped it was clear that I needed to be moving on. I appreciated his aid, but there would be a long plane ride back to the States soon enough for us to discuss things.

Assuming I wasn't completely passed out or worse.

Right now, I needed to get the rest of these people out.

"You ready?" I asked.

Chapter Eighty-Nine

In the guard's haste to make sure the rafters were clear following my escape, they had made a mistake. Strafing the ceiling with bullets might have been an easy way to make sure nobody was up there, but it had come with one enormous unintended consequence.

It had left me with plenty of holes providing both light and a visual into the world below.

Compared to my first trip into the rafters, this one was far easier. The temperature in the space had dropped quite a bit. Without the sun beating down from outside, most of the heat had leveled off, leaving me bathed in sweat as opposed to fearing sudden dehydration.

More important were the stray shafts of light extended up through the ceiling tiles. Thin arrows of illumination, they provided immeasurable aid as I inched my way forward, hands and knees wedged into the metal tracts of the rafters.

Moving along just a few inches at a time, I waited long enough to ensure Kolb was gone before heading past the wall of the second room and into the space above the third.

The bullets that went up through the ceiling were probably standard Kalashnikov rounds, meaning the holes they left behind were roughly the diameter of a centimeter.

Peering through them, I had a very narrow view, seeing nothing as I moved past the wall and made my way forward. White tile was all that appeared beneath the first three holes, a smear of blood visible beneath the fourth.

An untold number of times throughout the day, my pulse had surged, my adrenaline seeping in.

Fearing what an empty floor could signify, even more what blood spatter would represent, I kept pushing on. As I did, I felt my acrimony grow higher.

For the situation, for the people in it, for everything about it.

Tasting bitterness on my tongue, the thought spurred me on, moving a little quicker.

Not until the tenth hole did I see something positive, a pair of outstretched legs becoming visible.

The eleventh revealed something even better, the top half of the man coming into view, his eyes open, head moving slightly from side to side.

A jolt of electricity went through me as I forced myself to remain calm. To move slow. To not do anything hasty.

One stride at a time I worked my way onward, the next hole revealing more people. The one after that, more still.

Clustered into a circle, every person seemed to be sitting on the floor. In the center of them stood two guards, both facing the door. The all-too-familiar Kalashnikovs were held in the crook of their elbows, the barrels pointed toward the ceiling, ready to be pointed and fired in just seconds.

Halfway across the space, I stopped. There was no need to go further. I had seen what I needed to.

Pressing my palms hard into the rafters, I reversed course, moving back slowly in the opposite direction. Extending my strides just slightly, I kept a watch through the holes beneath me, careful to make sure none of the sweat dripping from my body made it through one of the openings.

Not until the last of the people had disappeared from view, nothing beneath me but clear white tile, did I stop. Pinning my knees to either side, I slid the bag from my back, squeezing it tight to keep the contents inside from making a sound.

In total, the sack weighed maybe three pounds. A fair number of the bullets I had started with were gone, as were the bolt cutters.

In their stead was two spare magazines, the night vision goggles, and the sat phone. None were items I was especially keen on potentially losing, but I didn't have much in the way of a contingency plan.

The configuration of the hostages was smart. The guards had known there was only one entry into the room, meaning they had effectively built a human wall to insulate themselves.

They couldn't let the people stand because that would inhibit firing. Instead, they had ordered people to the ground, allowing them to rise and lower as needed.

Then, all they had needed to do was wait out whoever was coming, having the patience to remain motionless through everything they had heard going on outside in the preceding minutes.

If I wasn't so full of loathing for everything they stood for, I might have been impressed.

The only flaw in their plan was the one I was now looking to expose.

Holding the drawstring bag in my hands, I hefted its weight twice. Praying it had enough density to do as I needed, I shifted it into my left hand.

With my right, I drew out a Glock.

Taking a deep breath, I sat suspended above the room.

Exhaling, I pushed the bag out as far ahead of me as I could, stray bits of light shining up through the ceiling catching the dark material as it passed by. For what felt an eternity, it hung in the air, the items inside rattling loudly, before crashing down onto the Styrofoam panel beneath it.

Given the number of bullet holes already striping it, the thin material was no match for it, the bag dropping straight down through.

Barely a second later came the sound of automatic fire, the guards jumping at my bait. The instant the bark of their weapons was heard, I jerked both knees inward, my own weight falling straight through the panel beneath me.

A plume of dust particles exploded around me as I fell downward, more than ten feet in total before my boots slammed into the floor.

With their backs to me, firing up into the ceiling, the guards barely even registered my arrival.

The first didn't even get his head turned as I put three rounds into him, his weapon falling silent as he pitched forward.

The second one did only nominally better as I finished him with a single shot, a round placed just above his ear that sent bone and brain matter skittering out across the far end of the circle he was standing in.

Chapter Ninety

The feeling of shock lasted almost a full minute. In the wake of my sudden arrival and dispatch of the guards, nobody said a word. Every person in the room just sat and stared my way, unsure how to react.

Many recoiled away from me. Others pulled back away from the bodies of the guards and the blood steadily spreading wide away from them.

Others simply looked like they may cry, sensory overload from the last eight hours finally setting in.

Taking advantage of their position on the floor, I did a quick scan of the place. Just like in the previous room, there was an impromptu lavatory in the corner.

Unlike the other, the bodily waste was held in check by the bodies of two men. Dressed in jeans and polos, they were near copies of the man that had given me the phone number earlier in the day.

If the CIA had been trying to be inconspicuous, they had done a terrible job of it.

Shifting my gaze away from them, I swept over the crowd. Best guess, there were more than fifty people all staring back at me, meaning they had combined the last two rooms together.

And that everyone was accounted for.

Seated along the far edge was Rembert, a healthy stripe of blood spatter covering the front of his shirt. The bottom half of his jaw looked swollen and misshapen, especially pronounced beneath his gaze boring back at me.

"You good?" I asked.

Raising a finger, he pointed to his jaw before nodding.

Reciprocating the gesture, I knew instantly what he was trying to tell me. The bone was broken. There would be no further banter coming from him anytime soon.

Damnation.

"We need to go," I said. Raising my voice and my gaze, I looked over the crowd. Very few people were as yet moving, seemingly uncertain.

Circling around wide behind them, I retrieved my sack from the ground, tossing it over one shoulder. I didn't bother looking inside as I did so, the equipment having done its job one final time.

"Now," I said. Reaching out, I snapped my fingers three times. "Unless you people want to sit and wait for more guards to arrive."

Rembert was the first to move, lumbering to his feet. Upon his activity, others began to follow suit, the low buzz of muted conversation coming with it.

Leaving the people to ready themselves, I moved in a quick arc for the door. With the Glock still in hand, I extracted the second one from my waistband.

Lowering myself to a knee, I cracked the door open and peered the length of the hallway. Just as it was when I last saw it, the space was empty save the two dead bodies on either end. Between them was a tangle of bloody footprints, their impressions like macabre hieroglyphics spread across the tile.

It was ugly, and it was unfortunate these people would be subjected to it, but it was all we had.

The last groups had made it through. These people would as well.

Keeping both guns trained on the door at the far end of the hallway, I sidestepped out into the hall. With my shoulders square to the door, I waited two full moments.

Nothing moved.

"Come. Now."

The first person to appear was a woman somewhere around fifty. With hair dyed an unnatural shade of cranberry, she paused on the threshold of the doorway, glancing between me and the hallway.

"Just go," I said. "Keep your head up and get to the stairwell. Once everybody is down on the ground together, we'll head out."

A quiver passed over her features, her bottom lip trembling slightly. Once more she looked at me, uncertain.

Not having the time or the inclination for such a thing, I could feel agitation rising.

"Come on. I'll walk you down there. They won't harm you."

To illustrate my point, I took a step forward. I was not about to lower my weapons, the simple gesture the best I could do.

There were fifty-some people that we still needed to get outside. Waiting on one was not something that I could abide.

Inching her way out, I could hear a small moan as she spotted the first body. Pretending I hadn't, I continued moving on. A quick glance over my shoulder told me she was following suit, the next in order doing the same.

One at a time they streamed out into the hallway, reversing the exact course they had first traveled eight hours before. Moving much slower than I would have liked, they filed past as I stood at the end of the hall, alternating glances between them and the double door behind me.

Not a single sound could be heard from within as the hostages fled. Not even as Rembert brought up the rear, passing by and disappearing down the stairs with nothing more than a nod.

Chapter Ninety-One

Eight minutes had passed since the last of the gunfire. Still tucked away in the office headquarters in the abandoned warehouse, General Renzo Clega had heard every shot fired.

The initial burst that had ended the life of his staff sergeant, the young man's blood now spread beneath the door he was staring at.

The follow up automatic fire from the far end of the hall that had slammed into the front end of the office.

The final rounds a few minutes later.

If the low din of voices and the repeated pressing of the release bar on the door outside was any indicator, the hostages had been retrieved. Their plan was over.

In the wake of everything, the world had fallen away to silence. Hidden away where he was, there was no way of knowing how large a force the Americans had brought in. Considering they had mowed right through his squad of handpicked men, he guessed it must have been massive.

Which was why he had not made a sound. Had not even attempted to join the fight. Wanted no part of stepping out into the fray.

There was a reason men like him were leaders. They had skills and expertise and were too valuable to be used as mere fodder.

Only now that silence had fallen, no attempts made to breach the office, did he dare take out his cellphone. Scrolling to the most recent call, he kept it off speakerphone, setting the volume low and pressing it to his face.

It rang just once before being snapped up.

"Salazar."

"Mr. President," Clega said.

A moment passed, Salazar reading his tone. "There's been a problem."

Nodding in the darkness, Clega said, "There has."

"Have the hostages been moved?"

"In a manner of speaking."

Staring out into the darkness, Clega could still see assorted airport personnel dealing with the accident that had occurred earlier. The flames were extinguished, but cleanup would be a long time in completing.

"What does that mean?" Salazar snapped.

Just hearing his tone, Clega felt his own aggravation grow in kind. If the president had let him extinguish all of the passengers like he had originally suggested, none of this would have happened.

Instead, he had insisted that only the agents be harmed.

And what they were seeing now was the aftermath. In ten minutes, the transport vehicles he had ordered would arrive. Somewhere beyond the reach of town, teams were ready to eliminate every last person.

Not that any of that mattered now.

Yet again, Salazar's indecision had led them astray.

"It means the Americans came and got their people," Clega said.

"What do you mean..." Salazar began, his voice trailing off.

"I mean exactly what I said," Clega replied. "They brought a damned army in here and took back what was theirs."

On the opposite end, he could hear Salazar sputter. "An army..."

"Yes," Clega replied. "Killed every last one of my men, too."

How much of the narrative was true hardly mattered. It wasn't like the president himself would be going anywhere near Bolivar for the foreseeable future.

So much came to the front of Clega's mind, ideas that he wanted to share, bitter retorts that he wanted nothing more than to fire at Salazar. One by one he bit them back. Unleashing them would do no good.

Certainly wouldn't change the fact that they were still strapped in this together, no matter how much neither wanted to admit it.

"Where are they now?" Salazar eventually asked.

Chapter Ninety-Two

S tanding on the landing outside of the door to the second story office suite, I had time to think. To consider everything that had happened in the preceding eight hours. Going back almost a week, if I really wanted to think about it.

Eight days ago, I had just pulled into West Yellowstone. Feeling light and free, I had arrived with the intention of opening the shop for the new season.

I would get there first, see to some paperwork and a few lingering issues. A couple of days later Kaylan would arrive, and we would go about the process of getting the place up to speed before customers began arriving.

All of that – and so much more – had changed with a single phone call from Rembert.

Now I was standing on a metal landing in a warehouse in a country I never would have thought I'd enter again. Strewn about in the vicinity of the place were a dozen bodies, lives I was responsible for ending.

Men I had never met, would have never even considered their existence, if they hadn't felt the need to pull us into some ill-conceived political power struggle.

As much as I wanted to believe that the return trip to the warehouse was simply about securing the hostages, I knew that wasn't entirely true.

The men responsible for this had taken myself and more than a hundred others and put us through hell. My body was aching, chunks of skin and tons of facial hair now left scattered in the area. Rembert's jaw was shattered. Several others looked like they'd been battered as well.

Four agents were dead.

While the blame for what had happened couldn't entirely be levied on this side of the ocean, they were the ones that had felt the need to bring us into it.

And that was an act I could not allow to go without recourse.

With my backside wedged tight into the rear corner of the railing around the top landing, I waited. Glock in hand, I allowed my eyes to glaze, staring out through the open front of the building.

In the distance, I could make out the faint shadows of people moving about, clearing the way from the destruction Manny had wrought.

Below me, there was nothing but empty concrete, the smells of fuel and cardboard I had noticed earlier now accompanied by tinges of smoke and soot. Blood and death.

All scents I had become far too familiar with over the years.

Somewhere nearby, over one hundred people were moving through the woods. If Ela had done her job, the first group should be arriving, ferried onto a boat, ready to be transported out into international waters.

Rembert and the others would be no more than a mile away, an easy gap for me to close once my work here was finished. Work I was prepared to wait all night for if necessary.

Work that ended up taking just fifteen minutes to arrive.

In the exaggerated silence of the warehouse, the sound of the double doors opening found their way easily to me, ripping me from my thoughts. Drawing my attention over, my grip tightened on the base of the Glock.

All along, I had known that the fat man with the mustache was waiting inside. No way would a guard have been posted up outside otherwise.

Which meant he had sat and listened as the fighting happened. He had even stood and watched as the hostages streamed past, disappearing around the side of the building and out through the hole I had cut in the fence.

Not once had he tried to enter the conflict, or even help his men. He hadn't called for reinforcements, nor had he put up the slightest opposition.

He had simply sat and waited, now hoping to slip away. A thought that only managed to heighten my anger.

The man had no compunction about ordering the seizure of passengers on a flight or the execution of foreign agents. Most likely wouldn't have thought twice about ordering every last one of us to be taken out into the woods and murdered, banished to unmarked graves.

But he damned sure couldn't be troubled to do any of it himself.

Recognizing the move as more of the governmental bullshit I had come to loathe over the years, my grasp on the gun grew tighter still. Tension extended from my shoulder down through my wrist, the weapon an extension of me, my psyche in metal form.

Rage pulsated through me to the point I practically vibrated. Standing resolute, I waited as the man wrestled away the remains of his guard. I listened as he muttered gasps and feigned indignance.

And I raised my arm as the door finally opened.

There were no words. No witty expressions. Just a split-second passing, long enough to let him register what was about to happen, before I pulled the trigger.

Part Five

Chapter Ninety-Three

In the wake of the situation in Venezuela, Charles Vance wanted nothing more than to sleep. To lay down and catch up on every wink he'd missed the last few nights.

At his age, bouncing back wasn't quite the given it once was. His joints ached. Dehydration left him feeling weak on his feet. Every so often he had to use rewetting drops to keep his eyes moist and clear.

But there would be no time for that.

Not yet, anyway.

In its stead, he was back in the small alcove in the rear of Director Horace Joon's office. On the screen before them was one last gift from Hawk Tate, one final thing that demanded their attention before they could hand things off to the higher-ups across the Potomac to do with as they chose.

Nothing more than an image taken from the camera on a sat phone, it was a close-up of a man lying flat on his back. Encapsulating from his upper chest to the top of his head, it showed a pudgy figure with hair and mustache both dyed a matching midnight hue.

Through his forehead was a red dot large enough to place a pencil.

On the ground beneath him was a glossy red amoeba, unmistakable against the white tile he was laying on.

Beside the image was a second window, this one from the CIA database. Stretched the entire length of the screen, it listed out everything that was known about the man.

"General Renzo Clega," Joon said. With his eyes pinched slightly, he peered down the length of his nose at the file. "Ranking Commander of the Venezuelan Army. Direct report to President Miguel Salazar."

Nodding, Vance grunted softly.

The news should not have come as a surprise, though he would be lying if he said he wasn't a little shocked. In the wake of the call from Underall, he would have assumed that Salazar and his regime would want to play ball.

After all, they were essentially offering to show up and eliminate the man's largest political opponent.

"Rogue leader or under direct orders?" Vance asked.

Already he knew the answer, though like a great many things in the preceding days, he had to ask the question anyway.

"Tate also mentioned that most of the men he killed had tattoos of the army insignia," Joon said. "It could be possible that he had put together his own counter faction within the army-"

"But more likely, this was a sanctioned event," Vance finished.

"Thinly veiled not to look like one," Joon added.

Again, Vance nodded. As little as a few hours earlier, the goal had solely been to shift the focus of Joon and Underall and get the hostages out of that warehouse.

That part had been accomplished with far better results that he had any right of ever even contemplating.

What they were looking at now was nothing short of a gift from above.

"What do you think the angle here was?" Vance asked. "What was Salazar playing at?"

For a moment, Joon was silent, contemplating the question. "Great question. Maybe Belmonte's not the only one that hates us. Maybe he didn't like someone else calling and telling him what was going to happen in his own country. Maybe he was going to try and play Belmonte's card, stir up some anti-American sentiment in his own campaign."

Considering it for a moment, Vance let it settle over what he knew, had been thinking for the last few hours.

"Hell," he added, "maybe the idea of us taking out Belmonte wasn't enough. He needed to show everybody how dangerous such a tact was, ride that to his next term."

Managing only a grunt, Joon nodded slightly. For a few moments, neither said anything.

Glancing at the screen before them, Vance again considered the picture of Clega and the repercussions it would have before flicking a glance down to the clock in the corner of the screen.

Five minutes until what was hopefully their final call with President Underall.

"Director-" Vance began. More than once he had played back the words he was about to say in his head. Gone through the apology, the supporting reasoning, everything.

In total, he made it through but a single word.

"No need," Joon said. "I will say right now and unequivocally that if you ever pull something like that again, I will fire you. And it will be ugly."

Turning to glare at Vance, he made sure that the last sentence registered.

Receiving the message in full, Vance bowed his head slightly in acknowledgement.

All things considered, he was just glad it was an eventuality he didn't have to deal with already.

"Good," Joon said, shifting his focus back to the screen. He minimized the photo of Clega and brought the online calling program to life, an oversized keypad on screen, waiting for him to dial. "Besides, you were right to bet on Tate. Might be someone we want to keep an eye on moving forward."

Chapter Ninety-Four

The official diagnosis was a concussion. The fall straight onto the concrete floor beneath the soccer stadium had rendered Edgar Belmonte unconscious for a number of minutes. It had gashed his forehead, leaving behind bruising and a scab that would take weeks to completely heal.

Not to mention the most intense headache he had ever encountered.

Back in his office at campaign headquarters, he was reclined in his leather desk chair. Not far removed from the hospital, he still wore the slacks and dress shirt from the night before.

Bright red droplets that had dripped down his chest were now dry, dark and hardened across the cotton material.

What had happened the night before was still being unraveled. Who or why the fireworks had gone off when they did was open to speculation. What had caused the security to overreact the way it did as well.

Throughout the night at the hospital, both Giselle Ruiz and Hector Ramon had tried to fill the time by doing just that. One after another they had tossed out ideas, all ranging from genuinely plausible to the utterly absurd.

One by one they had gone through everything they could think of, their continued banter doing nothing for the pounding in Belmonte's head.

The very same pounding that now precluded him from getting what he most needed at the moment - a glass of the strongest alcohol in all of Venezuela.

Just the mere thought of it brought a thin smile to his face, a look that lingered even after there was a slight tapping on his door.

An instant later it cracked open, a thin sliver of light appearing on the wall before him.

"Mr. Belmonte," came the familiar voice of Ramon, "you have a phone call."

Letting his eyes slide shut – as much to display his displeasure as for the bright light – Belmonte replied, "Take a message."

"Sir," Ramon pressed, "this isn't the kind of call you do that with."

Feeling his eyes crack open, Belmonte twisted his chair around. "What?"

"Sir, you really want to take this call. And trust me in advance, this is real."

Saying nothing more, Ramon retreated from the room. In his wake, equal parts incredulity and confusion crept through Belmonte. He sat and stared at the closed door for a moment before slowly shifting his attention over to the phone on his desk.

Taking up the receiver, he blew out a sigh before pressing the single flashing red button.

"Edgar Belmonte."

"Mr. Belmonte, this is President Mitchell Underall calling from Washington D.C."

Feeling his chest draw tight, Belmonte snapped his gaze up to the door. Through the blinds covering its glass, he could see Ruiz and Ramon standing shoulder-to-shoulder.

Both seemed to be wearing the same shock he now felt gripping his system tight.

Adjusting himself in his seat, Belmonte cleared his throat. "Mr. President, to what do I owe this unexpected surprise?"

A slight bit of static crept through the line, passing as quickly as it had arrived.

"Well, I wanted to talk about that campaign you're involved with down there," Underall said. "I'm pretty sure if you're willing to go easy on us, we can make sure you end up on the right side of things come this fall."

Epilogue

The Curacao International Airport was even smaller than Bolivar had been. Containing just two terminals, one was set aside for shorter flights to Aruba, Caracas, and Bogota. The other was where I now sat with the other passengers from LATAM Airlines, the space set aside for international departures.

If the board on the wall above me was to be believed, those consisted of no more than a couple of dozen flights a day. Amsterdam, a couple of places in South and Central America, and not much else.

The only trip arriving or departing on a regular basis from America was coming in and out of Miami, which was where the folks all jammed tight into the small stretch of the terminal were soon bound for.

Eager to get home – or to at least put as much space as possible between themselves and Venezuela – many were already lined up tight to the windows. Still more than an hour from departure, the looks they wore made it abundantly clear that they wanted to be away as fast as possible.

Whether any of them ever flew internationally again, or even at all for that matter, was something only time would bear out.

Though I wouldn't bet heavily on the notion.

"You sure you're not going with them?" Ela Ramirez asked. Sliding into the seat next to me, she looked to be every bit as exhausted as I was.

Fortunately for her, the return leg of her journey would be much shorter.

"Yeah," I replied.

"Looking to stick around? Maybe catch some sun?" she asked.

The boat ride from the coast of Caracas to the island of Curacao was just over one hundred and eighty miles. Taking most of the night, it had allowed for medical personnel to see to any injuries that were scattered throughout the group.

And it had given Ramirez and I ample time to debrief with Joon and Vance.

What would come of any of it, I didn't have the slightest idea.

All I knew for certain was I likely wouldn't hear about it, that sort of thing rare to ever make the papers.

Forcing a half-smile at the question, I shook my head. "Called in a favor. Getting my own ride home."

The last twenty-four hours had included more association with the CIA than I ever wanted to endure again. My last call on the sat phone was to Kaylan, having her arrange me passage from Curacao back to Montana as fast as possible.

I didn't even care that it went through Cancun and then Los Angeles before getting me home.

One of the points that Joon had made in the course of our discussions was that the Agency would be sure to be on hand in Miami when the plane arrived. He had couched it to sound like they would be there to lend assistance and offer a hand in the wake of what had happened, but I knew better.

Those people had seen and experienced far too much to be trusted back out on the street without proper vetting and debriefing. The full litany of what that would entail, I didn't yet know.

I just hoped they were gentle.

These people had been through enough already.

"How about you?" I asked. "Back to Venezuela?"

Flicking a glance my direction, Ramirez returned her attention to the crowd around us. "I think it's pretty safe to say my cover there is . burned."

Nodding slightly, I couldn't argue with her. Her time in country was over. Farkus's too, if they were smart.

"Back stateside. Congratulations."

"Thanks," Ramirez replied. Running her hands down the front of her thighs, she added, "Thank you for everything else, too."

Pausing, she held her mouth open for a moment, appearing like there was more to be added, before thinking better of it.

Instead, she gestured in the opposite direction, using her chin as a pointer. Following her motion, I turned to see Rembert inching closer. Carrying a soda with a straw in either hand, he was moving slow, as if the events of the last day had aged him in dog years.

"Looks like I'm not the only one wanting to say goodbye," Ramirez added.

Shifting to look back at her, I extended a hand. "Thank you for your help as well. Whether these people here ever realize it, you saved their life."

A flush rose to her cheeks as she accepted my grip. "You're welcome."

Pushing herself to her feet, she again made to say something before thinking better of it and moving on, swallowed up by the crowd.

In her wake, Rembert slid down into the seat she'd just occupied, his bulk spilling over, pressing against my shoulder. Extending one of the sodas my way, he flicked the top of his head toward Ramirez before shrugging his eyebrows slightly.

I picked up the hint immediately. "Naw, she was just asking about my new international fishing expeditions. Said she heard they're quite an experience."

Unable to respond, or even open his mouth, Rembert did his best to stifle laughter, his entire body quivering, small puffs of air escaping through his nose.

In all the time I'd been around the man, it was the first time I'd ever known him to keep a thought inside. Just thinking on that was enough to force me to chuckle as well.

The last day had been a long, long way from what was intended, but that didn't make his original projection while sitting in the Atlanta any less true.

As it were, we really were just two guys sitting in the middle of nowhere, enjoying the moment. After everything that had happened, I couldn't imagine anything better.

Hellfire.

Thank You

Aloha all!

As always, I am here to address you all directly by first saying thank you. If this is your first time reading my work, I appreciate you taking a chance on it. If this is a return trip for you, I am indebted for your continued support and willingness to continue.

For those of you that fall into the latter category, I'm willing to guess this isn't your first encounter with Hawk Tate. Arriving before Reed & Billie, this was a series that originally started from a very simple premise that came to me while visiting one of my favorite places in the world – Yellowstone Park.

One of the things that I love so much about it is the ruggedness that is presented in equal parts beauty and savagery. While never have I left without at least a few moments of having my breath ripped away, never is a visitor too far away from what could be a major tragedy.

A combination that would create an individual armed with both a honed set of skills and a mindset that might differ from the common person.

For this particular work, I wanted to get Hawk outside of his usual setting. While he has had some passing acquaintance with Venezuela, by and large this is a much different place than he is used to working in. Coupled with some of the real world events transpiring there today, and…well…

To wrap this up, if possible, I would like to ask one small favor from you. If you would be so kind as to leave a review, I would greatly appreciate it, and do take all feedback very seriously. That very thing is what led to the creation of this, the fourth Hawk Tate novel.

In thanks, please accept as a token of appreciation for your reading and reviews a free download of my novel *21 Hours*, available HERE.

Best,

Dustin Stevens

Free Book

Sign up for my newsletter and receive a FREE copy of my first bestseller – and still one of my personal favorites – *21 Hours!*
dustinstevens.com/free-book

Bookshelf

Bookshelf

Zoo Crew Novels:
The Zoo Crew
Dead Peasants
Tracer
The Glue Guy
Moonblink
The Shuffle
Smoked
(Coming 2021)

Ham Novels:
HAM
EVEN
RULES
(Coming 2021)

My Mira Saga
Spare Change
Office Visit
Fair Trade
Ships Passing
Warning Shot
Battle Cry
Steel Trap
Iron Men
Until Death
(Coming 2021)

Standalone Thrillers:
Four
Ohana
Liberation Day
Twelve
21 Hours
Catastrophic
Scars and Stars

Motive
Going Viral
The Debt
One Last Day
The Subway
The Exchange
Shoot to Wound
Peeping Thoms
The Ring
Decisions

Standalone Dramas:

Just A Game
Be My Eyes
Quarterback

Children's Books w/ Maddie Stevens:

Danny the Daydreamer…Goes to the Grammy's
Danny the Daydreamer…Visits the Old West
Danny the Daydreamer…Goes to the Moon
(Coming Soon)

Works Written by T.R. Kohler:

The Hunter

About the Author

Dustin Stevens is the author of more than 50 novels, the vast majority having become #1 Amazon bestsellers, including the Reed & Billie and Hawk Tate series. *The Boat Man*, the first release in the best-selling Reed & Billie series, was named the 2016 Indie Award winner for E-Book fiction. The freestanding work *The Debt* was named an Independent Author Network action/adventure novel of the year for 2017 and *The Exchange* was recognized for independent E-Book fiction in 2018.

He also writes thrillers and assorted other stories under the pseudonym T.R. Kohler.

A member of the Mystery Writers of America and Thriller Writers International, he resides in Honolulu, Hawaii.

Let's Keep in Touch:
Website: dustinstevens.com
Facebook: dustinstevens.com/fcbk
Twitter: dustinstevens.com/tw
Instagram: dustinstevens.com/DSinsta

Made in the USA
Coppell, TX
18 October 2021

64269923R00226